TINY
REVELATIONS
DEVOTIONAL

Beautiful Caroline !
Love you D

TINY
REVELATIONS
DEVOTIONAL

SUZANNE RICKETTS

TATE PUBLISHING
AND **ENTERPRISES**, LLC

Published by Tate Publishing & Enterprises, LLC
127 E. Trade Center Terrace | Mustang, Oklahoma 73064 USA
1.888.361.9473 | www.tatepublishing.com

Tate Publishing is committed to excellence in the publishing industry. The company reflects the philosophy established by the founders, based on Psalm 68:11,
"The Lord gave the word and great was the company of those who published it."

Book design copyright © 2016 by Tate Publishing, LLC. All rights reserved.
Cover design by Samson Lim
Interior design by Richell Balansag

Published in the United States of America

ISBN: 978-1-68333-359-3
Biography & Autobiography / Personal Memoirs
16.08.04

1

It's a SCOOBETY DO DAH kinda year! Happy New Year! Up at it and moving! Excited for what this new year holds! Welcome! Praying for some wonderful things in lives this year! Seeing God's hand move in people and on people is amazing! Continued prayer to have the eyes and heart to see the best in people and love like Jesus this year, more each day!

Change. It is a word that most people don't like to hear or think about. We are creatures of habit, and we tend to desire to keep things just as they are when all is good, and we are reaching and trying to usher in change when things haven't been favorable. And yet as much as we often dread change, there is much beauty in it. We cannot grow if we stay the same. We cannot move forward. And honestly, standing still, while we may think we are not "moving," change is going on all around us. The saying that change is inevitable is true. We cannot avoid it. We may say we want it, but we want "our version" of change.

So I am looking at the red maples in our backyard, which are a beautiful golden color right now. I love these trees because they are a visual reminder to me of the fact that change can be beautiful, and I should not run from it or try to avoid it but to embrace it. Some trees are green, then all the leaves just turn brown and fall off almost at once. But for red maples, this change is a gradual process. The leaves have gradually turned golden (and if it had been a bit colder this year, then they would have also turned red after the gold) then brown before they fall. And they do not drop all the leaves at once. So each morning, when I look out my kitchen windows, I am looking at these changing trees. Looking at my life what it looked like in my twenties, my thirties, my now forties (hanging on to the forties by a thread), and what God has still in store. I can see that I have been changing over the years. I did not just wake up one day completely changed. Yes, I am a new creation in Christ, but Christ is constantly doing a work in me.

Out with the old Suzanne, and in with the new creation. And so my leaves have gradually been changing over time. They are more beautiful now than they were before, but I know that God is continuing to sharpen me and move me, take me places where I could not have imagined for myself, and use me in such ways. So I am embracing this process. I pray that if God is calling you to change, then we will offer no more excuses. We will not put out our sign that says, "When we have time, God, then we will." That we will embrace change no matter what color it is, what time, what flavor. When He calls us to it, then it will be beautiful. The process is a letting go and trusting. Possibly some pain and hurt, but beauty in us is what He is calling out. Have a blessed new year! Love loud!

2

SCOOBER DEE DO! Up and slow rolling this morning! Late night last night, but all is well. I'll grab some extra sleep next week when I'm off. Amazing women's group meeting last night. God is on point. Always. He knows. I love my Beloved.

My honey comes home today, so I'm jumping for joy! Been too too long and can't wait to squeeze his neck! I can already see the smile he will have on his face. It speaks deep into me still.

So this morning, my heart is soaking in the freedom that revelation brings. When something is hidden from us, we do not see the beauty in it. We cannot understand it. We do not know how to experience it because we never have experienced it. Last night, our women's group traveled to France to order off a menu that was written in French. As we looked at the menu and language that none of us in the group could fully read, we could grab bits and pieces, and a few words were recognizable it become funny, and yet if I was in France and had to eat from what I ordered, I would be quite lacking and wondering. The foods we ordered were recognizable because we had an experience with that food at a previous time. We had tasted it before. And how would you describe a food to someone they have never before tasted? They could understand in part but not fully understand until they tasted it.

Psalms 34:8 (ESV), "Oh, taste and see that the Lord is good!"

God uses all five senses for us to experience Him. Revelation. God's breath. Revelation is palpable because it enlightens us to a God that loves us, draws us to Him. So when I am trying to explain God to someone who has had no experience (that they see) with Him is much like explaining a sunrise to someone that has been born blind. I can explain with my experience, and they can understand with their experience, but the two will never fully meet until an enlightening or awakening, a tasting. And once we receive true revelation on who He is, the freedom begins to unfold. Revelation can be flip of the switch or gradually like light in a sunrise, but it will change us.

Psalms 119:30 (ESV) The unfolding of your words gives light; it imparts understanding to the simple.

So today may we be enlightening. May we walk in the light and the words that the Lord has poured out for us, His very breath that we behold in our hands, His word, absolute truth. Love loud!

3

YIPPEE DO! Up and at it on this breezy morning! Much to get done today, and before I blinked, my weekend was full of places to go and people to see. Grateful for the opportunities God is putting in my lap with how I am spending my weekends sharing with others. Good stuff. I was reading in Hebrews this morning and thinking about the message that was being written to the Jews that had become Christian but, through struggles and trials and all the hard times, were wanting to return to Judaism. I was reading how the writer is trying to convey that Jesus came, and He is, was, and always will be the fulfillment of the prophesies. So the writer is pouring out all the ways Jesus is the one and for them to stay the course and see it through even in the struggle. So the struggle is real.

I know that it is human nature to return to what is familiar, even when it is unhealthy, dangerous, negative, pulling us away from God (or family or whatever is positive in our life); it is comfortable. That's what the familiar is, comfortable. Who doesn't like to be comfortable? I love to put on my pj's as soon as I can every night. Yep. I'd put them on at 6:00 p.m. if I could. But I can tell you this, as soon as I put them on, I'm done. There goes any desire to work or get things done around the house. Once the shoes come off, and the jammies are on, I'm in comfort mode. Relax. It's easy-chair time. It is wonderful to be content but can be dangerous to be comfortable. A little rest, a little folding of the hands....

So I am thinking this morning about the absolute struggle these people were in. Running back to the old stuff was easy—no persecution, no imprisonment and all the yuck. Let's just go back to trying to live out the laws, and even if we don't succeed, there is comfort in knowing what's expected and what's to come. So today, if you are in a place where the Lord is pushing you to grow and you are uncomfortable, it's not a bad thing. Don't leave it and run backward especially every time you start gaining ground against the enemy. He wants you to run back to the old ways, old habits, old people, old desires. He reminds you how comfortable you were there.

Easy. I gain nothing by sitting in my easy chair with my feet up. It's not a position where I can get much done, nor do I want to once I've pj'd it up for the night. If you are being pushed outside of where you are comfortable, God may be trying to grow you, may be trying to get you to walk away from things that are toxic and, instead, run to him.

He can fill all those voids and places that are longing and empty. Familiar is not always best. Stretch yourself some. Trust the Lord. Let yourself be a little uncomfortable, and wait to see if he doesn't bring you to a new and better place. Love loud!

4

SKIPPER DOODLES! Up and moving groovin' this morning! It's chilly like a frozen biscuit this morning! Ready for Friday! Free day! Freedom day! I'm doing some reading this morning in Isaiah about Zion and about the coming Messiah. Watched this awesome video last night that my friend, Katherine Cullins shared—love working with someone that who loves the Lord and we can have good discussions and sharing each day! I need to share the vid with my friends, but it was charging us, …reminding us about the "Great Commission"…go out and make disciples of all nations. So this morning, my heart has been about Jesus. …how wonderful is His love.

> The Spirit of the Lord is upon me, Because the Lord has anointed me to preach good tidings to the poor; He has sent Me to heal the brokenhearted, to proclaim liberty to the captives, and the opening of the prison to those who are bound. (Isaiah 61:1, NKJV)

Friends, I have lived a life in chains even after I knew Jesus. I thought there were places too dark for Him to heal, hurts too big, places I didn't want to release. I thought maybe I could handle it or do it better, in prison for sure. And even though I didn't choose to be hurt in some of those ways, I was choosing to hold on to that pain. I was choosing to not release it, lay it at Jesus's feet, and even deeper things I didn't even know. So over time and prayer and dying to myself, and letting Jesus reign, my heart is in process. He has cleaned up some messy places. He has freed me from dark rooms, and parts of me were hidden inside, thinking I'd never open those doors again.

Chains I couldn't break on my own, a captive in my own heart until I opened my hands completely, and my heart completely and asked Him to have His way. Quite painful to walk back through some doors and yet it was so freeing and peaceful to walk through them with Jesus. No more mourning. No more deeps and darks. He brought light into those places, healing in those places. He gave me beauty for ashes, and I was a heap of ashes for sure. Burned myself up. Restoration. Jesus is love, a love so deep that He can turn my ashes into beauty, my deep and dark uglies into a life that He is using. Crazy. I sit this morning, amazed and grateful beyond words. Joy to the full for Jesus! Love loud!

5

YABBA DABBA! Up and rolling this morning! Ready for a wonderful day! Game day makes it better. So I mentioned before that one of the words the Lord gave me this year for my family is *hope,* and I am continually being made aware of how we all need hope, and some days, in large doses. So this morning, as I prayed for God to reveal things to me before I opened my Bible, then I opened to 2 Chronicles 14–15 and read about King Asa. I am reading about a king with an army of 500,000 about to battle an army from Ethiopia of one million. Not very good odds from a worldly stand point. But I love King Asa's heart when he prays to the Lord.

> And Asa cried out to the Lord his God, and said, "Lord, it is nothing for You to help, whether with many or with those who have no power; help us, O Lord our God, for we rest on You, and in Your name we go against this multitude. O Lord, You are

our God; do not let man prevail against You!" (2 Chronicles 14:11, NKJV)

So today, I am thinking of all the hope this prayer offers. Asa cried out to the Lord. This was a prayer of, "Lord, hear me and help me!" No, gee, if you have time for this and that, but he opened his mouth and out came the desperate plea of his heart. Asa had complete confidence that God was powerful enough to do all things to aid his outmatched, outnumbered army and overcome the adversary. He had faith. "For we rest on You, and in Your name we go against this multitude." Gracious, resting on God, resting in God when we are faced with circumstances that loom large over us, it's where we need to rest. It's easy to say, but sometimes not as easy to walk. And Asa loves God and boldly declares, "You are our God" and we give this battle to the Lord because quite honestly, it is His battle.

So often we want to stand on our own and battle and swing and punch at the air and try and fight to win something, someone, whatever it is, but we are small in comparison as we stand alone. We weren't meant to stand alone. God wants these battles. He wants you to put your hope, faith, trust, confidence in Him. He wants you to have the courage to face the battle but also to know that He will be with you in the battle, and the odds don't matter.

Over and over and over in the Bible, God gives us these same situations where men have called on His name, had confidence in His name and the courage to stand in the battle (with bigger opponents) and come out victorious, not because we are big but He is big. Let us not forget that today. If you are in a place where it is bigger than you, where you are facing a multitude and you are alone, you are not alone. Cry out to the one who hears you and will be with you, and then rest in the confidence that He is fighting for you. God's math is better than my math. Rest on Him today! Love loud!

6

YEPPER DO! Up and at it this morning! I did some heavy weight today since I missed Monday, so my body forgot what it feels like. Ready for some good happenings today! Chapel is always a blessing for morning! Been doing much praying and discussion with friends about fruit—producing fruit. Good fruit. I was writing the other day about not tending the vineyard, about both people having a vineyard but the one who tends receives the crops. This morning, I am reading in Hebrews chapter 6, and I come to these verses:

> Land that drinks in the rain often falling on it and that produces a crop useful to those for whom it is farmed receives the blessing of God. But land that produces thorns and thistles is worthless and is in danger of being cursed. In the end it will be burned. (Heb. 6:7–8, NIV)

Over and over recently, as I am in quiet time and praying, I want to live a life of intentionality. I am looking at this as we have the land. It is available to all, but what we choose to grow in our garden is what we will own. And God brings rain to both crops, not just one. But the one that grows thorns and thistles is a crop that is neglected, a life that is lived for temporal, neglecting the eternal. So as the Lord brings the rain to us today, may we know that while He is offering nourishment to our souls, we must take the action to work the soil, pull the weeds, and fertilize the crops so that the fruit may be good fruit, eternal fruit. It is more work than temporal fruit. Temporal fruit is live for the now, the all about me, the feel good, the "if you feel it's right, then do it," the flesh, "the satisfy whatever want or desire you have because you can," it's your life. Yep. Temporal.

Just sit back and do what you want. Easy cheesy and short-lived and leads to death. So may we sow good seed in the soil and work the soil. May we do the work to bless those that the crop was meant to bless—others, not just us. And in blessing others and sharing that fruit with others, we bless the Lord. We bless others, and He returns the blessing. May we walk today seeing that we all get the rain but choosing today what kind of crop we will raise up. Love loud!

7

TOPSY-TURVY SWERVY! Up and at it this morning! Planned on a workout today but last-minute change of plans revealed a run for today. Nice to get outside this morning and feel the wind in my face, and it was a bit breezy. So this morning lots to think about! As I run, the wind is blowing pretty hard, and I am watching and listening to the trees. The oak trees stand firm and quietly whisper as the wind blows hard. Many trees are bare. The palm trees wave and bend and make lots of noise in the wind. When I came home, I was reading in Proverbs this morning.

> I went by the field of a lazy man, and by the vineyard of the man devoid of understanding; And there it was, all overgrown with thorns; Its surface was covered with nettles; Its stone wall was broken down. When I saw it, I considered it well; I looked on it and received instruction: A little sleep, a little slumber, A little folding of the hands to rest; So

shall your poverty come like a prowler, and your need like an armed man. (Proverbs 24:30–34, NKJV)

So as I am reading this morning, I am thinking about being "lazy" in spiritual terms, not physical. The lazy man had a vineyard. I promise you the diligent man has a vineyard too, but they probably look very different. God gave them both the same opportunity, but one man chose to be lazy. Before long, the thorns and thistles grow up. Even the stone wall that protects becomes broken down. A little folding of the hands. A day where I choose to be too busy to be alone with my Beloved, then two, maybe even three or four. You know, life is busy. Much to do! But am I looking after my vineyard? Am I pouring myself into taking care of that relationship, the one that truly produces fruit, harvest, bounty?

I don't want to become negligent of that relationship, and yet it can creep in and become so easy to do. I want to open my day with my Beloved, pouring upon my heart what it is He wants me to see, know, understand, do and love more today. And yet, and yet, life is happening. Will I slumber my relationship to thorns and thistles? Will I rise and meet the day and my Creator with anticipation? The choice is really mine and yours. I know that I don't want an overgrown, unkempt vineyard when the God of the universe had poured out the blessing for me to even have a vineyard. What have I ever even done to deserve one?

So as the wind blows today, we can choose. We can be the quiet oaks that stand firm and let the wind whistle through us, knowing we are firmly rooted in Christ. Why do we know we are firmly rooted? He tells us! And we spend that time weeding and letting him prune us, tree or vineyard, and we become more firmly rooted. And as the wind blows, we can be the palm tree, waving madly, attracting attention, and making lots of noise but letting the wind have its way with us. This morning, I want to be filled with God's quiet strength and wisdom. I want to spend every moment I can squeeze into my day by walking with Him and hearing His voice. Life is short, but our decisions are oh so long lasting. Love loud!

8

It's a YEPPER-DOODLES kinda day! Up and moving! Had a good finish to my day yesterday with softball. The girls are making some nice strides. Put some numbers on the board with timely hitting, and defense is picking up. Good to see my leaders stepping forward. So I was thinking this morning about puzzles. I'm not the biggest fan of putting puzzles together because they are so time-consuming and yet when I actually do sit down to work on one, I want to stay until I'm finished. I'm not a "walk off and leave" kinda girl. I stay the course even when it's hard, even when I can't make find the piece I need. I remember when I was younger, and I would work on puzzles that I would bang my fist on the pieces to make them fit together. I was determined that those two pieces must fit. Period. And they didn't.

I just ended up messing up the actual pieces with my selfish motive of wanting to get it done and that it must be my way. Fast forward many years, and I have learned a bit along the way. I am still not the most patient person in the world, but I have gleaned some understanding that my way isn't always the right way for sure. I have also come to see that forcing things that are not meant to be won't help either. It usually just messes up all involved or the situation, elevates it to a place of big mess instead of just existing. So I am thinking about coaching, parenting, leading, and all the other hats I wear in life. I am thinking about how I handle putting this puzzle together. For sure, we each have the puzzle sitting in front of us, and we can see a portion of the finished picture on the box, and if we work on what is in front of us that we can see instead of trying to fix the stuff we can't, then we will rest in a good place.

God sees the big picture, and He calls us to each task daily. Daily. We can make plans and have desires for where we want to be in two years, and for sure, I do! I know where I want to be in two years and what I want to be doing, but I must remember that to do this, I need to work to get to that place in two years. I must put my pieces together that are in front of me today. Not tomorrow's pieces. Today's. I don't need to bang and force the fit. I just need to patiently work to get the right pieces together. Stay in godly wisdom and close to His voice. And as the days pass, years pass, I can step back and look at what the puzzle is looking like. I cannot see the finished product this side of heaven, but I can see what God is doing with a mess like me and how He takes my mucky, bent pieces, and when in the big picture of the puzzle, He cleans them up and makes it all blend beautifully.

So today, let's look at the pieces placed before our hands on the table. Let's work on those and not get outside ourselves, ahead of ourselves, but patiently stay the course. The pieces are fitting together one day at a time. Praying that I will be amazed when I stand next to Him in heaven and see the finished puzzle. Love loud!

9

SKIPPETY DO DAH! It's a chilly and windy day! Up and moving and almost heading out the door to the softball field, more work to be done. I was doing a little reading and ran across this quote, "Every calamity is to be overcome by endurance" (Virgil).

And then I opened my Bible this morning, and I'm camped out in Philippians and 2 Corinthians, and I am hearing a theme of struggle and being under trial and persevering in adversity. Mark and I were talking last night about some of the struggles and trials we have walked through in thirty years of marriage. We were saying that at any time during some of those hard times, those times where the struggle was real, not just a trite saying that if either of us had given up and walked away, we would not be here where we are sitting today. We made the promise to each other when we first got married that the word *divorce* would never enter our vocabulary. That if we got in arguments (and boy, did we), that we would not give up on each other. And so enduring all these hardships has brought us to where we are today, a month or so away from celebrating thirty years of marriage.

Endurance, it is easy to stay put when things are great, life seems to be clicking along at just the right speed, and blessings are falling in your lap.

"Therefore I take pleasure in infirmities, in reproaches, in needs, in persecutions, in distresses for Christ's sake. For when I am weak, then I am strong" (2 Cor. 12:10, NKJV).

And so today, I think about our marriage and how all the trials and struggles and distresses have brought us closer, made us stronger, grown our love for each other. Part of that strengthening has come from keeping our love for God in the center of our marriage. We haven't always done the best job of this, but I know we have grown in this area tremendously, and it is pouring out into all areas of our relationship. We have been weak and worn, tired and struggling, not enough money to pay the bills and waiting for the next check, which was two weeks away; starting a business on borrowing money with credit cards; raising three kids, who are now twenty-five, twenty-four, and almost twenty-three; and trying to figure out which end was up.

We've walked the hurts and pains and been as weak as flesh can be. But our strength has come in Christ. Our strength has come from standing our ground and making a decision to endure together. The three-braided cord is stronger than each of the strands individually with God as the third strand. We are stronger today than twenty years ago. And today, we can look back and celebrate those sufferings, and today, we know that if we struggle now, that it is producing a good thing in us. Adversity is a process of hope. It can produce hope, but it is necessary for us to fight the battle and endure. So today, if you are walking in the fire and trying to figure out why or how or what is going on, you may not get the answer now, but keep walking. Endure. Love loud!

10

YEPPER DOODLES! Up and at it this morning! I heard someone once say that burpees are easy. I need this person to come workout with me and show me how they are easy. I must be missing something! Had a great day on the softball field yesterday and ready for more! Chapel this morning always starts my day off right! This morning, I was reading in Colossians, and I always find so much wisdom in such a little book.

> Beware lest anyone cheat you through philosophy and empty deceit, according to the tradition of men, according to the basic principles of the world, and not according to Christ. (Col. 2:8, NKJV)

I was thinking this morning about raising kiddos in today's world. About all the messages kids receive from TV, radio, music, movies, famous people, and just society norms thinking about how easy it is for us as parents to sit back and give the statement, "I'll let my kids decide what they believe." Really? Friends, if we sit back and let our kids, who are immersed in this culture and all the untruth of the world, all the messages the enemy has in the media and everything, and we think our kid is making the decision to believe the Bible? I pray that as parents we are taking an active role in what our kids are seeing, hearing, and being exposed to all around them. I'm not talking like "freak-out panic," but I am talking about being keenly aware that your message is heard by them so much less frequently than what the world is bombarding them with. And such is the enemy's plan. Our kids are swimming in a society of untruth and unbelief, emptiness. And the world is telling them to chase the next thing, the next material thing, the next bed, the next high.

What is being taught in universities as truth because it is science, and yet it leaves God entirely out of everything. My kids are grown, but I teach high-schoolers every day, and I pray that they are growing firm in their faith and knowledge that God's word is truth. You can stand on it. Because the world is not just right outside your door but inside your home, computers, TVs, etc.

So today, I am praying for all you parents that are in the battle of raising kids and teaching them, not leaving it to the world to make their path, but you are investing in our future, their future, their eternity. Love loud!

11

YEPSEE DO! Up and at it on this beautiful day! Summer rocks! Thinking this morning about the enemy and how he strives to knock us down, strives to steal our joy, strives to kill our spirit, strives to destroy our faith and trust. I find myself so many times in my life at places where I feel God strengthening me, speaking to me, moving on my behalf, empowering me to do more than I can do on my own, and I find that I am usually met face first with opposition in those moments. Sometimes the enemy is subtle, but other times, he is no holds barred in my face full-on assault, trying to crush my spirit or body or mind. Whatever he can get.

I am watching someone dear to me put the pieces together of their life, leaving behind brokenness and moving into a life of victory. I am watching this person find their self-worth in Christ and not in the world or what some person says about them or group of people say about them. It is a beautiful thing to see someone become a new creation again, to cast off all the old and yuck and muck and grab a hold of Jesus and not let go. And as I see this person's beauty emerge and shine out in who God has created them to be, I see the enemy has tried in subtle ways to sneak in like a sneaky snake, but it hasn't worked. So he doesn't quit. He comes back and attacks the body full on and brings enormous pain to this person's lower back. No particular injury or reason for the pain in the natural world but the spiritual world knows why.

This person makes their living in working out and being healthy, and so an attack to the lower back basically makes almost any movement painful and near impossible. Lower back pain can shut you down. The enemy didn't come to the front door where you could see but came around back to attack. The back (especially lower back) is the stabilizer for the body. Strong core is huge for movement. So the enemy attacks the backbone. He wants to take your legs out, make you immobile, and keep you in one place.

Oh, he has plans, but the power of Jesus can turn all those plans for pain and hurt and lying around into joy and power and strength! If the enemy is knocking you down because Jesus has big plans for break through and to use you to help build His kingdom, and the enemy has to try to stop you. Rise up today! Pray through! Know who holds the power over sin and death! Know who has the power to heal. Know that the enemy has already been defeated! Call out to Jesus. See your victory before you and then rise up! Pain, yes. But the Lord will bring you joy and victory through the pain. Come out of the dark room the enemy wants to keep you in. Rise up off the mat and walk in victory!

"Submit yourselves therefore to God. Resist the devil, and he will flee from you. Draw near to God, and he will draw near to you. Humble yourselves before the Lord, and he will exalt you" (James 4:7–8, 10; ESV).

Pray through! Victory awaits the humble and righteous! Love loud!

12

STORMITY DO DAH! Pull out your puddle boots! It's not here, but it's coming. Up and groovin' on this great morning! Ready to spend time in praise and worship and His Word this today!

Last night, I was checking my e-mail and saw a story on the server page "Python dies after swallowing porcupine." I laughed a little at the headline and then clicked on link to read the story. Turns out they think the python died because it fell and possibly the quills punctured something in its digestive system. I thought how interesting this is in regards to our lives. Pythons eat all kinds of animals, and even occasionally a porcupine, and it doesn't kill them. A python has independent jaws, not unhinging, so they can swallow things much larger than they are.

We live in such a world that the enemy is prevalent, and he tickles ears and puts all kinds of things out there for us. Things that will, in the end, steal, kill, or destroy us. We can hear things so much that even though they are not truth, we believe it. Why? Because we hear it everywhere. See it everywhere. It is in all the media, and our culture is swallowing these things without thinking of the end in mind. We can hear something so much that we begin to believe it. Truth is not a "each person defines their own truth," but truth is truth. And there is only one. Cannot be twenty or thirty or whatever feels good, or I like this or it fits me and too bad for you. So I was thinking about how this snake has consumed things for years that were bigger than him, and this porcupine should have been no different. Done it hundreds of times, so no worries eating one more, watching that one more time, reading that one more time, listening to that one more time. And we slowly change, and the world seeps in. And we become casual about things, not realizing we have swallowed a porcupine, but we think it's just another lunch, just one more.

No worries, right? And so one fall, one slip, one "Oops, I'm out of control here," and porcupine in belly, and we are punctured from the inside. We let the world inside often enough that the dangers were overlooked, and one wrong turn and twist, and we fall, a fall that we have had before, but this time, we are full of quills, belly distended, and we lose. World=1, you=0.

Today, as you rise, please consider what you are letting in. What you are listening to and believing? What you are swallowing? What we take in should bring us life, but too often, the culture causes us to be so similar that we find we swallowed a porcupine. Oops. Is it worthy of your life to be liked by everyone? Just one more lunch. Few quills never hurt anyone. Think again.

Praying that as we believe in one truth—that we speak that truth in love but that we speak it. Love loud!

13

YEPPER-DO! Up and at it this morning! Working out and running just after the mosquito truck sprays is quite the yuck! One thing for sure, oxygen in short supply. Ha! I have been spending more time in prayer during my forty-day social media fast, and yet I haven't always began my morning that way, which honestly has been a struggle. When I start my day in quiet time with my beloved then sit down and share a little. I find that my day is much more on track, and I am acutely focused on Him during the day. God is no side note or after thought, and yet we can push Him out if we aren't careful.

This morning as I wake up, and I read the verse of the day, "Let us hold fast the confession of our hope without wavering, for He who is promised is faithful" (Hebrews 10:23, NKJV).

My youngest son has been doing rock climbing for about a year now, and he has learned much and taught me a bit during this time. There are different types of holds and crimps and pinches. There are different ways to climb—free solo, lead, bouldering, solo, and others. It is something I can't do justice to in my limited knowledge for sure, but I have seen people climbing free solo, hanging on to this small little hold with one hand and having to stretch or swing themselves over to grab another hold. I think about watching the climbers in Yosemite climbing up the sheer wall of El Capitan. I think about holding on with one hand, all my weight dangling down. Even if I am harnessed in, that is not a good feeling to fall. I think about what is it like to hold on like that? What is it like to hold on fast like my very life depends on it? One hand. Two hands. Do I have the strength and mental fortitude? Do I?

What's it like to hold on like that, and let faith rise? It is amazing! My God is faithful, so I do not need to doubt or waver but remain. But hold fast. Our faith is not just a collection of words we say or share, but when we are hanging off the side of a cliff and our very life is at stake, faith, or lack of it, will speak. So this morning, I am praying for us that we would remember who is the Author of our lives and that He is always faithful. Promise—His promise, not mine. His is better. So let your faith arise with you, and hold fast to Jesus. He is the only thing worth gripping and worthy of clinging to. Faith speaks in actions. Be a blessing! Love loud!

14

WOBBLEY DO! Up and at it this morning! Legs are Jell-O but glad to be back at it! I was doing the wishy-washy on my workout this morning because the pillow almost won. Can't preach no excuses and then live with excuses.

This day holds much in store, and I know that the Lord has things prepared for me to walk toward today, so I am ready and walking in joy. Part of our sermon yesterday was about the power of the tongue, and I was doing much thinking about that as the kids and I were sitting around yesterday afternoon, reading some things on social media. I can tell you that I have fallen prey more times than I want to admit to spewing poison out of my mouth or worse on social media. I surely don't get it right all the time and would never say I do, but I am trying to spend time in prayer before I post something or if I am annoyed or angry. Well, I just work to steer clear of social media, so I don't leave my feelings out there for the world to see.

> Look also at ships: although they are so large and are driven by fierce winds, they are turned by a very small rudder wherever the pilot desires. Even so the tongue is a little member and boasts great things. See how great a forest a little fire kindles! (James 3:4–5, NKJV)

And this morning, YouVersion has Proverbs 13:3 (NKJV). "He who guards his mouth preserves his life, But he who opens wide his lips shall have destruction."

It is so, so easy for us to let our emotions get the best of us, to offer up that zinger, to have a "great" comeback, to "well she had that coming" comment, to "well, I'm just speaking truth" comment (despite the intent of the truth or tone), and more. I know it is too easy for us to speak the words without a filter. It is too easy to turn our filter off if we want to say it. But I am thinking this morning about self-discipline. About the tongue steering the body. I am thinking about words that I personally speak out loud over myself, out loud over my husband, out loud over my family, out loud over our home. The power of the spoken word is huge because its impact is powerful.

If we speak life, then so often, it is almost a self-fulfilling prophesy of what happens, what we become, what we see, what we do. And the reverse is true as well. So this morning, despite my huge reluctance to get up and move, I pulled my body into discipline. I told myself that it was happening, and my body followed suit. Fruit of the Spirit, self-control (self-discipline). So this tiny little tongue can soothe, heal, love, calm, bring joy, speak peace, offer wisdom, offer forgiveness, speak truth in love, offer gentleness, speak boldly, speak life, encourage, and many beautiful things, and this tiny member can undo, shame, gossip, lie, slander, insult, speak unforgiveness, speak folly, chaos, hate, death, slime, and filth.

And so our struggle is real to pull the tongue into discipline. But the tongue is like my lazy head that doesn't want to get up. It wants to do what it wants to do. So we, being filled to the measure with Christ, must give over ourselves, die to ourselves, give up the things within us that are us and become completely His. Then and only then does our language begin to change. Will we slip up? Yes. But our hearts will be in such a place where we want to be in alignment with God and so we will wrestle with that little member and bring it into discipline.

Hard? Oh yes! But when we begin to speak life and love and positive things into those around us, when we begin to hold our tongue instead of letting it control what is said, then we begin to see fruit. We begin to bear more fruit. So today, if you are like me, stand up and take control of that little flame thrower that is in you. Guard your mind for what thoughts are in there, and then filter and bridle the tongue. Bring it into discipline.

It may not be easy at first, but as you begin to control it on a regular basis, then you will find it a little easier. Never easy but easier. The enemy knows the power of the tongue, and that's the first thing he goes after. Before you write on social media, whoa, Nelly, bridle that tongue. Before you speak to someone who made you mad, take a deep breath. Bring life or at least gain control. We can do it. Let's set the world on fire today but not with ugly words. Ignite a fire for speaking love! Love loud!

15

SNAZZERIFIC! Up and at it this morning! It is been a wonderful week full of family, love, and food—too much of the latter and not enough of the former but just so blessed to see and spend time with so many dear ones.

So this morning I changed up my breakfast and had some grits with my egg, and I was thinking about grain. I read in 1 Chronicles this morning about the mighty men of David and a barley field.

> Now there the Philistines were gathered for battle, and there was a piece of ground full of barley. So the people fled from the Philistines. But they stationed themselves in the middle of that field, defended it, and killed the Philistines. So the Lord brought about a great victory. (1 Chronicles 11:13,14; NKJV)

As I read the incredible feats of these mighty men, I can't help but wonder if we have reason to look deeper, not just in terms of just men but in each of us. Here are the thorn in the side Philistines gathered together and ready for battle. This seems to be their stance frequently—ready to fight always. Have you ever met someone like that? They are always on edge. Always ready to pick a fight, war with words, get offended, have something they are always on the defensive about and just waiting for someone to walk close enough so they can begin the battle. Gathered and ready for battle.

And here is a piece of ground full of barley. Barley was a grain crop used in that time for bread, cereal, and livestock feed. It was an early harvest and came in before some other grain crops. So is it valuable? Yes, to have food for families, to have bread for the people who couldn't afford much, to have grain for animals and not having to wait a week or two or more until the wheat crop comes in. Barley bears value in this community.

And so the people run and flee. They see Philistines ready to fight. "Oh, here come those darn Philistine warriors again! Always on the attack." So they run and flee. Don't stand and fight…. Either from fear or just worn down from the constant fighting for things, but either way…, they flee. But not the mighty men. They plant themselves smack-dab in the middle of that barley field. Defend it, and kill the Philistines.

And as we sit this morning and get ready for a new week at work, we must ask ourselves, would we stand in the midst of the field and fight? What is our field? Do we know what we are fighting for? Friends, we are fighting for our family. We are fighting for our faith. We are warring against an enemy who is trying to wear us down because it is always offended and on the attack. We are warring for our future generations. So are we mighty? Mighty! Or do we run and flee? Do we realize what we are fleeing from and what fleeing can do to our society and our homes? Our barley is valuable. Our homes, our kids, our families, and our marriages are valuable. Will we plant ourselves in the midst of our field and stand under the attacks? Will we recognize the damage that running away can do to us and to our kids?

Will we be full of courage and see the value of what we battle for and then stand and battle for it? If we don't, who will? The barley holds great value as a crop and so do our homes and families in our society. Run and flee, or stand and fight. It is our choice, and there is so much riding on our decision. When you win the barley field, families are fed, homes are upheld, and the order is protected. See yourself as mighty, and stand in the midst. God is always passing through the midst. He brought about the great victory ever present and in the midst. Love loud!

16

YEPPER DEPPER! Up and at it, heading out the door for workout. A much needed one, I might add. I didn't kill myself yesterday. First time ever. Thanksgiving is not filled with the best food choices, so I am moving the body today.

I thought this morning about juice, about fruit. I prayed today about my life, my family's lives bearing fruit for the kingdom, thinking about the fruits of the Spirit in Galatians.

"But the fruit of the Spirit is love, joy, peace, patience, kindness, goodness, faithfulness, gentleness, self-control; against such things there is no law" (Gal. 5:22–23, ESV).

I do not spend much time on social media, but when I do, you know it is a good place to hear people's voice. I have heard people say that social media is a place where people like to "portray" their life a certain way like they want it to really be when in actuality, it is quite different. This is probably true for many people, and a very true statement that unless you live with someone, you do not know what is going on inside their four walls, yet. Yet I can say that no matter how often I have seen people put a front forward for what their ideal life/family whatever would be, this is truth: when squeezed, you will always find out their true self. I don't say this as someone who has never been squeezed because that is far from true, and I don't say it as someone who was squeezed, and what came out was not what I wished. So I write this as someone who, years ago, thought I was an orange—round, with dimples, a fruit no doubt.

I even painted myself orange so I would blend in. But when I was squeezed, and the enemy came at me and attacked me, when I was hurt and in struggle, squeezed. What came out was not juice from an orange but quite another color and not a fragrant odor. We can look like the fig tree. We can even bear figs, but are they rotten. You won't know until it's plucked and squeezed.

So as I look in the mirror now, at this season in my life, I have recently walked through some squeezing and with a much different result than in my younger years. So if we are His, and we are full of the Spirit, then when we are squeezed, it is good. Isn't it beautiful for the world to see patience coming forth when you are in a season of waiting and it is hard? Isn't it lovely to see and feel the love and joy pour out of someone that is under it, maybe even from you, and they pour out these sweet things on others? Isn't it soothing to see goodness, kindness, and gentleness stream out of a person that is lacking and hurting, and yet goodness and gentleness toward others in a tense situation is what they show? Isn't it a blessing to be around someone who is walking through something so weighty and heavy that it takes some people out, and yet this person oozes peace? A peace that no one understands them having in all this mess and yet they bear it.

Isn't it wonderful to see someone who when squeezed and pressured and the enemy hurls it all at them, trying to pull them off course and toward the world or whatever pit he can drag them to, to see this person flow in self-control? Walking away from something that could and would undo them at some point and yet should be so enticing but the fruits of the Spirit are abundant in them.

Friends, we have all been squeezed in our lifetime, and no doubt, it will come back around at some point, and we will be squeezed again, but really, when we are in these seasons, what comes out of us is truly a reflection of who and whose we are down deep. What's in the corners and crannies comes out in a squeezing.

> A good man brings good things out of the good stored up in his heart, and an evil man brings evil things out of the evil stored up in his heart. For the mouth speaks what the heart is full of. (Luke 6:45, NIV)

May we pour forth fruits of the Spirit when we are squeezed today—full to the measure, abundant. overflowing. Love loud!

17

SCOOBERIFIC day! Up and groovin' today! It is well with my soul. What beautiful words to speak but even more powerful to walk in. Thinking this morning about waiting and trusting. I almost laugh as I write these words because I am not a "sit and wait" girl. I was quite the opposite. If there is something to be accomplished, then I am all about that, and let's go and tackle it. Now. Let's go! I know there is nothing wrong with being driven and a go-getter, and yet there are times in my life where God has called me to wait. And in all my wanting to get it done, I have tried to make it happen in my own power, my own timing, my own way. Funny thing is, when I sit back and rest and trust, well, He begins to pull things together. He opens my eyes to what He has been doing. Doors begin to open that I with a huge crowbar could have never opened. Ha! So I was praying for myself yesterday for this very thing—to be able to wait well. This morning, I ask my Beloved where He wants to direct me today.

> Then the Lord answered me and said: "Write the vision and make it plain on tablets, that he may run who reads it. For the vision is yet for an appointed time; but at the end it will speak, and it will not lie. Though it tarries, wait for it; because it will surely come, it will not tarry. But the just shall live by his faith." (Habakkuk 2:2–3, 4; NKJV)

So I can tell you that God gave me a vision years ago, and so I began in my strength to try to make this vision come to pass. But it never was my vision. It was His call on my life, and I have come to understand that He will make the path, make the direction, and set the stage at the appointed time. And I sit here today as someone who received confirmation a couple of days ago that the vision that was given to me a few years ago is about to come to fruition. Not by anything at all that I have done or said. "Though it tarries, wait for it because it will surely come." And it has. And I can tell you that His vision will speak, and it will be for His glory. No one person could pull together the things that God has set in motion. I honestly have been in such a place of humility and almost shock these last couple of days, grateful beyond words for sure. So as it plays out and unfolds before me, I know I will be more in awe of how He pulls people together and sets things in motion. The best is yet to come. Faith in that!

So this morning, if you are in a place in life where you can't see what is going on and you are wondering, wait for it. And don't be like I was for so long. Wait well. God is faithful always. He is a God of fulfilled promises. He is a God who doesn't leave and abandon, especially if it is something He has put in your heart or a call He has put on your life. It will come to pass, but it will be at the appointed time. Not my time, not yours, always His, and let's be grateful for that since He is all-knowing. David wandered for years for his appointed time. Joseph endured much for his appointed time. Moses, Paul, even Jesus. So we are in good company. May you be encouraged. Wait for it, and wait well, my friends. He does not disappoint. Love loud!

18

SCRAPPER DOODLES! Up and at it on a pretty morning! Today is on its way to being a terrific one! God speaks before my feet hit the floor. Time with my Beloved, and time and breakfast with my honey.

I was thinking this morning about eyes wide open, about gaining a new perspective on things, about what we "think" we see and what's really there. Perspective is so huge in life. We can say things in a certain tone, and the receiver can take it in a way that we didn't mean it, and yet their perspective makes it a negative experience. We can sit and look through our windshield every morning, driving in to work, but after a trip down the highway with some major amount of bugs on your windshield, what you see will be limited. Washing gives a new and better perspective. Looking through binoculars the right way brings things far away into closer view, but looking through them with the big lens next to your eyes turns the perspective and makes everything close seem far, far away. That's really one of the keys. Seem.

We can base our perception on what we see, what we feel, what we experience, but that is not always truth. Truth is when we see with our eyes wide open. We are not limited. We have no blinders on. Our view is not shaded or jaded, but we get the full picture. I have experienced things in my life where I thought I knew what was going on. I thought I had an idea, but then God has spoken to me to move to a different vantage point or He has revealed something to me, an "eyes wide open" kind of revelation so when I do see. I have my breath taken away. I am in awe. I wonder how I didn't see it before, and yet I was limited in my view or knowledge or vantage, and it seemed like I had a picture of my reality.

This morning, still reading 2 Kings and wanted to share an eyes wide-open experience. The king of Syria is wanting to make war with Israel, and Elisha keeps speaking to the king of Israel so they are eluding war. This makes the king of Syria angry, and he wants Elisha hunted down. He sends out an army to get Elisha with horses, chariots, a great army, and that great army surrounded the city in which Elisha and his servant were staying.

> And his servant said to him, "Alas, my master! What shall we do?" So he answered, "Do not fear, for those who are with us are more than those who are with them." And Elisha prayed, and said, "Lord,

> I pray, open his eyes that he may see." Then the Lord opened the eyes of the young man, and he saw. And behold, the mountain was full of horses and chariots of fire all around Elisha. (2 Kings 6:15–17, NKJV)

So you might be in a place where you are looking all around you and wondering if someone is for you? If someone is even there? You might be looking hard. You might be straining your eyes to see, and all you can see is the enemy camped all around you. Masses like an army that is bigger than you, outnumbers you, more powerful than you. And if that is where you are, then I pray that you will pray for the Lord to open your eyes, for you to gain new perspective. The army around Elisha was already there, and Elisha knew it. He could see it. But the servant didn't gain those eyes until Elisha prayed for him to have his eyes opened. You might not see the army of God camped all around you today, but I was reading in Psalm yesterday where David was praising God that the angel of God never left him and was camped around him.

This is while he was being chased and hiding out from Saul. Friends, God can open your eyes for new perspective. He can reveal things to you that have been going on right under your nose, and yet you didn't see. You didn't have that perspective yet, and your eyes were not yet fully opened. So know that the one who is for you is greater than the one who sends armies against you. God is more powerful, and He camps close to you. Even when you cannot see Him,

He is fighting for you. Had my eyes opened last night for something I have laid at His feet years ago, and He has been working right under my nose and putting things together. Last night was when I was standing like the servant, and all of a sudden, my eyes were opened. I could see something I had never seen before. And it was amazing! Praying for an eyes wide-open day for you. Know that He is for you and is camped all about you and working for your progress! See the new! Love loud!

19

YABBA DABBA DOODLES! Great stuff happening today! Don't know all, but ready with a positive attitude and eyes focused. Starting my day talking with my Beloved before I get out of bed and feet hit the floor is always a good way to begin.

Thinking this morning about love, reading about it in several places in the Word this morning and then spending time with my honey and Josh and Courtney and other couples I know well and watching love in action. The Bible has much to say about love. Love covers a multitude of sins. They will know you are my disciples by your love. Love one another. Love is patient, kind, not jealous or boastful, not rude or evil, doesn't rejoice in iniquity but in truth. Love is enduring. Love bears all things, believes all things, hopes all things. Love never fails. Love your enemies. Love must be sincere. There is no fear in love. Love comes from God. We love because He first loved us. Greater love has no one than this that he lay his life down for his friends. Husbands love your wives as Christ loved the church and gave up His life for her.

Of all virtues put on love, which binds them all together, a friend loves at all times. Let us not love with words or tongue but in action and truth, whoever does not love does not know God because God is love.

I stop there because that's a big chaw of verses—much to chew on and could take some deep thinking about all each little one has to offer. There are more, but this is a good gathering. So as I am spending all this wonderful time with my honey since school is out. I am reminded even more so of all the reasons I love him. And all the reasons I have loved him for thirty years and how that has grown. I watch both my boys with their girls and can see a deep love in their relationships, and I enjoy as a momma, how much they love each other. So am I writing about love today because it is so near and dear to my heart. It permeates our home, and we have raised our kids to love, and the Bible has much to say about love.

I think about the years of marriage and being in love. Love is not an emotion. Emotions come and go, ebb and tide. So if we love based solely on emotion, we are in for a short-term relationship. Mark and I have had arguments, disagreements, frustrations, annoyances, and so the list goes on. We have experienced this with each other over the course of a lifetime as well as anyone in a long-term, committed relationship. I am writing this today because I see and hear so much on FB that if you don't agree with someone, if you don't condone their lifestyle, their choices, their whatever, then you aren't loving.

Really? I can tell you that Mark and I don't always agree, but we do love. We care enough to speak truth to each other and get gut-level honest with what things are looking like, and then we love our way through the process. I can tell you that I haven't always agreed with the decisions my kids have made, but my not agreeing with them never meant I didn't love them. I have experienced relationships where speaking truth in gentleness to someone maybe not at that exact moment, but over the course of time and continuing to pray and care for that person has brought about healing, and they have spent some time with God where He has revealed things to them. We could never have long-term committed relationships with people if we didn't love.

And people who we encounter each and every day, we are called to love. Love them because _____ (fill in all the verses at the top of this writing). Not because we know all the answers. Not because we get it right all time. Not because we think we are better (because we aren't). Not because of anything other than the fact that when Christ is in us, we want good things for others. We love. The Holy Spirit convicts and reveals and heals, and we love. Not unconditional agreement but love. So today may we love those who don't love us. May we love well. Gentle and truthful. Love works wonders. I know. My mess was redeemed by a loving God that convicted my wrongful choices and loved me back to His ways. Marriage is full of these times. Friendships are full of these times (true friendships). Reach out a hand today to someone who needs to know they are loved. Love is God's nature, and He is good. Love loud!

20

YEPPER DO! Up and groovin' this morning! Getting lots done today. At least that's my plan. Ready for all the Lord has purposed in this day as I step into it. Yesterday, I was able to get lots of things done but had a nice break in my day when my honey took me to lunch and then we ran in Bed Bath & Beyond to grab a couple of things, most especially a new pillow for him. I haven't been pillow shopping in a while, so yesterday was an adventure of sorts. I stood back and watched him shop. I looked at the whole pillow section and all the choices. Scads of choices! Different sizes, standard—queen, king. Different fills—down, bamboo, poly, non-allergenic, and more. Different sleeper positions—side, back, belly. And honestly, I am probably shorting each section from some of their selections. I was laughing because Mark started and was ready to give up because there was so much, and it is almost an overwhelming experience, but he stayed the course and came out with a pillow he likes. At least he slept well last night, so I think it is successful.

So I am thinking about our daily walking in life. See when we go to choose a pillow, we are not just choosing that pillow for one night's sleep, but we are choosing it based on what we think will give us many good nights of sleep. We are trying to look ahead and make an informed decision based on the information at hand labeled on the pillow and what our sleep preferences are, and then we are choosing something for the long haul. When my youngest was two, we bought him a really nice down pillow, and he named it "peelow," and peelow went everywhere with us. By the time he was leaving for college, I had bought a few different pillows for him to sleep on because peelow was used up, smelly and dirty despite many secret trips to the washer.

He finally got another pillow he liked but kept peelow in his bed for a year or so after he didn't sleep on it. So this pillow thing is personal. Maybe for you it's not as personal as it was for Jake, but nonetheless, there are some things to be gained in all this. We make choices each and every day and probably more times than we care to admit, the choices are not looking ahead. We can make choices based on limited information. We can make choices just on what feels good in the moment. We can make choices based on the fact that we just want to do something and many other reasons. And if we are not examining our choices before the decision is made to act, then we can end up with a useless pillow, a pillow we don't like and wasted our money on, one that sits in the closet or one that we are forced to sleep on and costs us many sleepless nights.

I am in a season at this time where I have some big decisions on my plate, and part of me could just jump right in and act. Jump in, no forethought other than what I want and buy the first pillow because it looks fluffy. But there is much at stake in my decision, and it is not a decision just about me. They never are, so therefore, I must lift up the choices in front of me to the Lord's throne, and ask for some guidance and clarification. I can't let the immediate fluffy pull me in for a quick buy and then cause me many sleepless nights or be a decision that I want then have to put it on the shelf in my closet because I don't like it anymore. Choices are what we are presented with each and every day. Decisions are the action way we put our choices into play. So as you sit today at your desk or in your car, look ahead. Don't be overwhelmed by the whole process of making decisions, but see that the decisions you make today will have an effect down the road. Belly, back, side sleeper doesn't matter, but make the decision based on God's will and guidance and not just what you want. You are with that pillow for a while, so choose wisely. Love loud!

21

YABBA DABBA DOOZERS! Up and at it this morning! Good workout and wobbly as I left, so good stuff! Have much to get done this week.

So this morning, I woke up to a wonderful YouVersion verse that always makes me smile.

> The members of the council were amazed when they saw the boldness of Peter and John, for they could see that they were ordinary men with no special training in the Scriptures. They also recognized them as men who had been with Jesus. (Acts 4:13, NLT)

I love reading this passage! I love how Peter was the one denying Jesus a few months earlier, and now he is bold. Now he is different. He had been ordinary, but his in filling of the Holy Spirit and time with resurrected Jesus made him extraordinary! These religious leaders are looking at them and can't deny the miracles being performed, and they can't explain it, but they know and recognize them as "men who had been with Jesus." So today as we walk about in our daily everyday shoes, daily routines, daily chores, daily regular same old same old, just wondering if we look at ourselves and ask the question, "Are we recognized as someone who has been with Jesus?" Are we different? Are we changed? Did we used to be ordinary, no special training, no pedigrees, no five degrees to our name with cum laude at the end, and now we are bold? And now we are speaking with boldness and confidence, and it is apparent to all around us that Jesus is all over us, all in us and coming out of every pore?

If not, why? So I am seriously, no joke, looking in the mirror at myself and asking these tough questions today. I don't want to walk around doing the same old things I did before I was in a relationship with Christ. How is that different? If I don't recognize sin or turn and run from it but continually run to it, then I am not living a life that has Jesus at the center. I don't want to be consumed by rules and regulations in a way that I can yell and holler Jesus things, but I am a legalistic fool.

If Jesus is in us we love, not shout, not worry about religious leaders, we just do as we are called. Jesus in us should evoke such a change within us that the old has gone—that we are bold by what we live and walk out and what we speak. That someone knows when they have been around us that we are different because of Jesus. So today, let's walk in bold confidence that he is doing a work in us, and we are no longer the same! Love loud!

22

SCOOBER DOODLES! Up and moving this morning! So ready to spend some of this day in my Beloved's house, worshipping Him, praising Him, hearing His word and where His Spirit fills the room. Being in his presence is one of those experiences that you can't wait to get back to. I am in His presence in my private worship but love it when it's thick in the corporate setting. Such a sweet experience.

So this morning, I was reading in Nehemiah when this Psalm 69:32 verse came up on my news feed, and the two tied together beautifully. God always has a plan.

In Nehemiah 2, he has gone before the king (as cupbearer) and laid some things out that are on his heart, but here are two of the things with that chapter that grabbed me this morning. First, he prayed before he requested anything of the king. Second, after the king grants all the requests, he gives credit to God.

> Then the king said to me, "What do you request?"
> So I prayed to the God of heaven. And I said to the
> king. (Neh. 2:4, NKJV)
>
> And the king granted them to me according to
> the good hand of God upon me. (Neh. 2:8)

So as I was steeping in this passage and reflecting on my life and how I need to be more consistent with laying things before His feet, being in His presence before I embark upon some quest and on making sure that I always give credit where credit is due. As I am in this place, one can't help but be humbled. Reflecting on all God has done and is doing in your life, thinking about when I pray to Him before I begin something and ask Him to be in the center of it, asking Him to move on my behalf, asking the request to be His and not mine that I don't want to "own" it but that all glory will belong to Him, well, it just makes my heart smile.

I can see His hand on my life in so many places and times and things I never could have done in my own strength, things I never could have dreamed or imagined, things I thought were great for me, and He redirected me elsewhere, and I have found that He is right, always. So as a coach you always teach your team that when they take the focus off individual accolades and accomplishments and focus on the greater cause (which is bigger than self, amazing things happen. When we stop worrying about getting credit for things or lifting ourselves up then we can find that it is much easier to see God's hand on us and then give the credit to Him.

"I told them of the hand of my God which had been good upon me, and also of the kings' words that he had spoken to me" (Neh. 2:18, NKJV).

Right after this, they say let us rise up and build. So this morning, as we can be in all different places and seasons of our lives and yet we are always in the season of needing to lay things out before the Lord, needing to lift our requests up to Him before we speak to others about our needs or wants or desires. His hand of favor and blessing upon you is amazing, and then turning to speak about His good hand, speak to others about it, and give God credit and glory for what is happening. It is encouraging. It is amazing. It makes hearts glad! Today, lift up things, big or small to Him, and watch as He moves, watch as the puzzle pieces come together in ways you never thought possible. And then be humble enough to remember to give Him the glory. He deserves all the honor and glory and praise. His hand is mighty! Love loud!

23

YAPPLE DAPPLE! Up and moving on this beautiful day! God's glory is all around! Lots going on today and all of it is good.

This morning, as I sit before my Bible and ask God where He is leading me today and what He is wanting to share, He takes me straight to Philippians chapter three. There are so, so many good things in this chapter, but truly, the word that grabbed me as if in bold letters was *rubbish*.

> But what things were gain to me, these I have counted loss for Christ. Yet indeed I also count all things loss for the excellence of the knowledge of Christ Jesus my Lord, for whom I have suffered the loss of all things, and count them as rubbish, that I may gain Christ. (Phil. 3:7–8, NKJV)

So this morning, I am thinking about what do I count loss? Do I lay everything down at His feet? Do I hold certain things closer to my heart than Him? And if so,

Why? For if I count something as loss, then I must hold it loosely in my hand, ready to let go if He asks it of me and not cling so tightly that my white knuckle grip makes it apparent what I really value. So rubbish. So I count all these temporal things around me as rubbish, waste, food fit for dogs, litter, worthless, useless. This morning, I am looking hard and fast at the temporary things in my life—cars, home, money, accolades, things I cannot take with me, things that will stay here and rot, and yet we often grip these like there is no tomorrow. Ha! Funny thing is that if there is no tomorrow, then what is the real value in these things? In my attic, I have three boxes full of trophies, worthless and collecting dust. One is almost as tall as me, and yet it is in a box in my attic and should probably be in the trash instead of taking up space in my house. Compared to my life in Christ, all these things are worthless, waste.

My relationships with people—these are of value because those have eternal worth. My pursuit of Jesus and my relationship with Him is of eternal value. Not trash. Not sitting in boxes in my attic. I hope we don't put our relationship with Christ in a box in our attic and occasionally pull it out to look at it. Tell a couple of cool "old glory" stories about it and then put it back in the box until some other time, month, year passes. So today is a look-in-the-mirror day for me as to what is rubbish in my life? And if I cling to anything too tightly, over my relationship and pursuit of Christ, then am I boxing up

Jesus to sit in my attic? May we have God stories today! May we not cling to temporary and boxed-up Jesus, and may we encounter Him everywhere today—fresh and refreshed. No more rubbish! It just stinks up your heart and mind. Let it go. Love loud!

24

HIPSTER DEE DO DAH! Up and at it this morning! Skeeters are out in force and about carried me away so moved the work indoors today. Ready for all that God has in store for today! So last night, Mark and I were talking and just so much of our conversation centered around this verse:

"But seek first the kingdom of God and His righteousness, and all these things will be added to you" (Matt. 6:33, ESV).

And this morning, I am looking ahead at my day, all that lies before me that I can see and even things not yet seen. I want to live in such a way that I am seeking God in all places, all times, all circumstances, all deeds, I want to seek Him in all things I put my hand to in all seasons. Am I going to get it right all the time? Heavens no. But if I am truly seeking him first—His kingdom and His righteousness, then I will walk differently than the rest of the world. I will not place a focus on myself. I will not worry about awards or accolades or putting myself up in high places. No need. I will walk in humility and seek God. Gracious! There is such satisfaction in that place!

"And whatever you do, whether in word or deed, do it all in the name of the Lord Jesus, giving thanks to God the Father through Him" (Col. 3:17, ESV).

So all that I do, may it be done by a Jesus girl who is running hard after Him and doing it all in His name for His glory, giving Him thanks and praises. I don't want to run after earthly things—lust of the eyes, lust of the flesh, pride of life stuff. Just that, stuff. Stuff is fluff. Just like the stuffing in a stuffed animal, taxidermy or build a bear. I don't care. Stuffing doesn't put life into anything. It's just stuff. It's empty. It's shallow. It doesn't bring life but only fills up space. And as I look in the mirror this morning, I want to examine what I'm filling myself with? Is it Jesus? Am I running and pursuing life with Him and giving all of myself to Him? Or am I running after the stuffing? Empty, shallow, filling but not satisfying. Praying today to chase after my Beloved and seek him first. Love loud!

25

TOO-RIFIC TOO-DAY! Up and groovin' in the sunrise! God is good! Meets me when I roll out of bed, looking haggard and messy and meets me with all my messy and loves me in spite of it and through it. Grateful heart! Ready for a day filled with Jesus! So this morning, I am still camping in the little epistle of Jude, and I'm camping in a funny place considering all the urgings in his letter and valid points.

"To those who are called, sanctified by God the Father, and preserved in Jesus Christ: Mercy, peace and love be multiplied to you" (Jude 1–2, NKJV).

So I am looking at the first five words, "To those who are called," what does it look like to be called? So all this cool technology has afforded us the ability to look at our phones and decide if we want to answer a call. We see who it is from, and then we make a decision based on who is calling. So today, we are reminded in this little verse that we are called and who has called us. I am looking back to a decision I made about ten years ago to pick up my phone and answer a call. Truly, I won't bare out all the details here but I will tell you that I was sitting at a stoplight by the school where I taught and had been sitting at the light for some time. It wasn't a frequent green light because it was a side street. I would occasionally run the light if I sat there for more than a minute and no traffic was coming. Yep. I admit it.

So one day, I had been sitting, and I was annoyed it was taking so long. I was in a hurry. I need to get somewhere, and time is short. I am talking to the light to hurry, and my phone starts to ring, ring, and ring, and it is a number I do not recognize. I pick it up and look at it while sitting at the light, and while holding it, I decide to answer. At that exact moment, my light turns green. I can shoot off from my extended stay at the light, but something holds me there— the phone call. No one on the other end is responding to my answering. I cannot hear a voice. I put the phone down and just as I put it down a car going about 70 mph crosses in front of me. I barely even see the color it is going so fast. If I had been my usual self and hit the accelerator when the light turned green, I'd be dead. T-boned by that car and would not be sitting here writing this today.

I immediately called the number back and was told it is not a working number. I sat there for a while and just cried. Wake up, Suzanne. I was called that day. I received a phone call from God, and though I didn't hear a voice on the other end, He left no doubt in my mind that He saved me. So this morning, as you are out and about today and I wrote about a "phone" call this morning, don't forget that your life has a calling. You have been called by God to walk out your time here in His will and doing what He has purposed you for. It isn't more me time or more self or more I want to be the best me. It's all for Him. His work. His glory. His honor and praise. Don't ignore that call. Don't look at what you've been called to or who called you and walk away. It matters. Love loud!

26

YEEHAW! Up and moving this morning! So this morning, I am out cleaning the pool. Jake shocked it last night, and this morning, I decided to scrub the walls. I could only really see a couple of places where there was a start of algae, but oh, once I put that brush to the walls and started sweeping, *bam*! Pool was looking a little cloudy. It was definitely a workout for my arms and even used my legs in a few places but had a good sweat going by the time I was done. Got all the nooks and crannies and hard-to-reach places. So as I was doing this, I was thinking about my walk with Jesus. At first glance, I can look fairly clean, just some patchy areas to clean up. Sure. I'm okay. But the brush is the test. Put the scrubber to my life and how it can expose some places that I didn't know were holding grime. And Jesus doesn't just want to clean one wall and then walk away and leave the rest dirty. Nope. He wants us to shine. It is tasking for us to get clean.

I'm not talking, just asking for forgiveness, but clean in a sense of opening ourselves to Christ and exposing areas maybe we didn't know were dirty until He reveals it to us. And then each and every day to get alone with Him and let Him reveal these places in us and for us with the Holy Spirit work on ridding our lives of any sin patterns or harboring unforgiveness or resentment or slander or selfishness or any type of sin. Anything that keeps us from having a deeper walk and deeper love of Jesus. So we are a work in progress. I will have to scrub the pool again. It will not stay clean. If I keep up on the certain things that work and keep it clean longer, then those help, but I will still have to scrub again. And dirty dirt will come out of the crevices. Yikes. But how freeing when that dirt is revealed and you offer it up to Him, asking Him to remove it and cleanse you. We all hold the muck and grime, but the fact that Jesus is making us new in our time with Him, time in His Word, time in the fellowship of other believers that sharpen us.

All these things help us as we work to walk well. I don't want to neglect all these things, and before long, I will be full of grime and the water so murky that no one would want to dip a toe in. No one would want to be around me because I would be too full of the world and myself. So unappealing.

"Here is a trustworthy saying that deserves full acceptance: Christ Jesus came into the world to save sinners—of whom I am the worst" (1 Tim. 1:15, NIV).

Amen.

So funny because I honestly wasn't going to write on this today. I had read another passage out of Jude and was going to write on that, but my Beloved had a different thing in mind. So today, may we not be afraid to lay some things bare. May we not be afraid of taking a scrub brush to those areas, and may we be ready for what Christ will reveal in other places where we need work. So grateful for a Savior that saves the dirty and mucky people and loves us where we are but doesn't leave us where we are. Blessed to be His! Love loud!

27

YEPPER DEPPERS! Up and hustling this morning! I forgot to set my alarm, so I got ready at high-octane speed this morning. I had a fun time with the women last night at group. It has been a semester full of blessings, joy, tears, struggles, triumphs, and grace. This morning, I have much on my heart as this will be the last women's group I lead for a while. I am not a seasoned veteran by any means, but in the few or so years, I have been exclusively leading groups of women. I have gleaned a few things for keepers. I have watched women walk through the doors of my home in emotional bondage, wrecked, torn up and torn apart. Puddles.

I have watched women in chains of bondage of what a man has spoken over them or whispered in their ear or shouted at them, beaten up not physically but emotionally. And what a toll it takes on a person. My heart has been wrenched and poured out for these women, and I have seen some powerful things. I have seen what a collective group of praying women can do. The power of God called down and out upon a soul is like no other. And that's what I am writing about today—the power of God and the amount of power you let Him have in your life.

I can write this not just from an observation point but from a woman that has walked in emotional bondage. So this does not come from a place of haughty but a place of seeing and living out what God has spoken over me. My dear ones, we can be in emotional bondage and a wreck if we choose to let someone have that much control over us. People will treat you the way you expect to be treated. If you command, respect, and walk in dignity, then you will be treated with such. If you hold your head in shame and shrink back into a corner, then people will treat you that way. When we let someone speak into our lives, we are allowing them to have a direct link to us, and if we internalize what they say, good or bad, it will affect us. So here we have the opportunity each day to let God speak into our lives to open His word and let him pour into us, and we have the choice each day to rise up and put on the armor. We can empower ourselves with His word, and we will find that we are being strengthened from the inside, and it will manifest itself outwardly.

I watched a good friend one year ago, stand in such a place where she was in emotional bondage in a relationship and watched her completely step out in faith, empowered by what she put in her mind (the Word), what she spoke over her home and in prayer, what a group of women prayed for her. And today, I see this woman claiming victory in her life. God stepped in and provided and answered prayers in that situation. Some even before we prayed them. It can happen. So today, we need to take inventory of who we have in our lives and what message we let them speak over us. We can stand up and walk on our own, or we can let someone else speak negative, damaging, bondage statements over us and watch our chains hold us in every area and then watch that person move us about like a puppet. So today, if you are in a dry place that feels empty and you feel alone, please know that you are not alone. He is with you. May you recognize His presence, and empower Him to speak into your life. He is the only one truly worthy to have that place and power. Rise up. Lose the chains. Stand on His strength, and you will begin to find yours. Love loud!

"Submit yourselves then to God. Resist the devil, and he will flee from you. Come near to God and He will come near to you" (James 4:7–8, NIV).

28

SCOOBY DOOBY! Up and groovin' this morning! Ready for a great day! God is good, and He has the places I walk before my foot even steps there today. So can't help but share the little photo card I posted yesterday:

> Moses couldn't follow God without standing in front of Pharaoh.
> Noah couldn't follow God without building an ark that would bring ridicule from his neighbors.
> Daniel couldn't follow God by praying to Him alone without being thrown into the lion's den.

Can't help but feel this morning that this is a message God wants so many people to hear and grasp today. Sometimes, we are called to tough places. Sometimes when He calls us to obedience, it usually isn't the popular thing or the easy way. Sometimes when He calls us to places where we are standing face-to-face with something that we fear, we need to get rid of, a sin pattern, a stronghold, an obstacle, an idol we worship, and as we stand in these places and these times, we are called to be different, called to lay things down, called to walk toward Him, called to lay ourselves bare before Him and in our laying it all down, we stand.

If Moses had run from the call, he never would have learned to stand. If Noah had ignored the call, he never would have stood. If Daniel had lived in fear, he never would have been able to stand. So as we look at these men and countless others in the Bible and even friends around us today, what separates the person who is able to stand from the one that runs or ignores or hides in shame or lives in fear? Obedience. Friends, when we walk in obedience, then even though the world may hate you, those around you may point fingers and say things about you, the world will make you out to be a scapegoat, casting everything upon you and running you out on a rail, and yet if we stand in obedience, God has us.

He takes us and calls us to obedience and then blesses us for standing in obedience. So today, if you are in a hard place and trying to discern things, praying for clarity and right thinking and godly wisdom, His wisdom is true and right, so go there and follow hard and fast. We are called. Obedience becomes a blessing! Love loud!

29

SCOOBER UBER! Up and slowly moving on a beautiful morning! My pillow won the battle this morning and kept me in bed a little too long. Much going on today and ready to see what the Lord has in store!

Doing some reading and thinking this morning to back when I was a kiddo and back to when my kiddos were little and they used to "set the table" before a meal, took extra time, extra preparation. It meant being intentional and thoughtful about each person who would sit at the table and what all was going to be needed for that meal. It also took some forethought, making sure you covered everything so no one would have to get up and go get something after everyone sat down to eat. I was reading in Proverbs 9 this morning about wisdom and folly and have written on this several times but not from this point.

> She has prepared her meat and mixed her wine; she has also set her table. (Prov. 9:2, NIV)

> You prepare a table before me in the presence of
> my enemies. (Ps. 23:5, NIV)

So I am thinking this morning about what is laid out before us today. I was reading about folly, and she sets no table and prepares nothing. She invites you into her house to drink stolen water and eat in secret. What's done in secret is always revealed, and what's stolen or taken can only bring about death. The enemy is the ultimate deceiver, and he is all about stolen water and doing things in secret. But today, I am thinking about a God that prepares a table before me. Setting the table takes time, and intention. And, friends, God does this for us. He wants good things for us, but notice that wisdom is part of that preparation.

If we are full of folly and just skip about life, things will not fall into place as we wish. Through wisdom, we will add to our life. We will gain wonderful things, but it is because the preparation has been done. "For through wisdom your days will be many, and years will be added to your life. If you are wise, your wisdom will reward you" (Prov. 9:11–12). So I am looking at my season of life right now and pondering if I am setting my table and am I setting it well. Am I being intentional with what I put before me, what I put in my mind, what I see with my eyes, what I let my ears hear and my mouth speak? Am I praying for wisdom and then sharing that with others? Am I worried only about myself, my wants and desires? Am I preparing?

See, we all go through seasons in life, and when we walk through a good season, we want it to last, and we can usually look back as we walk through that season and see that preparation was done to set the table for what we are currently walking in. Same with a bad season. As we walk through it, we want it to end soon, but we can usually look at where we are and look back and see that we have not been intentional about setting the table, but more like folly, we have just happened along and now wonder why we are in this place and how can we get out. Been there. Lived it.

Please understand that some seasons are brought about by tragedy, and I am not speaking to those, just ones we place ourselves in. So today, our challenge is to look at today, and embrace setting the table before us. Love loud!

30

YEPPER DO! It's an up-and-at-it fun day! Ready for lots of good stuff going on this week, so let's get it rolling!

So this morning, I was sitting on the thoughts about yesterday, thoughts about Lot's wife looking back at Sodom as they were fleeing for their lives, spared and yet held captive. After years of teaching kiddos how to throw or how to shoot a basketball, a good part of teaching has been about what the eyes look at and how that is huge in hitting your target. There is lots of science to confirm that about shooting free throws and all those things, about how the eyes focus, and then it sends a signal to the brain, and the brain tells the arm and hands how and where to release (and distance) the ball. It's all amazing, but without the eyes, the rest of the process wouldn't work well at all. So am I thinking about what I am looking at as I rise up this morning to start my day? Am I focused on Jesus? When I am, He will guide me, help me choose life-giving words, turn my sorrow to joy, turn doubt to faith, stand in strength in areas I am weak and so much more.

It is so wonderful that He can do all these things and more when we are fixed on Him. What happens when we aren't? What happens when we even receive the blessing of being rescued and yet we keep our gaze fixed behind us on the life past? On the things that somehow still hold us captive. Yet why? Think about Achan in the book of Joshua, who could not let go of all the spoils he gained from the war. Clinched fist. I am thinking this morning about what my eyes are fixed upon because honestly, friends, that is what our heart is fixed on. You can look at something and look away. Oh, but that second look that calls you back, then it calls your eyes to stay. And when our eyes keep looking at something, then our heart desires it.

Lust—lust of the eyes, lust of the heart. Achan lusted, desired the riches and spoils of war so much that he took a chance that it wouldn't cost him his life. He didn't think he would get caught so that treasure kept his gaze, and it killed not just him but his entire family. Lot's wife felt the need, the desire to look at Sodom one more time. What happened there that drew her attention back? We don't know, but she knew the result of looking back, and she still took that chance. I have been in times like this in my life. Times where I thought what I wanted was better than what God could hand me. Things I would cling to so tightly that could cost me everything, and yet I'd cling. Open your hands. Fix your gaze on Jesus. Get it off the world. The enticing and alluring glamour it offers is a shallow and temporary fill and ultimately death if we stay there long enough and visit it too often. Take off that yoke the enemy is trying to put on you this morning, and cast your eyes upward. There is freedom in Christ, no slavery, no bondage. Lift your eyes to the only one worthy to fix your eyes on. Jesus. Love loud!

31

UPSIE DOODLEY DO! Up and at it this morning! Quick bam of a workout but still sweat like a wooly mammoth in August. Excited to spend time today with dear ones I love! Breakfast with my honey, lunch with sweet friends, then dinner with the family. Missing Sis, but I know she is having a blast in Cali!

"Therefore we must give the more earnest heed to the things we have heard, lest we drift away" (Heb. 2:1, NKJV).

Sitting at Bible study last night and hearing a teaching on the ten virgins like none I've ever heard before, taught in such a way that my eyes were truly opened and new things revealed, which made perfect sense, and yet I wondered where I have been all these years? I do not spend enough time in my Bible and studying His word the way I should. I do not spend as much time as I would like in quiet prayer with the Lord. And so I must do some things in my life to prioritize these because they are very important to me. I have to be intentional, and I have to be careful to not drift away or lessen priorities, lose focus or commitment, or passion or discipline. We hear the things of God frequently, and yet do we always steep ourselves in what we read or hear? I don't want to lose focus and drift away, become casual about the things of God, and without even meaning to, it can happen.

Then one day, we wake up, and I've heard people say they haven't heard from God in years, or they can't hear His voice. So we were praying for our family last night to draw near to God. Pull in close, so close, each and every one of us so that we may hear Him whisper, hear Him breathe. James says draw near to God and He will draw near to you, and yet too often in our lives, we get busy with the busy, and we push God back. Again, without meaning to do so and yet it happens. Then little things slip in, little things of the world we give way to. Again. Then again. Then once more. And the tiny little things begin to add up, stack up. And before long, we have built up a wall, and God is on the other side, which is never where we intended Him to be, and yet we put him there. We are a well-meaning Christian but not following well. Been there. Done that.

So today, as I get my day rolling, I am looking to stay close, draw near, keep the things of God close to my heart and in my mind. Drifting away happens when we aren't intentional, sitting on the raft and just waiting for where the water takes us. The world has a path for you, and without intentional rowing or fighting through, it will pull you with the current that leads to destruction. Float along with the world, or draw close to God, and let Him empower you to battle the current flow of the world. I chose Christ. No drift, just drive. Love loud!

32

YEPPER DOODLES! Up and at it on a beaut of a day! Going on a couple of errands with Jaker and Bible study tonight. Honey is working in Waco today, so he was gone when I got up this morning. Ready for a new season. Sitting out here on the back patio, thinking about time. Thinking about each one of us and how we spend our time here, what we spend our time doing, if it is what we want to be doing, if it's not what we want to be doing, then why are we still doing it? Are we looking back two years ago, and seeing that not much has changed in our today and two years down the road, will we be still sitting in the same "today" as now? I have lived a bit over 18,000 days. I look back two years ago in my life, and not much is different today as it was then. Oh, I am older. My kids are older. They are progressing forward with things in their lives. I am deeper in my faith and walk, but honestly, not much had changed until recently.

I decided to take some steps of faith in a few areas of my life, and God showed up in each one of those areas and has begun moving me (and Mark) to a vision beyond ourselves. Dreams we've had for years are beginning to come into vision with clarity—visions and dreams for our kids, for our family, for our finances, for our faith, for things we only dreamed about when we were young. It is crazy because I had bought into the same idea that so many also walk through in their lives. Just sit back, and take life as it comes to you, which is quite funny for me because I'm a "get up and get after it" girl. And so we as a couple have begun to take these steps together—new business, new church home.

God has been true to the promises He placed in each of us. We, however, had to take the step. There was no fulfillment to the promises if we just sat back and stayed comfortable. And so I am challenging you today. If there is an area of your life that God is calling you out, calling you into the uncomfortable, then step out into that area. It may just be for a season, but the joy that comes once you get uncomfortable and see the amazing things that happen in that zone will keep you returning. Don't settle. Today is number 18,076 for me. I may not have 18,077. I don't know, but I do know that I am put here for a short season, and I don't want to leave it and say, "Oh well, it's done. Too bad I didn't _____." Yep, God has called me out to a new place, so I won't ignore it or push it down. No promise of tomorrow, so get after it. Joy in being uncomfortable. Find it. Love loud!

33

HOOPETY DO DAH! Sitting here writing this afternoon—a rare privilege I get to enjoy these days, and thinking back to when I was a little girl, I was so independent. I wanted to do everything myself, for myself, by myself. No help. I thought I could do anything. And I still have a pretty long streak of that running through me. While it is good and has been beneficial in many areas of my life and circumstances, I can tell you that there are truly times when I have needed the shelter or protection or just dear friendship of someone.

I used to fight my mom when I was little to let me do at all by myself. I didn't want her help. Stop trying to do it for me. And yet I can remember being lost in a store a couple of times. I remember hiding in the clothes racks while my mom was shopping. I was trying to get away from her, and before I knew it, I really had. She was looking for me, and I didn't know where I was. The fear and panic that strikes through the heart of a little one that is lost is almost overwhelming. Stricken with terror is probably an understatement. I was trying to be silly, trying to do it all by myself and show my momma that I could hide somewhere where I couldn't see her and still be okay—that's what I thought. And then I found myself emerging from the center of a clothes rack, and Momma was nowhere in sight. Then I knew fear and how much I needed my momma and how much I loved her and wanted her right in front of me.

So I think about how many times in my life I pushed back on God. How many times I told Him, "I can do this by myself. I don't need Your help." Oh, sometimes I didn't utter those words, but my actions shouted it loud and clear. "I got this." And I can tell you, more than once I have stood, wondering what on earth I was thinking and crying out to God to rescue me and please scoop me up and tell me, "I am right here and I have you." I think we all need to be reminded of this very thing from time to time. Even if we walk with Him and share the most intimate details of our lives with Him, sometimes we just need to have our Daddy hold us close and remind us that He has us in all things and in all times.

There is nothing wrong with us standing up and walking on our own two feet, but may we be mindful of the Beloved who created us and how our souls long for Him, even when we think, *I've got this*. And so I don't hide out in clothes racks anymore, but I have tried to hide hurts and pains and run away from things I didn't want to face. And as I emerge from those places, there is a Father who is standing and smiling at me, letting me know that He has been right here and ready for me to take this step. Let go of all the fears and things of this world that can bind you up and send you running or hiding. Let go of fear (which is from the enemy), and step out into a faith that is more real and tangible than any false sense the enemy can conjure up. Spread the clothes and step out. Faith is waiting to wrap His arms around you and welcome you. Love loud!

34

SNAP-A-DOODLE! It's an up-and-at-it great day! Can't tell you how glad I am to finally have a true week off this summer! No workouts, no camps, just time with my people, much needed time with my people. Yesterday was such an incredible day. Blessings are still running over into my today. This morning up and workout while my honey swims, breakfast with my parents, lunch with some of my squenchers, then church softball tonight watching my boy—full day of activities and love.

> But as it is written: "Eye has not seen, nor ear heard, nor have entered into the heart of man the things which God has prepared for those who love Him." But God has revealed them to us through His Spirit. For the Spirit searches all things, yes, the deep things of God. For what man knows the things of a man except the spirit of the man which is in him? Even so no one knows the things of God except the Spirit of God. Now we have received, not

the spirit of the world, but the Spirit who is from
God, that we might know the things that have been
freely given to us by God. (1 Cor. 2:9–12, NKJV)

I just love this! I am quite honestly at a place, a season, in
my life where I am watching things unfold before my eyes
that are more glorious and amazing than things I ever could
have imagined, things that are way beyond me. I remember
when I was in elementary school having friends who were
in junior high and them trying to talk to me about algebra.
It was way beyond me. Not forever but for where I was in
that season. I hadn't experienced anything on that level, so
I couldn't understand all the things that lead up to that,
which made algebra quite strange for me. Letters in math?
What? What? Fast forward to high school, and then my
previous learning and experiences had caught up, and I was
equipped for algebra.

Without the Holy Spirit, we cannot grasp a corner of
the wisdom of God. We will never in our limited human
form understand God, but we cannot even make heads or
tails of godly wisdom without the Spirit. When we have
the Spirit, and God imparts things to us, we are in awe
of the depth and magnitude of His being. The things of
this world we think we understand although we are still
learning things about this earth, and we are still discovering
and uncovering mysteries of this planet, and every time we
think we are more intelligent and above God, He reveals
something new, something we thought we had right, but

we find out that we were off and now have to readjust what we "thought" we knew.

I love that God freely gives us His Spirit, and we can study His Word in depth, and His Spirit can reveal things to us that we think we know (in our human knowledge), but His Spirit reveals deeper meaning and understanding, revelation. Friends, God is about revelation. He loves to reveal Himself to us in ways we cannot imagine. He loves for us to turn a corner and His revelation hit us smack in the face. What? That's been there the whole time! How did I never see that? He loves to see our eyes opened. He loves when we look with our hearts and let His Spirit reveal wisdom to us.

I am in a church now where I am in the "What? Letters in math?" haha! Learning so much about the Hebrew and Greek and the depth of the Bible and God's revelation that I leave each week and wonder why I sat so long and only understood one or two levels of understanding. I've been missing out, and He has revealed much to me in this short time. Now watching things in my personal life elevate to a new level and watching God pull people and things together on a vision He gave me years ago, now it's coming to pass but in a huge way, more abundant that my little mind ever thought. And such is God more than my little mind ever thought. Soak in quiet time with His Spirit today, and revelation will come. He is a God of revelation. Love loud!

35

YABBA DABBA! Up and at it this morning! Good workout, and my honey did his workout in the pool. Always love when we exercise together! So glad to be off work today and spend time with loved ones! Much on the list today, but God puts good stuff in each day. Errands and grocery store (grocery store is not good but necessary), lunch with good friends, more errands, men's group tonight, and I'm getting together with some of my friends at the same time. God is good. I am grateful.

Reading this morning in James 4 and then on through to James 5. Can't help but grab a hold of one of the messages about being patient in the struggle and praying.

> Therefore be patient, brethren, until the coming of the Lord. See how the farmer waits for the precious fruit of the earth, waiting patiently for it until it receives the early and latter rain. You also be patient. Establish your hearts, for the coming of the Lord is at hand. (James 5:7–8, NKJV)

> Is anyone among you suffering? Let him pray.
> Is anyone cheerful? Let him sing psalms. (James
> 5:13, NKJV)

Thinking this morning about the struggles of life. Lost a dear sweet girl, one of my athletes in 2011 on this day. She was fourteen. This was a struggle. Big one. Thinking about all the trials and fires and storms and pits and muck I have been in, some self-inflicted, and some by the push or actions of others but no less in them. So when the world is pushing back on you, holding you down, cutting you off, boxing you out, putting you underneath or in a dark place, then we must find a way to make it through. How? Pray. Prayer is our life source as believers. We have no deep strength or ability to stand for long periods and battle something larger than ourselves unless we pray through.

Looking at the farmer being used in these verses and thinking about growing plants. A seed has to exert force to grow. It has to work. For work to be done, you need a force and a motion. Moisture triggers the seed to begin its growth process. It has to split. The roots have to push downward, and the sprout has to push upward and out of the soil. And the soil is pulling downward (gravity) on the seed. It's a lot for a tiny seed to overcome, and yet, it does. So we are planted. We are placed in this soil around us, the earth, and the ruler of this world (the enemy) is constantly pushing against us and fighting us to gain ground. But when we pray, we have a lifeline.

God pours out moisture. Rains on us, and we are triggered to grow. We grow through the process of the struggle and the prayers as He is nourishing us and nurturing us at the same time. And the world pushes against us. And we fight and find out that what is within us is strong, and with the prayers, we are strengthened, and the push back of the world even though it means to keep us dormant and underground. It actually helps us fight and become strong enough to break through. I can say that there were times in my life that I lied dormant and let the enemy have me, but when I found myself on my knees and began a serious prayer life and walk, I changed.

I found strength I never had before for the struggles and was able to push through. Grow upward and out, and establish roots at the same time. God is good. If you are in this midst of this type of season right now, know that time with Him is like rain to a seed. It triggers growth and strength that could never happen in a dormant, dry, prayerless life. Lift your prayers up today. He truly hears. I am walking proof of a hearing, listening, and responding God. Love loud!

36

SCOOBER DOODLEY DOO! Up and at it with a tight back but no excuses. Gotta work if I expect results. Ready for a great one today! Last day of volleyball camp, lunch with my honey, time with a sweet friend, and, finally, getting a chance to cook dinner for the crew. Holding hands with my Beloved today throughout my day as we walk together, at least that is my plan unless I wander off and lose focus.

I am reading in the book of 1 John this morning and thinking about the power of the Spirit, the power of Christ, and how the enemy is such a deceiver.

> We know that we are from God, and the whole world lies in the power of the evil one. (1 John 5:19, ESV)
>
> Little children, you are from God and have overcome them, for He who is in you is greater than he who is in the world. They are from the world; therefore they speak from the world, and the world listens to them. We are from God. Whoever knows

God listens to us; whoever is not from God does not listen to us. By this we know the Spirit of truth and the spirit of error. (1 John 4:4–6, ESV)

So I am thinking back to a time in my life where my faith fit neatly in a tidy little box with a big pink bow on top. I could keep it on the shelf and look at it from afar. "Oh isn't it pretty?" I could take it down once in a while and open it up and then put it back for the majority of the time. I could say the right things, but they were neatly packaged as I pulled them out of the little box and then put it back. Many years ago, this was the "tidy box" faith I had. What changed? Life. Things happened to me and around me that were way beyond my control and what I wanted—things that were ugly, things that were messy, things that were big, things that I didn't want, and my "tidy box" faith couldn't handle them. It was way, way too small and trite to handle real life. And so I found myself on my knees. I found myself pouring into the Word. I found myself in lots of quiet time with God, talking and crying and listening.

The world was bigger and "badder" than anything I could handle, and I wasn't ready, and my box was too small. So I am reading this morning about the whole world, "Lies in the power of the evil one," and yet today, that doesn't undo my "tidy box" bow, and it doesn't undo my life. Why? Because my faith now is bigger and way, way beyond me! It's way beyond a "tidy box." The God I worship today is the God that has overcome. He is greater than he who is in the world. He doesn't fit in tidy boxes with pink bows. He doesn't fit on a shelf no matter how much or many times we try with all our might to put Him there.

All we really do in that case is imprison ourselves because we are worshipping a god who is too small to fight our big battles, and if we worship a small god, then, friends, it is not *the* God. We may not understand how large and mighty He is, but if we can put Him in a box, then we are self-worshiping. Our pride of me is bigger than He. So today, I pray that we can look deep at our faith and be real with where God abides in our lives. No more tidy boxes with bows for me! Celebrate the one that is greater than anything we battle and anything we imagine! Love loud!

37

YAPPLE DAPPLE! Up and groovin' this morning! Ready for a day filled with outdoors, heat-index warnings, lunch with sweet friend, family time, Bible study. Whew! Love summer days! Filled up with all the things I love! I have been in a season for a while now of learning more and more about the Holy Spirit from reading books by Robert Morris, Danny McDaniel, Jack Deere, the Bible, and more, and I have had numerous encounters in praying for friends and my own quiet time. So I was reading this passage yesterday in 1 Samuel 19 about Saul pursuing David to kill him. Relentless pursuit. When David was anointed in chapter 16:13, "The Spirit of the Lord came upon David from that day forward." I am reading this passage in chapter 19, and I will share.

> Then Saul sent messengers to take David. And when they saw the group of prophets prophesying, and Samuel standing as leader over them, the Spirit of God came upon the messengers and Saul, and they

also prophesied. And when Saul was told, he sent other messengers, and they prophesied likewise. Then Saul sent messengers again the third time, and they prophesied also. So he (Saul) went to Naioth in Ramah. Then the Spirit of God was upon him also, and he went on and prophesied until they came to Naioth in Ramah. (1 Sam. 19:20–23, NKJV)

I love how I have read through this before and never really grasp the power of the Spirit. The Spirit comes upon men, and they prophesy but also that God's plan will prevail. Saul thinks he has this thing figured out and keeps sending wave after wave of people to find David and every time they arrive, the Spirit comes upon them, and they prophesy. Saul sends more. It happens again. Finally, Saul must think he is sending weak men, and he decides, "If I want this done right, I have to do it myself!" and he is met by the same Spirit of God, and he meets with the same end result, but the Bible goes further to say that after that Saul strips his clothes off and lays naked all that day and night. I want to share one more verse that I read this morning that ties this together.

"And the Spirit is the one who testifies, because the Spirit is the truth" (1 John 5:6).

So we can run. We can hide. We can push our own agenda. We can tell everyone we rule, and it's only our way that matters. We can think we have outsmarted God, but clearly we see that God is on the throne. His Spirit is truth, and as these people receive the Spirit, they speak truth and prophesy. They are no longer under the power of man and his rules, but God's truth covers them. David had the Spirit come upon him, and don't you imagine that is what kept him strong all those sixteen years that he tended sheep and was chased and hunted by Saul? The Spirit is truth. And God will advance His kingdom in truth no matter what man's plans or desires are.

When He fills you with His truth, you no longer have your own agenda or angle or bitterness or anger or malice or hardened heart. Why? Because He will strip you just like He did Saul. I would not want to lay naked all day and night out somewhere, but you can believe that your dignity would be lying out there bare with you. And so God does this to get rid of our flesh and pour out His truth on us and in us so that we will be all about His Kingdom, His truth, praying that today we may throw off the flesh and be filled with His truth and spirit—the same Spirit that today can empower us to advance His kingdom no matter what the odds look like or no matter how many waves are coming at us. Spirit of truth. Receive it. Love loud!

38

SKIPPER DEE DO! Up and at it this morning! Ready for an amazing day! Sitting here, thinking about how grateful I am for each step, each season, each victory, and each struggle in my life. Honestly, if God had sat down with me ten years ago and given me the map of my life, the road ahead, the mountains, the valleys, the potholes, the beautiful, the windy roads, the traffic, the quiet two-lane highways. Not sure I would have taken that from His hands and said, "Okay, let's go!" There has been so, so many blessings and amazing things that have happened, and there have been some deep hurts and pains, some detours, some pits I wasn't sure there was a way out.

Yet I realize that each and every one of these things I have encountered and been through in these days has made me the person that I am, has strengthened me, has made me resilient in some places, has softened me for others, has grown my love for God, has increased my faith in leaps, and I know that if, if I had the opportunity years ago as I sat with God, if I had the chance to look at the map and say, "God, that's looks rough in some places. Here is your map back. I will pick mine," I realize that there still would have been pits and struggles, but I know that my steps are ordered, and in that, how could I even spend a second of my time here in worry or doubt?

Honestly, there were times where Mark and I were pouring over scripture together crying, praying for one of our kids, all of them or our family—times when the hurts were so much bigger than us and our family that God was/is the only one we could rest in. So today, if you are looking at the path you are on, and it is a rough patch of road, bear it out. Know that God is in the midst and is with you in this. It doesn't matter if it is bigger than you; it is not bigger than Him. May we be sharpened and strengthened in the process. May our experiences serve to bless others. May we recognize that even the struggles are a victory!

> For everyone who has been born of God overcomes the world. And this is the victory that has overcome the world—our faith. Who is it that overcomes the world except the one who believes that Jesus is the Son of God? (1 John 5:4–5, ESV)

Praying today that we would not stress and worry about what the map ahead looks like but realize that if we have given the wheel and the vehicle to the One who created it, that He is driving, and we are shaped in such a way to bless this broken world. He's got the map, and may I trust, just keep my eyes on Him. Love loud!

39

UPSIE DO DAH! Up and at it this morning! Running out the door, tying my sneakers. Much to do this day but holding my Beloved's hand through it all day. I had a wonderful day yesterday between church and time with kiddos.

So this morning, I am reading in Joshua chapter one. Good stuff in this chapter. very empowering.

> "Have I not commanded you? Be strong and courageous. Do not be frightened, and do not be dismayed, for the Lord your God is with you wherever you go." And Joshua commanded the officers of the people, "Pass through the midst of the camp and command the people. Prepare your provisions, for within three days you are to pass over this Jordan to go in to take possession of the land that the Lord your God is giving you to possess." (Josh. 1:9–11, esv)

I have read this passage many times, and this morning, something different stuck with me. Joshua, who has just had a conversation with the Lord, commands his officers to "pass through the midst of the camp." So I am thinking about how many times in my life God has walked through the midst of my camp and given me directions, guidance, encouragement, so many things. How many times does God walk through the midst offering us something? Something we need, something we need to hear, some step we need to take to move further, gain ground. Gracious! For most of us, I imagine this is His typical way through the midst. He usually doesn't stand far away and shout at me, usually not on the outskirts of my life trying to offer me things, things from far off. Nope.

God is in the midst. He brings people into the midst with us and uses those around us, those with wisdom and courage who will follow close. He walks through the midst and give us steps, helps us prepare, encourages with uplifting words or words of correction, but stand and know that He is in the midst. Could Joshua have been that bold to give the officers the instructions (to walk through the midst so all the people could hear) if he had not just received a word from the Lord?

So today, let's open our eyes and ears, and realize that God is in the midst with us and offering more than we can imagine, not on the fringe but in the midst. That's where the instruction and encouragement and boldness lies. Love loud!

40

SCOOBER DO! Up and at it in the heatness! Moving, groovin', and shakin'! Ha! Mucho great things happening in my world today! God is good and so blessed and ready for today and that He is in it all, every part!

So I was having a great conversation a couple of weeks ago with a dear friend who attends a different church than my family. In our conversation, we were talking about how our friendship is still strong, and we still love each other even though we attend different churches. We talked long about the struggle of so many of us as Christians to realize we are on the same team—Team Jesus, not church 1 and church 2, and you are red and I am blue (Dr. Seuss is my friend). I have been coaching for years, and as a coach, you have many things you want to accomplish, but getting a team to unite and understand how to play together, how to put self back and put the agenda of the team first is probably for me the biggest.

I love to win, but honestly, winning is short-lived and won't last if the team chemistry stinks. The lack of team chemistry will show up. You can count on it, and it usually will show up in the big game. On the other hand, team chemistry can take a mediocre team far, far beyond its capabilities as individuals.

I have a nine defensive positions on my softball team. I have a catcher, pitcher, shortstop, third baseman, center fielder, and so on. So my catcher cannot play each position. There are certain duties as a catcher, certain capabilities in that position that not everyone on the team can do. Same with center fielder. Same with shortstop. Same with pitcher. So I am thinking this morning what would it look like if we truly stopped being negative about differences and realized that is part of our roles on the team and embraced them? Embraced that your church is different than my church and her church and his church, and that each church fills a role for that person, and each church fills a role in the body of Christ, in moving the gospel out into the world, outside the four walls of the building and into the community, the world.

I am praying today that we see and embrace our team and our positions, and then we work at our position so that God is glorified, not us but the entire team. The entire body looks like a team. Unify Team Jesus, and stop driving wedges in the body that should be united. It's hard to win a game when the team is missing players, or players are playing injured. Encourage. Edify. Unify! Love loud!

41

TOASTY POSTY HOT! Up and a little slow this morning. Had to take my son to airport early and tried to nab some extra sleep when I got back but just tiny catnaps, which makes you feel like you didn't really even sleep. Ha! Heading out to get much done today. My list is growing as summer is shrinking. I wish it didn't work that way, but what I get done, is what happens. Praying today for my brother and his family as this is the anniversary of his son's death. You may not know my nephew's story, but he was a pretty amazing young man and was murdered when he was twenty-three years old. Today, we have candles lit in our home to remember this day, but he will always be remembered in our hearts.

I was reading in Proverbs this morning and came across so much but sticking with this today. "Faithful are the wounds of a friend, but the kisses of an enemy are deceitful" (Prov. 27:6, NKJV).

I can look back on many past relationships in my life, and God has brought me through some hard lessons along the way. I have sought after people before who never had intent on being my real friend but only used me for a time, for what they needed and for their gain. It happened to me a bit when I was younger because I wanted friends and would not always see the situation until I had been stung repeatedly. I remember once when I was a kid, banging on a fence post, and a swarm of yellow jackets came out and stung me. I was running around and screaming and trying to get away from the stings, but they were relentless. They finally got tired of chasing me, I'd run too far away, so they stopped, but I sure had the welts and pain to show for my misfortune. I sure learned not to bang on metal fence posts, but I also learned that the yellow jackets don't stop stinging until they are done.

So today, if you are in some relationships that give you a constant "sting," take a good hard look at the relationship. A true friend will speak words of truth to you in love, and it might have a bite to it, but if you are "friends" with someone and being constantly hurt in that relationship, but they smooth it on the surface like sugar, well, open your eyes. Sugar doesn't make wasp stings or yellow jacket stings better. It tastes good to the tongue but doesn't heal. Flattery from someone who doesn't love you may taste like sugar, but it will be like poison. You will just keep drinking it in because of the taste when it is ruining your body from the inside.

I honestly don't know why I am writing on this today because I am surrounded by some incredible friendships right now in my life, but please know I have lived the rotten end of this. Trust the true ones and run hard and fast away from the yellow jackets. Their kisses hurt. Love loud!

42

SNAZZERIFIC! Up and at it on another beautiful day! Look around at a world full of blessings! May we be the ones with eyes to see all the glorious things about us and not lock eyes on all the negative swirling about us. The negative is always there and will not leave, so may His beauty, His majesty, and His power capture our attention today.

Much to do today and lots of people to see and love on, which makes it good stuff before it even gets rolling. Having lunch with my faves today. All my crew except my honey bear who's gone. It's been too long since we all sat around a table and laughed and shared a meal. Sitting here on the back patio and just truly amazed at how God meets me here each day. How He renews me. How He pours strength and wisdom in me. How my faith has grown leaps and bounds, and I pray is still moving forward. Last thing I want to do is become stagnant or stationary or dry. Sometimes, we can be in such a place and not even realize how starved we were until we move on. So reading this morning in Lamentations, and it honestly just lifted my heart. I know that a lament is generally not a heart lifter, and yet it brings me face-to-face with the reality that God loves me and is more than enough for me despite all my ugly.

> Through the Lord's mercies we are not consumed, because His compassions fail not. They are new every morning; Great is Your faithfulness. "The Lord is my portion," says my soul, "therefore I hope in Him!" The Lord is good to those who wait for Him, to the soul who seeks Him. It is good that one should hope and wait quietly for the salvation of the Lord. (Lam. 3:22–26, NKJV)

As I sit and soak this in, it is like sitting in deep waters when I really take it all in. Jeremiah wrote some of these same things about the Lord's great faithfulness, His new mercies, and His unfailing compassion. I am looking at my swimming pool and thinking about standing in my pool where the water is all around me, deep soaking, deep healing, deep soothing. I woke up this morning to see a God that has a pool full of new mercies for me today—mercies I will need. And they will be all about me, surrounding me and touching every part of my life. He will not fail me. The water will not fail to hold me up, suspend me even if I am heavy and burdened. He does not leave me, does not get busy. The water doesn't forsake me and say, "Hey, we are busy with this other person over here, so we can't surround you right now. We can't hold you up. We are leaving and will be back soon, so hold on."

When I am soaking in the pool, it is constant. When I am in His presence, it is a constant. God is a constant, faithful, and full of mercy and grace. And you and I, friends, are surrounded by it right now, wherever you are. So this morning, I soak in the presence and faithfulness of a God that is bigger and more incredible than anything I could fathom. My hope is in Him because nothing else can offer true hope. Beloved, if you are flailing about in the water and think you are drowning, can't swim, tired of treading water, thinking you are done for and can't do it, rest in Him.

He surrounds you. He is and will hold you up. He will not fail, and He is faithful. He has more mercy than you have mess. I know. I've got enough mess for many. Let go, and stop working so hard on your own, and let Him have you completely, and watch your life change. Your words. Your walk. Your sight. Your heart. Your mind. Love loud!

43

SCOOBER DOO! Up and at it this morning! Loving the sweatfest! What a beautiful morning it is to sit with my Beloved! Had an awesome day yesterday and looking forward to all that God has in store for today! Much to do today, including lunch with a dear and sweet friend along with all the joys of work and time with my kiddos! Working for that forever summer in my life so I can pour out and bless others each and every day.

I was up until one-ish last night in deep conversation with the kiddos about God, about how they love His presence and are just seeking Him more each day, about how we are watching the depth of our love and longing for Him in deeper places, about how we are amazed at the depth of love and mentorship and pouring out of God at our new church home. My boy is surrounded by men of valor who walk deep in faith, not just words but actions, and it shows up in their families, wives and kids, how they lead. Love-late night conversations because I can't get to these places. God leads us there.

So as I rise this morning and camp in Romans 12, I have much to soak in.

> I beseech you therefore, brethren, by the mercies of God, that you present your bodies a living sacrifice, holy, acceptable to God, which is your reasonable service. And do not be conformed to this world, but be transformed by the renewing of your mind, that you may prove what is that good and acceptable and perfect will of God. (Rom. 12:1–2, NKJV)

We have probably all read these verses a hundred times and know it like we know the back of our hand, and yet I was just sitting with a few thoughts this morning. Thinking first about living sacrifice, thinking about offerings and how a sacrifice is supposed to cut a little, dig down a little, not a sacrifice if it doesn't sting a little, and you have to give up something. So as I think this morning about each and every day, what do I sacrifice for Christ? What do I give up? What do I lay aside and say, "For you, Jesus, I will throw it off even if my flesh pulls me." I don't want my every day, every month to turn into a convenience, my following to just be "easy," and my life to just be the same and just for me, living each and every day, minute hour as I am giving up myself empty, pouring out the Suzanne, sacrificing and being filled with Christ.

Thinking about not conforming, not making the "easy" decision because it is popular, because the world doesn't like it when we don't agree, because we want to blend in even though we were called to be set apart. Conforming is easy. So I have to ask myself if following Jesus is easy. Is what I stand for easy? Does it mean that I change what I believe based on who I am around? Do I conform so I have lots of likes on FB or want the crowd to think I'm awesome? Paul calls us to be transformed, changed, different from the inside out.

I think back to one of the early years I lead FCA, and we made shirts that we had printed inside out, tag on the outside, seams on the outside. And on the shirt, it said, "Inside out." Those shirts were always big conversation starters because someone would see the seams or tag and tell you that your shirt was inside out. And then it gave us all the chance to explain what exactly "inside out" meant. So I am thinking that if Jesus changed the world, turned it upside down and inside out, then why is it we want to fit in? Putting myself in that inside out-mind frame today, letting the Spirit renew my mind and keep it fresh and on being inside out for Christ. Walk in your place today with a power of transformation and living as inside out as you are called. Love loud!

44

YAZZLE DAZZLE! Up and at it in the sunshine! Glorious sunshine! Love, love my summer mornings! So much time with my Beloved and with my honey. Just does this heart good. I recently have been on a couple of trips, and I usually end up being the navigator, which is quite humorous if you really know me. I am not a map reader, so my iPhone has become the greatest techy thing I've ever had. When I am driving, I am very aware of where I am and usually watching signs like a hawk. I watch mile markers, exit signs, landmarks—anything that will help me determine where I am and what is around me so that I can recognize where I need to be and what I need to be doing, such as moving lanes, exiting, turning, going straight, and all that jazz.

When I am a rider, I am not as observant, but as a driver or navigator, I am on full attention and taking the job quite seriously. Exit 29b, got it. So this morning, I am reading in the book of Daniel about some of the prophesies.

There are so many prophesies about the Messiah in the Old Testament, and it is always amazing to me that Jesus fulfilled every one of them. But it was interesting to me this morning as I read about the prophecy of seventy weeks to rebuilding the city of Jerusalem and about the angel Gabriel telling Daniel that 483 years after that decree, the Messiah would come. Catch that, 483 years from the time of that prophesy. Exactly 483 years later, Jesus comes to the city of Jerusalem and presents himself to the people as the Messiah (David Jeremiah). This is in Daniel chapter 9. So I am thinking that if I am the driver or navigator and leading the way, the one with the directions in hand, I sure need to be looking for that 483.

I really shouldn't miss it. Not on the phone, not changing radio stations, not talking to someone and fly right by 483, and yet the navigators of the people of Israel, their religious leaders had directions in hand, GPS on, blinking, Siri telling them in her annoying voice, "483, here he is boys," and they missed Him. They studied the Word more than anyone and yet. Whether on purpose or accident and that's not what I'm here to discuss but just that they missed Him. Exactly 483. not 482. not 486 but Jesus hits the mark, 483.

I have friends and family that have all the information in front of them, map in hand and still are missing Him. Can we point the way? Yes. But we cannot make anyone believe or hear us or follow. My daddy used to always say, "You can lead a horse to water, but you can't make him drink." And it is true. We cannot turn people's heart toward Jesus. We cannot make them see, but may we continue to point the way with our lives by what we say and what we do and how we love and pray and trust the Spirit to move them. It is a beautiful thing when He does. So be grateful this morning that you saw the directions, and keep praying and living in such a way that others around you might see the 483 as well. Be a blessing! Love loud!

45

YABBA DABBA! Up and groovin' this morning! Ready for what God has for me today! Day is jam-packed but always room for God in every part. He's like ice cream. No matter how full you think you are and your day is, He fits in all the cracks and crannies and just makes things right. I laugh because I'm not really an "ice cream" girl anymore but used to be. You get the gist.

This morning, I was reading in a few different places in the Bible and camped out in 2 Chronicles for bit. I was reading about Asa and his prayer to God in chapter 14. Asa was up against an army from Ethiopia that was a power house—one million men and three hundred chariots. Asa had an army of 300,000, and from the tribe of Benjamin 280,000. There were some great things in this passage that grabbed me for my walk today. First, the beginning of the chapter talks about all the work that Asa was doing in his kingdom to establish God as the God as well as all the building and fortifying of his cities. Second, when describing the army of Asa and Benjamin, it finishes with "all these were mighty men of valor" in verse 8.

Lastly, when this army that is twice as large as Asa's comes out against him, he doesn't back down and in corner and say, "Poor me," "We're done for," "Now we're all gonna die," or anything along those lines. In fact, he says quite the opposite. He cries out to the Lord,

> And Asa cried out to the Lord his God, and said, "Lord, it is nothing for You to help, whether with many or with those who have no power; help us, O Lord our God for we rest on You, and in Your name we go against this multitude. O Lord, You are our God; do not let man prevail against You!" (2 Chron. 14:11, ESV)

Asa cries out and then states his commitment to God, his confidence in God, and his courage because he knows the Lord is with him and for His people.

So today or any day, when you are up against it, open your eyes and look. Have you established God as your leader and cleaned house of all the other gods? Have you been busy working, establishing and fortifying your home? Where you work? The environments you are in? Are you standing with mighty men of valor and women who are warriors for the kingdom? Or are you standing with ones who are running about, doing the world's business and ways? What is your outlook? Do you see God in all things?

Do you know that He is for you and He is good? Are you confident in Him and your commitment to Him shows because it is who you are through and through and not just what you show up to do once a week?

Is your courage in battle founded in Christ and what He has done for you, in you, and how He has empowered you? Do you have concern for God like Asa, or do you not care if the enemy advances and is gaining ground, possibly your ground? Today, may we be sure of who we stand for and confident of His strength and power. May we face battles that are larger than us, and rise up and know that we are called, but may our confidence be in God and not ourselves, courage in Christ and love of Him, His kingdom. If you are up against it, cry out. He hears you and will respond. His ways and His timing is not always to our understanding, but we can rest and know that we are His, no matter what. What are you establishing today? Be blessed and gain ground. Move forward. Love loud!

46

YABBA DABBA! Up and at it on a muggy morning! Lots to do today! Reading this morning and thinking about wilderness and glory. Sounds weird, I know. Yesterday, I was reading about how John the Baptist was to be in the wilderness until it was time. Jesus went to the wilderness for forty days before He began His ministry. Moses and the Israelites wandered in the wilderness for forty years before entering the promised land. So I know that I have walked through wilderness times in my life, and just like these few examples I gave, much was gained in the wilderness. Not many distractions in the wilderness. Sometimes looking around and wondering why are you here and sometimes knowing why you are here but what are you lacking. Not lacking in a sense of "I need a new car" lacking, but lacking in a sense of I need more quiet or intimate time with my Beloved. More time to hear His voice. More time to listen and not just talk. More time to be alone and have some deep reflection about why I'm in this, and where my heart needs to be.

Sometimes people think that if we are Christ followers, we will not have valleys or sufferings, but that is far from true. But our sufferings do not define us, and that is the difference.

> And since we are His children, we are His heirs. In fact, together with Christ we are heirs of God's glory. But if we are to share His glory, we must also share His suffering. Yet what we suffer now is nothing compared to the glory He will reveal to us later. (Rom. 8:17–19)

Take heart! Love loud!

47

YAPPER DOOZIES! Up and moving! So glad to be home! "Home sweet home" is ringing true in my bones today, even though we had an amazing time with some incredible champions on the cruise. Sitting outside and looking at our red maples having finally changed color and the quiet breezes blowing through them and the egrets soaring around the lake together. What a beautiful scene to come home and experience.

"As you do not know the path of the wind, or how the body is formed in a mother's womb, so you cannot understand the work of God, the Maker of all things" (Eccles. 11:5).

Stood at the front of the ship yesterday with Mark as we sailed over calm waters. Yesterday was probably the calmest day we experienced on the waters during the cruise, and yet standing at the front of the boat and just watching the deep blue rolls. Roll, roll, roll over and over. Thinking about when God came upon the face of the waters and how it must have rolled under Him. It looks so deep and mysterious. Thinking how in Job He speaks of when He created each thing and the mystery of the waters and all they contain. Thinking how we think we have so much knowledge (and we do) and yet there is still so much mystery and undiscovered under the seas and still even places on land that we don't fully have knowledge or eyes have not seen. He is vast. He is deep. He is beyond all we can comprehend. Yet He is love. And in all His vast ways, He desires and takes delight in us. Amazing.

Amazing as I behold all that is before my eyes right now—the beautiful, serene outdoors; the seas that were deep and vast and that were calm and rolling one day and tossing us around another day; the winds that are blowing through the trees, the winds that move the waves and boats and all these things.

And He is in the midst. His thread runs through it all. All connected. Do we understand? No. We don't need to. Behold. Friends, to behold is to receive revelation. May we sit back today and rest in His presence and realize we are in His presence and behold Him. He is beautiful.

48

YEPPER DO! Up and at it in the groggy foggy this morning! My legs are feeling my workout this morning, but today, my hands are also feeling it. Did dead lifts this morning and increased my weight, working to put on some muscle, but my hands are really beginning to get some calluses. I remember when I used to work on hitting back in the day when I played or when I was working with my son on hitting and how we would both get blisters. Maybe they would open up, but eventually, we got calluses from working so much. Today, I am going to be working on our softball field, digging holes, putting in bases, moving more dirt in wheelbarrows, and all that jazz. And you know what? I will get calluses today even if I wear gloves. So I am thinking this morning about God being a God of work. When He created the world, He worked six days then rested. He loves to see us put our hands to work and not sit around and think "we deserve" or "we are owed" something. And so as we roll up our sleeves, we gain so much when we learn to work, much more than just calluses. But our calluses, while painful in the work stage, can produce a place where we are stronger so that the next time we are called to that same labor, we are a little tougher, a little more able to withstand the pain or struggle.

> He said, "Thus says the Lord, 'Make this valley full of ditches.'" "For thus says the Lord, 'You shall not see wind nor shall you see rain; yet that valley shall be filled with water, so that you, your cattle and your animals may drink.'" (1 Kings 3:16–17, NKJV)

So when God speaks to Elisha and tells the king to get his people to dig ditches, He is saying get up and work. Make straight the path. Get up and work. God will meet us where we are at, no doubt, but He expects us to make some roads straight. He expects us to dig the ditches. If the Lord had brought all that water and no one had picked up a shovel to dig, all that water would have been wasted. Or God would not have brought them that miracle. Sometimes, for us to see the miracles, we have to have the faith to dig so God can show up. Friends, such reward when we have the faith that we can put ourselves to work, and God will show up in our midst. Water without ditches is a flood and wasted. Ditches are hard work, sweat, and calluses but the reward is worth the faith. Love loud!

49

SCRAPPY DO DAH! Up and at it this beautiful morning! Whoo! Get out and feel the air and love the weather! As I ran this morning, thinking about all the years I've coached baseball/softball and teaching kiddos. Yesterday, we were working on base running, especially running through first and then breaking it down quick. I have seen lots of types of base runners in all these years, and it had me thinking this morning because my Beloved kept telling me Philippians 3 this morning as I ran, so I had to get home and see what was there. I promise, these verses mesh with the base running thing.

> Brothers and sisters, I do not consider myself yet to have taken hold of it. But one thing I do: Forgetting what is behind and straining toward what is ahead, I press on toward the goal to win the prize for which God has called me heavenward in Christ Jesus. (Phil. 3:13–14, NIV)

So I don't know if you've ever watched kiddos play baseball/softball, but for sure, there are certain things some of them do once they actually hit the ball. Some kiddos hit the ball and just stand there, maybe amazed that they hit the ball, maybe not sure of what to do next, so they just freeze. Some kiddos hit the ball, and they are the ball watchers. They run to first, but they cannot get up to full speed because they are more in tune with where the ball went, and is there a play being made on it. Some kiddos run a good speed, but they have to slow down a little before they reach first because they want to stop on the base. And some kiddos hit the ball and just run all out, not watching anything other than the coach and listening to that voice, running full speed, past the bag, and then breaking it down.

So I am thinking about these base runners in our daily walk today. Some people hear God and are just so amazed that they hear Him speak to them that they just freeze. They stand there and don't move into the action that God has called them to. They are frozen. Sometimes, people hear the Lord and know the path they are called to run, but they are so distracted by the circumstances around them, the looking behind, looking around at the world. World watchers like the ball watchers that they never get up to full speed and frequently get out, don't truly fulfill their purpose in Christ.

Then other times, people hear the Lord and don't get distracted by the world, not a world watcher and yet they have their own agenda in mind, not the agenda of the team, not the agenda of the coach, not God's agenda but a selfish motive. We want to stop on the bag. It doesn't matter what others want. It doesn't matter that we might get out or never fully get up to speed in our calling, but we want what we want. And lastly, there are times where people are keenly focused. Not worrying about what is behind, where the ball went, what the world is saying or doing, not their own agenda and motives but all about Christ's call. These people hear the call, make the connect with Jesus, and are out of the box on fire, heading down the line hard and fast pursuing our Beloved, listening to His voice as He coaches us down the line and not slowing down until after the finish line.

So today, as we rise to greet this world for another day, may we be aware of how we approach this day. May we be aware of what kind of base runner we are today, what kind of Christ pursuer we are today. I want to be out of the box on fire for God! Listening to His voice and not slowing down a lick until I pass the finish line. Today's the day! On fire and pursuing the prize! Love loud!

50

ZAPPER DOODLES! Up and at it this morning! Hit the legs hard this morning and moving like a mean streak. Pursuing this day with some passion! Ready to see what God has in store and encounter Him in the moments, small and big places. Talking with my girls a little bit yesterday made me spend some reflection time at home thinking about passion. One of my prayers for my family this year has been that God would ignite a holy passion within each and every one of us, so I am thinking about the way I am made.

Some people are quiet; some are loud; some let the world step on them; some want to rule the world—all kinds of people in this world for sure. And I know this: God has made me a person full of passion. I don't do things halfheartedly. I don't give just part of myself to whatever the endeavor. I'm an all-in kinda girl, which is funny that we kicked off this year in Advocare with that motto for our challenge. So I am thinking that passion is an action word. Verb. It's whatcha do. So in this short writing on this today, I'm just going to hit a couple of thoughts. Passion moves. Peter is a man of passion. His "feet first jumping into things" gets him into messes sometimes (as I can identify), but he moves with a hungry pursuit of whatever he puts his hand to, even if it's climbing out of a boat into the water to walk to Jesus.

Moving with passion—a passionate person also pursues. Think about David and how he pursues God with all his heart. He is an all-in kinda guy. No "meet me halfway" with David or Peter. I will have time to give more reflection tomorrow, but school mornings cut me short. So today, I am looking at how I coach, how I lead, how I teach, how I reach out, how I meet people and especially my relationships. How am I pursuing God? Am I? May we pursue Him with all we are. All in! No part-time job and no part-time pay on this one. It's big.

> And whatever you do, do it heartily, as to the Lord and not to men, knowing that from the Lord you will receive the reward of the inheritance for you serve the Lord Christ. (Col. 3:23–24, NKJV)

So today, may we chase after God. May we pursue Him with passion with all of ourselves down to the very core of our being. Completely His. I can't get there with a casual, occasional, part-time faith and love and walking. May we all be all in today and move with passion after the only One who is worthy of our hearts! Love loud!

51

ZIPPETY DO DAH! Up and at it this morning! Little wobble in my walk after killing my legs this morning but much needed. It's crazy how quick your body will run back to a weaker form of itself. Just take a couple of days off and see what I'm talking about. Ha! Yesterday was a special day, simply blessed.

So this morning, as I am working out and dying, I thought about how my body runs back to complacency as fast as it can. I took a short run yesterday, about ten minutes, and Saturday didn't want to get up that early on a nonschool day to hit a workout, so I missed Friday and Saturday, and yesterday was light. So my body says, "Slump, clump, easy cheesy. Let's do this 'sit and take it easy' thing." And as I did my workout this morning, it was a good one, but it wouldn't have been that hard on me a few weeks ago. Bringing our body into discipline is an ongoing task. Yes, a task. As soon as we rest a couple of days, then our body is fine and happy with that. Complacency.

And so as this year begins, and January is well on its way. We will all be tested throughout the year. Will we stay faithful to eating right and making good choices? Will we stay the course and keep finding time to get in some type of exercise? Because our bodies and minds will tell us that they are just fine if we don't. They are fine if we get too busy to prepare food, to carve out even fifteen minutes of exercise. Yep. Have I been here. Yes! Each day is a challenge in itself to bring my mind into discipline and my mind to tell my body that it is going to follow suit.

Discipline is not easy. It is hard. It is "every day, every hour" hard. I have been reading in Hosea and Micah about the Israelites who struggled to bring themselves into discipline. Struggle to do what they know they should do, but it is so much easier to do what is convenient. I get it. So get it! So when I apply this to my spiritual life, I don't want a life of convenience and complacency. That doesn't move me in the right direction. That doesn't show up in the world as being any different than the rest of society. Discipline is not easy but so worth it. Sometimes I do it kicking and screaming. Yes! But I am watching my heart change over time to where the discipline isn't as hard anymore.

In fact, it actually becomes a want to but only after time and submission to it. I am looking at Israel as they forgot what it is to be loyal in love. I have been here too, forgetting to put God first in all things and putting myself before Him or others. No discipline sometimes.

So today, if you are in the place where you are trying to stay focused and intentional to changing your body, what you put in it, and how you move it on this week in January, take charge of your mind, will, and emotions. Pull them into discipline, and you will see and feel changes occur, and if you are in a place where you are spiritually struggling to see through the fog, lots of dirty windows, and low visibility, well, clean the windows. Grab a hold of the Word of God, and submit yourselves to what God has to say to us. Then let's be loyal to our love for Him. When we remember our love, it's much easier to be loyal.

So here we go! Time is moving. Grab hold, and keep moving if you are already doing so. Keep firmly planted in discipline. Water it daily. It will grow. If you are spiritually making baby steps forward, then keep moving. Forward is a good direction, no matter how small the steps! Discipline is not easy, but it can be yours. No osmosis. No DNA. No inheritance. Get up and grab it, then go! Have a blessed day, and stay the course, friends! Love loud!

52

SCOOBY-DOO! It's just that kind of up-and-at-it morning! So blessed to be alive and kicking and feeling awesome at forty-nine. Where did the time go? I don't know, but I am going to reflect on the past, learn from it, and move ahead with intent and passion and conviction! Moving with purpose in my life because let's face it, we honestly don't know how many days we have on this earth, but I know when it's all said and done, I don't want to stand before the Lord with a pocket full of wishes. Committing myself to grow in intention each day, living for Him and sharing hope with others.

As you read this, I want to offer you some hope, some freedom, some wake-up call, and see what the Lord has in store. I don't know about you, but I have had places and times in my life where the darkness was so much bigger than me. When the circumstance I was in was more than I could handle, in fact, it handled me—darkness, being alone, struggling, suffering, feeling like a burnt piece of toast.

(Those are not eaten in our house.) This morning, Mark and I are reading in Daniel, and I want to share it with you.

Daniel 3:19–25 is the story about Shadrach, Meshach, and Abednego being cast into the fiery furnace. I want you to see a couple of amazing things. First, they were "bound in their coats, their trousers, their turbans, and their other garments" and the guys who cast them into the furnace were burned up. Talk about hot! In verse 23, as our boys were cast in the fiery furnace, they "Fell down bound into the midst of the burning fiery furnace." And third, King Nebuchadnezzar is amazed to see them. "Look! I see four men loose, walking in the midst of fire; and they are not hurt, and the form of the fourth is like the Son of God."

Well, here we go! Our boys are bound up, tied up, held captive, and in all their clothing, so we know it's gonna be a hot time in the fiery furnace tonight. You ever been there? Let the enemy bind you, completely tie you up with no chance for escape (at least you feel that way)? And as they are cast into the furnace, they fall (oh, and they are still bound). Tied up, falling down, and in a fiery furnace—yep, I think these guys had it worse than any of my yuck and muck and dark places. Could they unbind themselves? No. Could they do the Batman/Robin show and miraculously get untied and beat up the bad guys? No, this is real life. So inside the furnace is where they meet Jesus. Where it is bigger and hotter and more fiery than ever? And there is Jesus. He unbinds them. He sets them free. Are they still in the furnace? Yes. But they are walking in the fire with Jesus, and they are not being burned. Has He rescued me? Oh yes! I have scars from my mistakes, but I am not consumed and burned up, and I look at those scars and remember my mistakes and not to go that road again. Or let the enemy have me like that.

Here's a bonus that I just caught this morning (Yes, I'm slow). King Nebuchadnezzar recognizes the Son of God! I've read this many times and seen that there is a fourth person, possibly "Son of God" stuff but never wrapped my mind around who is doing the recognizing. This guy who is a mess, the guy who threw them in there in the first place, this guy who doesn't celebrate and worship our Lord. Yep, this guy recognizes the Son of God. So I am thinking this morning about all our friends and people walking around in our lives who haven't recognized Him yet. May they come to see Him and know Him this year! May their eyes be opened! "Look!" Just like the king's. He sees men who are free. He sees men who are walking in a fire and not being burned. He sees Jesus. May we live our lives out in front of this hurting and lost world. Are you bound up right now? If so, let Jesus set you free, and through that process and living it out in the fiery furnace with Jesus beside you, others will be enlightened. Jesus doesn't leave us in the hard times. We might not recognize Him, but if the guy who set all this in motion can recognize Him, then others in our lives can too. He frees. He saves. He lives. He enlightens. Give Him the keys, and let Him go to work in your life. Love loud on this beautiful day!

53

YEPPER DO! Up and moving this morning! I love it! Seeing some sun this morning, yay! Oh, how I have missed it! Glad for today and all that is in store! God is beautiful!

I love this morning. As I sit here and look out the windows at the sky, the trees, the water, and how the light is just gently lighting the view. I am thinking back to when Mark and I were dating way back in the day in 1983. I was seventeen years old, and I came to this blazing realization that I loved him. I wrote him love letters, told him I loved him, baked cookies and cakes for him, longed to be next to him. If I could just be in the same room as him, even if he was busy, then I was happy. So today, as I sit across the kitchen table from this man and look at him as he is reading his Bible, well, I'm more in love today than I was when I was seventeen. I know this is the case for people who have long marriages, who in going through the storms and trials and ups and downs and not two pennies to rub together to stairstep kids and all that jazz. That in those places and times is where love grows. Love grows in the cracks and crevices. It abides in the easy places and flows there, but in the nooks and crannies and hard edges is where it is sharpened, and it gains strength. So I am looking at my relationship with the Lord this morning and thinking about how much I love Him but so, so glad that He first loved me and showed me what love looks like.

My love for Him has had the places and times where all is well, and I am so grateful for those times as love is flowing and abiding in me and around me, but I can so recognize how much I value the struggles, the times that I'm in the nooks and cracks and crannies and God's love pours into those, right where I am and fills up those places, and I am left with complete love. I feel what it is like to love wholly. I honestly wish I could say that I recognize this all the time or that I stay filled up with His love, but I fall short. I am so glad for the times I abide there because I know what it feels like and long to get back. I long to sit in the room with my Beloved, even if it is just to be in His presence.

"And we have known and believed the love that God has for us. God is love, and he who abides in love abides in God, and God in him" (1 John 4:16, NKJV).

God's love and ours. Let it be who we are today. Loving others and His presence. Love loud!

54

ZIPPERTY SKIPPERTY! Up and groovin' today! Can you smell it? What you ask? Well, here I stand. It's actually not the first time I've stood here but the biggest time I've stood here as a parent. It is not an easy place to stand, I might add. It's a place I've been in the last few weeks, a place of standing and watching. I am in this place, and maybe you've been here too, watching a door close before my son, a door that he cannot open.

So what is it like to get so close to something that you can smell it? I think about how when I am baking the house fills with the aroma of whatever is in the oven, and if the front door was cracked open, someone standing at our door could smell it too. Well, in this place, I am working through watching my son stand at a door—not just any door but a door that he has dreamed of walking through since he was little, a door that has dreams behind it and a young man that has passionately pursued his dream with fervor and intent and talent, and then to stand so close to the door that he could smell what was on the other side, and then it closed.

I would be dishonest if I said that I have not struggled with all this. I have been on my knees, on my face in all postures and pouring out to the Lord, seeking understanding and yet knowing that there are things that I am not meant to understand or grasp on this side of heaven. I could ask myself all kinds of questions. Maybe I didn't pray enough. Maybe I didn't do this or that, and here we go. Trying to put human parameters to God's plan. Is it easy to watch from this place? No, but it is part of being a parent. I can't change it. He can't change it. But I can rest on the truth that I have hope. I have faith. And I know that God has my son. Period.

I have been doing much reading in scripture through this process and, a couple of weeks ago, came across this: "And to the angel of the church in Philadelphia write: 'The words of the holy one, the true one, who has the key of David, who opens and no one will shut, who shuts and no one opens'" (Rev. 3:7, ESV). And I worship and serve and love a Savior who can open any door, and once He opens it, no one can close it. And He can also close a door that no one can open. I know that God never closes one door without opening another, not always at the exact time He closes one door, but He does provide another way, another path, another opportunity.

So, my friend, if you are in a place where you were standing in front of an amazing door and things were lining up in such a brilliant way that as you stood there you could smell it, and it was amazing, I pray that you get a chance to walk through that door. But if not and it closes on you, do not dismay. We pray for God to show himself in amazing ways. We pray that He will leave us amazed and perplexed, not understanding how He did such an incredible thing. Let us remember that the "perplexed" doesn't just apply when things go the way we want. Sometimes, we are amazed and perplexed by His answer and a door closing. I can say that my son's strength does leave me amazed, and even if he or I don't understand it all, I know that God is shaping him into a man who is strong and passionate for Him. So I know that soon, another door will open, and I will stand and watch him walk through. Love loud!

55

YEPSEE DOODLEY DEE! Up and at it this beautiful morning! Sky is clear and a little breeze. All is quiet. It makes for some good workout/quiet time with my Beloved. Icing on top is having your honey workout with you. So excited and ready for today! Ready to worship! Sitting and soaking in His word today!

This morning, I'm working out and listened to a few songs on my worship playlist, and "Multiplied" by NEEDTOBREATHE comes on. I am standing there, working out and listening deep to the words of song. There is a reason this song is one of my personal favorites.

> Your love is, like radiant diamonds / bursting inside us / we cannot contain / Your love will, surely come find us / like blazing wild fire. singing Your name / God of mercy / sweet love of mine / I have surrendered, to Your design / May this offering, stretch across the sky / These Hallelujahs, be Multiplied.

So I am sharing this with you this morning because this song always, always brings me to my knees. Radiant diamonds bursting inside us we cannot contain. Friends, I have seen with my own eyes, visibly seen the change in someone when they surrender their heart to Jesus. It is not just a walk down the aisle and say a prayer and I'm done. No. Far from it. If there has not been this complete surrender, life will go on as it always has. Oh, but when you see the person change before your very eyes, it is no less than amazing! One cannot contain this shining forth, and they radiate Jesus out of every pore. It is beautiful! I have recently seen this in two dear ones, and I can tell you that it is so visible and beautiful that it makes me cry. His love will chase you down and find you wherever you hide, whatever pit you are in. He will find you. But the question for us always remains is what will we do when He finds us?

Oh friends, when we surrender to his design, the Hallelujahs are multiplied! More lives are touched, changed, surrendered. It stretches across the sky, a horizontal chorus of hallelujahs. It reaches in the deep and dark places where the enemy tries to hide people and keep them under his thumb, but the change in us that radiates forth can find people in the darkness. God does the changing, but we must be faithful to surrender each and every day. We can get distracted, so we surrender again and again, we can radiate His glow and glory, and it penetrates walls, breaks chains, and brings down fortresses the enemy has erected.

How God works in us will always amaze me, but I can tell you that I will never grow weary of seeing His visible change within someone, a change that is within but comes out of us in all we say and do and think. We are so blessed to have a God who loves us so deep that His love can penetrate those walls and sever chains and free us right where we are, and then we shine bright like diamonds for Him. Love loud!

56

ZIPPETY DO DAH! Up and at it this morning! Saw a light show this morning by the wonderful hand of God! Ready for a busy day on campus, and hopefully, I can stay dry today.

I stand amazed at the Lord each and every day. He seems to always find new ways to amaze me or remind me that He is right here. Of recent, we have been dealing with some attacks from the enemy, each and every one of the family in our home right now. We can each recognize it for what it is, and we discuss and encourage and pray for each other during this time. We also know we are being tested as to how we will handle these attacks. I'm not a give-up girl, and yet sometimes, the frustrations loom large. Without a strong family environment and quiet time with the Lord, these seasons would be extremely difficult, and yet I know that in this process, I am growing and moving to a place of stronger faith. It can be foggy, and I can get bogged down in the muck and mire if I am not careful and not diligent to pray and seek deep friendships that pour life and truth into me. I pray I am the same for others.

So yesterday, I was at work and reading in Deuteronomy about blessings and curses. Mark and I have been speaking blessings over our family since these attacks have increased in intensity, and we are standing in faith knowing that God is good, and He is with us. Yesterday, we received an unexpected blessing that was almost more than I could have imagined. It was one of those that makes you cry because it is big and beyond you. Here's the best part: that major blessing came straight on the heels of a huge attack on my husband, a direct attack from the enemy. The kids and I were diligent to pray for Mark and this situation. God shows up, friends.

> The Lord will grant that the enemies who rise up against you will be defeated before you. They will come at you from one direction but flee from you in seven. (Deut. 28:7, NIV)
>
> The wicked flee when no one pursues, but the righteous are bold as a lion. (Prov. 28:1, NIV)

So this morning, stand and be bold! Know that God fights for us! When enemies rise up to strike you or trample you, know that they will be your foot stool. No weapon formed against you will prosper. Be bold as a lion! He is the King, and you are a child of the King! Love loud!

57

YABBA DABBA! Up and at it in the early! First day of school for lots of kiddos! Lots of excitement, lots of hustle and hurry, lots of anxiety, lots of nightmares of traffic flow, lots of "what to wears." But all in all, today will be a great day! New beginnings are great. How do I know this? Because each morning, his mercies are new and fresh and fall on me, which I need, by the way. Sometimes I find myself in a pickle, in a mess, in a "why on earth did I say that?" "Why on earth did I do that?" "Not sure how this will turn out" way, and lots of other situations—situations where I have slipped, situations where I have stumbled, situations where I need a "mulligan," and Jesus meets me in these places every time, and so when I rise in the morning and spend time with Him and in His presence, I realize that I am equipped for the day ahead. Just like a kiddo heading out the door for school who has all the new notebooks, pencils, pens, new shoes, and all that good stuff, I too am ready. Having to pray this morning to be on guard. To put on His armor. To guard my thoughts, words and actions and to be His in every way... to bring praise and honor and glory to Him.

I don't always get that right, so I need those new mercies. I rise to a fresh new day. I am a new creation and ready to not only receive His grace and mercy but pour it out on others. Honestly, because you might need a "mulligan" as much as me, some days. Friends, if you need a "do over" or a "mulligan," that amazing grace is found at the feet of Jesus each and every day. Fresh and new. So this morning, if you are looking at your yesterday like me and finding some rough patches, today is fresh and new. Be guarded in all you think, do and say. And lavish His love and grace in all the places you walk. Love loud!

58

SCOOBER DOODLES! Up and at it this morning! Great workout and heading out the door for some getting stuff done tonight! Ready for all the Lord has in store on this amazing day!

Been having some great conversations in our home about discernment, about wisdom, about God's power of healing and restoration and love. Always love all the insight and things shared. Always love that no one in our home thinks we have all the answers but that God and His righteousness holds the answers but always lots of discussion that bring good things to light.

> When wisdom enters your heart, and knowledge is pleasant to your soul, discretion will preserve you; understanding will keep you, to deliver you from the way of evil, from the man who speaks perverse things, from those who leave the paths of uprightness. (Prov. 2:10–13, NKJV)

I have done much writing on wisdom, not because I am this incredibly wise person, although I daily pray for wisdom but because of all the places the Bible speaks of wisdom and what wisdom looks like. Things of this world are temporary and fleeting. Things of folly are things that are worldly, and yet each one of us can get caught up in these areas. We can hear the calling of folly and not even realize we are slowing inching toward her until we are in her gates and on her porch. She calls and pulls in subtle ways. If she is too brash and loud, she will draw in just the lost and wandering, but she instead will sometimes whisper and be subtle as to pull the righteous one off course, one step at a time over and over. Just a little here, just a little there. And so folly doesn't need to shout at us, for she is clever and subtle.

She may call to our lusts, our fleshly desires, our pride, our selfishness (which is pride), our things we do in secret. She is clever, and so wisdom must enter our heart. Wisdom is what saves us from the calls and guiles of folly. Wisdom is beautiful as she gives us the discernment to see with clarity the subtle ways of folly, and she preserves us. Wisdom gives our heart vision, and faith puts the feet to that vision. So today, if you have been in a place that you wish you never travelled, a place off the path of unrighteousness, at the gates or in the home of folly, all is not lost.

Our God is a God of redemption and restoration. Our God is a God of healing and power. Our God is a God who will pour out wisdom upon you, into your heart so that you may see where you are standing, and if it is in folly, then turn and run the other way, and our feet of faith will help us rise out of that folly home and move out the door and out the gates and back to the path of righteousness. So may we ask for wisdom today. May we seek godly wisdom. It is the only true wisdom. Love loud!

59

HOPPETY BOPPETY! Up and at it this morning! Sun is up, and I am groovin'! Much to get done today and some celebrations as well—work stuff and home stuff. The list doesn't get shorter no matter how late I stay up. Moving to make some changes to that situation. Ready for all the Lord has in store for today and so excited!

Yesterday, I was talking with a dear one, and they have been under some strong attacks from the enemy recently. We talked and prayed, and I know that brings peace, and yet there can still be wounds from the hurt. Healing takes not only time but also takes the Lord and some complete submission. The enemy hasn't changed in all these thousands of years. He is the father of lies. He comes to steal, kill, and destroy. He walks about like a roaring lion (*like* because we all know the real lion is, the lion of Judah). He wants nothing more than to separate you from God's love and truth. The enemy is timely in his attacks. He comes to hit us when we are weary and worn, and he comes to attack when we are getting ready to step into a great calling. So this morning, I am still camped out in Nehemiah and the building of the wall.

> Then Judah said, "The strength of the laborers is failing, and there is so much rubbish that we are not able to build the wall." And our adversaries said, "They will neither know nor see anything, till we come into their midst and kill them and cause the work to cease." (Neh. 4:10–11, NKJV)

And so the adversaries come when we are weak, when we are distracted and surrounded by other tasks, when we aren't expecting, when we are up to kingdom work. The enemy plans to attack you and destroy you so the work of God will cease and so that all the influence and life and truth of God you are bringing to this broken world will not happen. And so he stays predictable and yet he still catches us off guard at times.

> Verse 14 And I looked, and arose and said to the nobles, to the leaders, and to the rest of the people, "Do not be afraid of them. Remember the Lord, great and awesome, and fight for your brethren, your sons, your daughters, your wives, and your houses." (14)

The enemy turned away at this point as they heard that Judah was aware of their plan and that God had brought their plan to nothing, so they didn't attack. And so the plan proceeded that half the men would build the wall, and half the men would stand armed and ready to fight. So often, we can get discouraged in these seasons of attacks, and yet I love this divide and conquer. I love how the Lord shows up when we pray. I love how Nehemiah kept a guard up and proceeded with building the wall. That strikes a deep blow to the enemy. Now we are guarded, and we are able to continue in our work and calling despite what the enemy planned to do. So if you are in a place of attack right now, don't forget how mighty and great and awesome your God is.

Don't forget that if He has called us to something, then He will equip us for that calling and give us legs to stand in that calling and in that attack, but we must remember we can't get caught up in the attacks in the words of others, in the circumstances, in the mess, in the battle. Our focus must be on the greatness of our God and in that place we will battle and stand.

"Resist the devil and he will flee" (James 4:7). Give him reason to run. He has no hold on you unless you don't stand with sword in hand. Like a lion is not a lion. Like anything is not the full and completeness of what it is *like*. Remember the awesome power of God. There is no other! Love loud!

60

YABBA SKADDABA! Up and at it this morning in the humidity! Giving a shout out to my honey who has been up working out with me every morning (no matter how early) for the last three weeks! Way to go! So proud of you! Ready to get things done today! Had an amazing night last night of being poured into by some incredible women. Iron sharpens iron.

So this morning, I am reading in Ephesians and Nehemiah, thinking on building.

"And in Him you too are being built together to become a dwelling in which God lives by His Spirit" (Eph. 2:22, NIV).

So reading in Nehemiah about all the things that happened and put in place to rebuild the wall, about plans, about how certain people were negative were not put to work on the wall because they were shrinking back, about how people worked on the wall close to their home, and all the details that went into this rebuilding process. So today, we have been born in sin. We are sinners, and yet once we have Christ in us, we are being rebuilt. We are being built together in community. We are being raised up for a purpose and a time. We are building and fortifying the walls close to our homes. If we are diligent, we are building up ourselves, placing people of godly influence around us and our families, placing the no-showers to the side, placing the naysayers to the margins, placing the people that speak truth and encouragement and power into our lives right next to us.

Friends, we are all in process, in the building process. We can build up walls that keep people out or fear in. We can build up others. We can build up idols and worship empty things. We can build up our love for others and empathy. So this morning, may we remember that we are building, and we are in process of building ourselves together, building ourselves to be a temple where Christ dwells, building lives that impact and influence others for the kingdom. You are building right in your own place not in a far-off land but right where you are. What are you building for? Love loud!

61

ZIPPY SKIPPY! Up and at it this morning! Ready for all the Lord has in store for this glorious day. How do I know it will be glorious? Because I know who sits on the throne and who rules and reigns in my heart so that things may come crashing down around me, but I will rest and be settled in Him. So a glorious day it is! Much on my heart about my family and all the things I see God doing in each one of them—my honey and each of the kids—and I have so much to be thankful for and so much to continue in prayer about. This morning, I read the verse of the day and soaked on it a bit during my workout, and then when I came in, I asked the Lord to show me what He wanted to reveal today before I opened His word, and it ties beautifully to the verse of the day.

> But from everlasting to everlasting the Lord's love
> is with those who fear Him, and His righteousness
> with their children's children—with those who keep

His covenant and remember to obey His precepts. (Ps. 103:17–18, NIV)

And Solomon loved the Lord, walking in the statutes of his father David, except that he sacrificed and burned incense at the high places.

> At Gibeon the Lord appeared to Solomon in a dream by night; and God said, "Ask! What shall I give you?" And Solomon said, "You have shown great mercy to Your servant David my father, because he walked before You in truth, in righteousness, and in uprightness of heart with You; You have continued this great kindness for him, and You have given him a son to sit on his throne." (1 Kings 3:5–7, NKJV)

So this morning, I sit as a parent, thinking of what kind of legacy am I leaving to my children? I am a praying momma, but am I walking in righteousness? Am I walking upright? In truth? So as David obeyed the Lord's precepts and had a heart that chased after God, so he leaves blessing upon blessing to the next generation. So as it reminds us, "with their children's children," on down the family line. We can pass many, many things on to our children and grandchildren, but our question today is what do we want to carry down through the generations? Pain? Addiction? Laziness? Complacency? Gentleness? Love? Compassion? Giving? Faithfulness? Greed? The list is endless, and so we must ask ourselves what we are speaking over our children and loved ones, into them, about them, and praying over them? Are we calling out the best? Are we on our knees in fervent prayer and living out our calling?

David, while a broken man, was a man who loved the Lord deeply and sought to do His will and he left a legacy for years to come. His obedience and righteousness gave his son the blessing of having the Lord ask him what he wanted, and it would be given. I know that I have received so many of the blessings in my life because of the prayers of my parents and probably even grandparents. And so I desire to bless my children and grandchildren as I walk and live and I pray that I am walking in truth and love and righteousness before a loving and merciful God. Bless your family. Leave a legacy of obedience and love, and watch God show up on down the line. Love loud!

62

SCOOBER DEE DO! Up and rolling slow this morning! Great day back at school yesterday seeing all the beautiful people I work with and getting out and coaching. Been awhile. Ready for another day of learning and teaching.

I got much going on in my life right now, and to say my plate is full would probably be an understatement. I think the biggest struggle I have in seasons where my plate is overloaded is that I don't do everything with the level of excellence that I expect from myself, so I wear myself down quickly, and I get frustrated. Had a word spoken over me yesterday, and part of it was that I am always running, and I need to slow down. Working on that part too.

So as I am talking about the fact that I am always going ninety miles per hour, and I am not a rester, it is just part of my DNA that I struggle in the area of patience. I have grown leaps and bounds in this area, but I am still someone who is driven and wants to get things accomplished so when something moves slow, I am not the best "sitter."

This morning, reading in 1 Peter, something just came alive for me. God says, "Hello, Suzanne. Do you see this? I am talking to you." Haha!

"When God's patience waited in the days of Noah, while the ark was being prepared, in which a few, that is, eight persons, were brought safely through water" (1 Pet. 3:20, ESV).

As I read this, I am seeing that God has patience—God, the God, the only God, the God of the universe that can make anything happen at any time He wants. He is patient. What? Haha! Yes! So the Lord, who gives Noah the instructions for building the ark, sits and waits on it to be carried out. He is patient. He waits for the building to be completed so that He can save people. He can bring us through the waters. So this morning, if you are in a place where you have been waiting, stay. Be patient. God is patient. Noah was working and being obedient to what God had called him to do down to the last little detail, and in that obedience and God watching and being patient, Noah was saved. Noah and his family were brought through the waters. They did not perish. Did not get swept away and overtaken. Ridiculed? Yes. Mocked? Yes. But when the waters came, which they always do, will you have proved out obedient?

And to think that Our Father is patient. He waits for us. He doesn't want us to perish. So if He, who can move and do all things can be patient when He doesn't have to be, I think I can do a better job of resting and being patient as well. Have a blessed day! Love loud!

63

YEPPER DOODLES! Up and back at it this morning! Back to working out in the dark but still beautiful! Kicking off some on campus working and meetings today, then first game of the season today. Ready to see what these ladies can do!

Reading in Ephesians this morning and just thinking about how much of my life has been devoted to "team." Whether it has been as an athlete on a team, a coach leading a team, a mom building a team (family), a member of church, body of Christ, leader in business, wherever! So many facets of all our lives move around being together. God wanted us to be community, and yet sometimes, it can be difficult because we are not all the same. We can move differently, look differently, act differently, think differently and so on, and yet we are called to be together and function as one body. So I am reading in the fourth chapter and thinking about being held together.

> From whom the whole body, joined and held together by every joint with which it is equipped, when each part is working properly, makes the body grow so that it builds itself up in love. (Eph. 4:16, ESV)

So Christ is the head of the body, and we are each one, parts that are meant to function all together. That doesn't mean the same way or moving exactly the same, and yet the overall function of the body should be unified. I was struck by "joined and held together by every joint with which it is equipped, when each part is working properly." The body has different types of joints—ball and socket, hinge, pivot, saddle, gliding, and more. And each joint, though it moves differently, it joins and holds together as well as moves the body to function properly.

So Christ is our head, and we get so hung up sometimes that some other part is moving differently than our part. We don't like it. It just can't happen that way, don't they understand, and on it goes. We forget that God has not only created each part to function and carry out a certain purpose but that the way that part moves and operates within the body is all part of the plan as well.

Christ should be the glue that holds us all together—the joints, not only the head. He determines the way the part moves and functions, and then if operating within the purpose it was created, then the whole body can carry forward. A gliding joint cannot and will not operate the same way as a ball and socket. So may we set aside the fact that all parts are not the same, and all parts do not operate the same, but all parts when working properly will glorify Christ. Don't get caught up on the differences today. Glorify Christ as the body moves as one! Love loud!

64

YEPPER DEPPERS! Up and at it this Friday morning! Work 'em out and heading out of town today. Still need to pack, so better get moving!

Woke up last night with four *W*s on my heart—want, work, wait, will. Thinking about what each one of them entails and not enough time to write on all four this morning but going to touch on will. God's will. There have been times in my life where I have wanted, times I have worked, times I have waited, and times I have been in God's will. I have chased after wants, solely things that I desired, not for the gain of anyone other than myself. I have worked my tail off for things, things that would be good for me, good for my family. I have also spent time waiting, waiting for what I worked for, waiting for what I wanted, and best of all, waiting for what God wanted to call me toward.

I can tell you that we can want, we can work, we can wait (and sometimes it seems like forever) for something, but when we seek His will for our lives above everything we want, work, or desire, then things can line up. That doesn't mean easy. That doesn't mean no bumps or waiting. What it does mean is perfect peace in the situation. Not trying to make His will happen for us but resting in His will, knowing that He has us, and we can trust Him, and if we truly trust Him, then we won't press and push and force and make it fit in our package.

We might have a tiny box of dreams, and God has a huge box for us, but we can only conceive so much. Without trusting His will, we will always limit ourselves because we limit God. So even patience in the waiting shows Him that we trust Him, His will, and His timing, and His placement completely. Walking in His will is what I want for my life these days. I don't want to push my agenda. I have dreams, yes, but they are dreams that God has called me to and continues to reaffirm in my life. I only received these when I stopped pressing the Suzanne agenda and desires.

The dreams and plans He has shared with me are so much bigger than me, so full of blessing others that I am overjoyed because that honestly is mine and Mark's heartfelt desire for our marriage and for our family generationally. So this morning, if you are pressing and trying to break through, nothing wrong with want or work or waiting, but stay in His will, and watch the Lord work for you. Love loud!

65

ZIPPER DEE DO! Up and at it this morning! Moving and groovin' today! Much on my heart and mind about choices and desires.

Thinking this morning about being hungry. There aren't many times these days that I get physically hungry like my stomach is growling, and I'm ready to eat a side of beef. Mostly these days, my body is conditioned as to what time I usually eat, and since I eat about six times a day, I can feel when it's time to eat, but I don't know hunger like people in third-world countries know hunger. I was thinking about since we live mostly on appetite today here in America, we can get conditioned. We can grow complacent and just eat pretty much whenever we want so we don't experience hunger.

So I was thinking about when we walk through our daily lives, what do we really long for? What do we hunger for? Is it just a passing feeling, just a wish, just a want to, just a tiny temporary fix for today? So often I have discussions with young people that say they want something and yet they don't hunger for it. They want to nibble, or they want to be a picky eater and just choose the parts of life they like and then throw away the "work" areas.

They want someone to bring room service to their door. They want someone else to cook, feed, and clean up. I say this not because I have never been in this place because I have, but I learned at a young age that if I wanted something, I had to get up and go after it. And was my want a hunger or a wish?

> I spread out my hands to You; my soul longs for You like a thirsty land. (Ps. 143:6, NKJV)
> Blessed are those who hunger and thirst for righteousness, for they shall be filled. (Jesus' words) (Matt. 5:6, NKJV)

I was looking at myself and asking what am I hungry for? I have a few things on my list that I am fast and relentlessly pursuing, but honestly, I am not pursuing anything as deeply as I am pursuing my Beloved, my time with Him in prayer, in His word, to listen, to see Him in others, to speak what He puts in my heart. I hunger for Him. He truly does fill us. I was reading in Deuteronomy chapter 11 this morning.

> And it shall be that if you earnestly obey my commandments which I command you today, to love the Lord your God and serve Him with all your heart and with all your soul, then I will give you

> rain for your land in its season…I will send grass in your fields for you livestock that you may eat and be filled. (Deut. 11:13–15, NKJV)

I love that! We know it to be true, and yet some days, we hunger and pursue things that will never fill us, not completely. They will be like food that passes through the body a temporary filling. But loving God with all that we are fills us, brings us to a place where we desire what He desires. We wake up hungry for Him, and if we hunger for Him, then we know that He will fill us.

May we prioritize those things we are hungry for, and put God not only at the top of what we long for but mingled in with all the other things we pursue. He deserves not only top place in our lives but to be in the midst of all we say and do. His presence is perfect. Love loud!

"I am the Lord your God, Who brought you out of the land of Egypt; Open your mouth wide, and I will fill it" (Ps. 81:10, NKJV).

66

SCOOBER DEE DOODLES! Up and moving slow this morning! Gracious! Need to get rest to keep my body moving!

Thinking this morning about what a joy it is to know the Lord. What a joy to walk close, to read His word that speaks to me, to spend time talking with Him and listening to Him, just a joy to be in His presence. I think about how amazing He is, about all the things He has done. I am reading part of Job this morning and thinking about the power of God on display, about who He really is and how often we forget how big and mighty He is, and we brush Him aside. We somehow think, without really meaning to, that He can't do something or something is too much. We might not speak it but somehow the fact that we don't expect Him to show up is making Him tiny. We don't expect miracles. We expect the mundane. We expect the every day. I want to go throughout my day expecting miracles, expecting God to show up.

> For you formed my inward parts; you knitted me together in my mother's womb. I praise you, for I am fearfully and wonderfully made. Wonderful are your works; my soul knows it very well. (Ps. 139:13–14, ESV)

The verses continue on and talk about our frame not being hidden when we were being woven together and that our days are written before we were formed. I have a bachelor's degree in kinesiology, so I have learned much about the human body and movement of the body, about how absolutely amazing it is, and how intricate and finitely detailed. God doesn't miss a detail in making us. He doesn't take shortcuts. Everything He does is with excellence and intent and purpose. So as we stand and walk and breathe and eat and sit and throw or catch or climb stairs or climb rocks or jump or score of other things, our bodies were designed to do these.

We can do them without thinking about how amazing our bodies are, and yet may we sit back sometimes and enjoy the miracle of the human body. I have always loved this chapter, but I want to pull out part that most people run over without thinking. "Wonderful are your works; my soul knows it very well." Beautiful. As we walk about in our miracle bodies and behold the miraculous intricacies all about us each day, our soul knows it very well.

We may deny that God is in the details. We may ignore that He is in every single thing created, but our souls know it very well, and so our soul will keep calling to us to find Him and run to Him. Our bodies and minds might deny and look in lost places to fill the voids and empty places, but our souls know His wonderful works very well. Let us open our eyes to see, and let our souls soak in the joy of knowing God's wonderful works and miracles are all about us, including us. Have a miraculous day! Love loud!

67

SKIPPER DO! Up and at it in the beauty! Some days, I feel like I'm a "struggle-o-lumpus" like I'm living in a struggle. Ha! Yet worry does not hold me or burden me.

> And after you have suffered a little while, the God of all grace, who has called you to His eternal glory in Christ, will himself restore, confirm, strengthen, and establish you. (1 Pet. 5:10, ESV)

Goodness! Much-needed good word today! Thinking about some things, I am in the midst of at this moment and holding fast to this truth. In 1 Peter, here I find that while we have suffered a little, God will restore, confirm, strengthen, establish us. I don't know about you, but in such a place of trials and suffering, I am dealing with some struggles. I find such a peace and comfort in reading the Bible. God is a God of restoration, bringing us back to a place "like new" but even better. Why? Because now we have the experience, and when God restores, He always goes above and beyond just returning to the original state. I don't know about you, but being confirmed is a big deal. Talking with a dear friend Dori Phillips awhile back when we were both not sure of where all the ministry stuff was leading, she said that being affirmed by your pastor before you take on a role in ministry is important. Love that!

A pastor who affirms His people called into ministry so God will confirm us, stand behind us, back us, assure us of who we are in Him and that we are His. He validates us. Love that God strengthens me. When I am too weary and worn, His strength finds me and fills me. Not just a smidgen but He pours in enough to get the job done and then to continue standing—a God of abundance and provision, not just squeak by.

Lastly, He will establish me. Gracious. I am watching this whole scenario play out in another area of my life, and I can honestly tell you this is the order. And to watch God establish you, it's breathtaking. Why? Because it is something you couldn't do on your own no matter how hard you tried. You could try your best to lace it all up and even tie it in a pretty, neat bow and just sit back and watch it unravel before your very eyes. Oh! But when God reaches down to establish you, then the foundations of the earth cannot shake or move what He has brought together. He establishes His plan.

So if you are in a struggle like me today—waiting, waiting, waiting—and things you are counting on are letting you down, step back and see the big picture. If you are doing His work, then He is letting you wrestle a little bit like Jacob in the night. But the payoff is coming. God is establishing you, friends. Count on Him. Love loud!

68

FLUFFY DO DAH! Up and at it in the sunrise this morning! Heading out early to serve locally today. Always does a heart good. I don't do it near as much as I desire but love when I'm in it.

There is a general rule in our home. When you hear Mom blow drying her hair, don't come in. I am deaf in that moment and can't hear your knock or your voices. I am naked because I'm hotter than a firecracker after a shower and then a hot blower. Therefore, if you make the mistake of coming in the bathroom to grab something you forgot or to ask me a question, well, the show *Naked and Afraid* is applicable. I am naked. You will run away, afraid. There. I thought of the title of that show long before it came out. Lived it. I'm a having a little fun, but I also have had times in my life where I have been naked before the Lord. I held on to things that I thought were too painful to bring up, too ugly to share, too much dirt, too much shame.

I would have to come face-to-face with what I feared the most, and that was what I thought God would think of me. Misguided thoughts that somewhere along the way, forgetting about the power of the cross, forgetting that Jesus forgives and died for my sins, not just everyone else's sins, thinking somehow that my sins were bigger and nastier than anything Jesus could forgive. How could He love me? Me? And in those lies, I was negating the power of the cross. I was, without intending to, saying that my sins were so great that not even Jesus could erase them. Oops. Yep, that is what that says, and yet so often, we are so steeped in the enemy's lies that in our shame, we can't even see the truth that is staring us in the face.

So I finally found such peace in laying myself bare before God, in humbling myself, in recognizing that sharing with Him was the beginning of my healing and change, and I didn't need to be afraid of lying bare but that I could trust Him with it all, even the dirty, filthy rags in the back corner of the hidden closet behind three doors—even there.

"And no creature is hidden from His sight, but all are naked and exposed to the eyes of Him to whom we must give account" (Heb. 4:13, ESV).

So this morning, if you are living in a dark place and trying to hide, get naked. Yep. You heard me. Get naked before the Lord, and give Him all the junk! He can handle it. He will love you through it! I promise. Love loud!

69

HOPPETY DO DAZZLE! Up and at it on this fine summer day. I'm looking forward to spending some time with my honey today. God is good. Always. So this morning, I am thinking about God being with us, in us, all about us. I am thinking about how I can run about my day and miss His presence if I am not careful. I can forget that He is with me. I was reading this morning in Ezekiel and a few other places and wanted to share:

> And the name of the city from that day shall be: the Lord is there. (Ezek. 48:35, NKJV)
>
> Have I not commanded you? Be strong and courageous. Do not be frightened, and do not be dismayed for the Lord your God is with you wherever you go. (Josh. 1:9, NKJV)
>
> Be strong and courageous. Do not fear or be in dread of them, for it is the Lord your God who goes with you. He will not leave you or forsake you. (Deut. 31:6, NKJV)

And gracious, I know there are countless places in the Bible where God speaks and tells us that He is with us or Jesus reminds us of the same thing. But I can tell you that there have been times in my life when I've been skipping along and then something major happens, and I find myself broken and on my knees. There have been times where I forgot He is with me everywhere, every moment, every circumstance, every you name it. I can forget to look around and see Him in the nature and beauty around me. I can forget that even when I am driving on the freeway in traffic and my neighbor cuts me off, I can forget that they are also created in His image, and the world is not all about me and my schedule.

I can forget that when someone hurts me or says something unkind that He has me in it, and His words about who I am in Him are what and where my focus needs to be, not on the negative. I can forget that He is there when my circumstances are huge and looming large over me. No, for me, I find it easier to lean in hard in those times. My struggle is can I see He is there in my day to day, my minute by minute, busy, scurrying about, chores, to-do lists, and work kind of days.

Yep. It is such a blessed reassurance that He is there in all the hard times and times we are struggling to keep our head above water. Yet I find complete resting faith in the fact that He is here with me right now and the next moment and that this day won't pass without Him being right here. May we stand outside the door of our homes and look forward and say, "The Lord is there." May we walk into our jobs today, each day, and say, "The Lord is there." May we not forget The Great I Am is past, present, and ahead of us. May we just have the eyes and tender heart to see and feel Him with us, in us. Take hold of your path today wherever it leads and see. The Lord is here. Love loud!

70

YABBA DABBA! Up and groovin' this morning! I'm ready to be back on campus today and not traveling in a car, although I did enjoy driving out of town despite the weather. Ready for all God has in store for today! Already enjoying the view of fog on the lake this morning.

So I am thinking this morning about promises, about God's promises. He is faithful. He is truth. He doesn't lie or deceive. So we can trust, right? So easy to say, and yet at times in my life, I have struggled to walk it out well. I'm a slow learner and am in a place now where I know that some promises are not meant for my "now" but later, and may I work while I wait and may a stand in faith knowing that He delivers on His word. Faithful but thinking this morning about Abraham and his promise of a son. A promise that he believed and yet thought he was supposed to "help" God out and speed up the process, but finally, God delivers. Isaac is born to Sarah—a promise kept, a promise that had feet and ran about, a promise that brought such joy, overwhelming joy. I can imagine that when Abraham hugged him, he thought he might squeeze him too hard. So in love and amazed.

I can imagine he watched him play, so proud of him, smiling so big he was probably laughing out loud. God had delivered and in such a beautiful way, better than anything Abraham could have imagined. Then I read this verse this morning and want to camp here with your heart for a moment:

> Then God said, "Take your son, your only son, Isaac, whom you love, and go to the region of Moriah. Sacrifice him there as a burnt offering on one of the mountains I will tell you about." (Gen. 22:2, NIV)

And here we are. God tells Abraham, "Take your son, your only son whom you love." Such powerful words! God could be casual and tell him to take Isaac with you up the mountain, and there you will sacrifice him, but God pulls all the heartstrings and reminds Abraham just how valuable and who Isaac is to him. Isaac is the seed through which Abraham will be the father of many nations. And here stands the Lord telling him to take his most beloved promise and lay it on the altar. Sacrifice his promise. Lay it down. Even beyond that, God does not have someone else to put the knife in their hand to kill Isaac, but He has Abraham himself raise the knife. Kill a promise that was spoken by God seems crazy, seems impossible to imagine.

But somewhere down deep, Abraham might have held on to Isaac a little tighter than he should have. He might have had such a tight-fisted grip on him that His Father was a little less in his heart. Just maybe. Just maybe God was revealing something to each one of us about His promises. He is faithful to deliver, but all things operate in His time and for the benefit of His kingdom. When we let go of those promises, when we stop trying to control the outcome, when we truly lay it on the altar of God and let Him have the promise, sacrifice our promise to the very One who spoke it into existence, then we find our promise can grow. Our promise reaches a new level of fulfillment and God knows where our heart is, and we know where our heart is too tightly holding a promise to the point of worship. So open your hand and let it go.

So today, if you are holding on to a promise that God has spoken in your heart, don't white-knuckle grip it and not let it breathe. Lay that promise on the altar of sacrifice, and God will do some amazing things with that promise. Do you imagine that Abraham had any idea how massive the promise "Father of many nations" meant? God can do more with tiny seeds and promises if we leave them on the altar of sacrifice. Let go. It is His promise, and He is faithful. Love loud!

71

SNAZZLES DAZZLES! Up and running under the trees this morning. God has my steps ordered, so I am marching through the day knowing I am His with each step.

So honestly, where my heart has been is on the reveal of the tree image that God gave me the other day—the fallen tree in the woods that I wrote about. I have been listening to many conversations round and about and always looking at things people post on social media. I am thinking about the state I was in when I was the fallen tree in forest—fallen, bug infested, slowly rotting away with no chance of raising myself back up or putting new life back in dead wood. I remember the subtlety of the enemy. He didn't come in with chainsaws after me. I would have recognized that. No, he came at me with tiny messages about my unworthiness—tiny, creepy, crawly things that slowly invaded my body and my mind, turning my outlook, turning my mind-set, capturing my thoughts and attitude. Invasion.

The world tells us it's okay to have sex with whoever, whenever, wherever as long as you "feel" something for that person. The world tells us it's okay to hurt others if they were going to hurt you, or if they hurt you. The world tells us it's okay to say whatever you want and speak however you want based on your emotions and what goes through your mind.

The world tells us that our lives are our own; live how we want and little else matters. The world says we are our own gods because we are the ones with the final say, and we are in control of what we do and say so we have no one to whom we are accountable. We rule. And so these creepy, crawly messages can soak in and infest a sound mind, a mind not guarded, a mind that has slipped too far away from the truth and too close to worldview. It is easy to do, and it is easy to lay on that forest floor and wish life was more. And while it is easy, it is painful. It is painful because you can, somewhere down deep, know that you were created for more, and yet the struggle and question of how to rise can be daunting.

So we lay there, and the world infests us, and before long, we no longer look like who we once were, but we are a spitting image of worldview, and truth is being eaten away by the worldview/enemy that invades us daily. I know this place. I have lived here. I have watched others visit here. I have watched as some stay on the forest floor longing for more but not ready to give up all the world is offering—

death and infestation. Sounds enticing, right? Rotting away our valuable time and lives, living a life that is a gift, and we lay rotting on the forest floor, fallen victim to worldly things and the enemy's flashy false promises. This is a dark place to lay. It is not a place we have to stay.

"No love of the natural heart is safe unless the human heart has been satisfied by God first" (Oswald Chambers).

So let us put our minds on things above, not on earthly things. Let us lift our eyes and hearts to the one that is the Word and the Truth and the Way. Resurrect us? Yes. Redeem us? Yes. Restore us? Yes. Renew us? Yes. So our question is why would we continue to lay on the floor in filth and lies when the Truth is before us and offers abundant life? Only you can answer for you. Where have you placed your heart? Whose hands? I promise you it is in someone's hands. Who will guard it and protect it and love you? Only one Lord. Who is like our God? None. Love loud!

72

SCOOBER DO! Up and at it this morning! Ready to be back in the groove today! Really, really ready for my honey to be home! This week looks to be busy like most weeks, like most of us, so may we get after it!

I had an incident this morning with Snicker's food bowl, enough of one that I had to share. This process of growing my hair out and waiting for it to get "useable" is quite a struggle within itself but to get to this morning. I do not own a straightener, but I decided I would give it whirl this morning and went up the stairs in the dark to turn on Jess Ricketts's straightener. I did not bother to turn on the lights as most of the house was dark, and my eyes were adjusted. After some time, I headed back upstairs to use the straightener, and as I left her bathroom, remember the rest of the house is quite dark. I was hustling, and my foot found the edge of the dog bowl, which proceeded to flip up and pound my shin, and tripped me at the edge of the stairs, no doubt. I grabbed the banister, which kept me from tumbling, but I can assure you that no matter how much I work out, I found new muscles this morning that no Anatomy book has named yet. They were undiscovered. But I now know where they are. I feel them.

I am sure this would have been quite a sight to watch, and I was laughing after the pain went away. Shin has a big knot, bleeding, and new muscle soreness I had not expected. Quite an adventure to start the morning, all for straight hair. Too much trouble, I've decided. Haha! Anyway, despite all the funny and the pain, I can honestly say that I have spent time in my life thinking, "I know the way," or "I can see well enough to navigate this," and do you know what has been the overwhelming result of times when I've lived like this? Dog bowl in the shin, bleeding, almost falling down a flight of stairs, and finding new soreness and muscles I never knew existed.

It is amazing what light can do! Illuminate our path. Help us to see obstacles and objects we were not meant to encounter if we only use the light to guide us. Jesus is the light of the world. He lights our path set out before us, but we can choose to remain blind or close our eyes to where and what He is leading us toward. A little light would have helped this morning. A lot would have made this whole adventure totally avoidable. May we walk through our day not only with our eyes open, but remembering the light is within us. Don't hide it under a basket. It is meant to shine! Love loud and shine today!

73

YEPPER DEPPERS! Up and at it this morning! Ready to spend time in worship and praise of our Beloved and with some dear ones. Think I'm up before normal on a Sunday because I am beyond excited. I am always, always ready to hear what pastor prepares to bring from his study and quiet time with the Lord. But today, there is extra because a dear one will be leading worship. I'm asking for seconds today. Can we have a round 2 of worship and praise, please? God is good. I love how the broken are being healed, and I am part of that as well as watching it happen in others.

So the Lord kept this one recurring in my head last night as I was asleep. Too often, I can't get them back when I awake, but this one stayed and even began again when my eyes opened, so I know this was meant for more than me.

I love trees. Love them. If I could live anywhere I wanted, and money was no object, I would live on a couple of acres of land, moderate home, but the place would be full of trees.

I grew up in such a place, and I would love to have trees all around me. They are beautiful.

The question came in my mind this morning, "If a tree falls in the woods and no one hears, does it make a sound?" Yes. Yes it makes a sound. How do I know? Have the trees whispered things to me? No, but I am such a tree. I have been a Christian since I was young, but I was a weak one. I lived on my terms most of the time and God's terms when it "fit". I was being undone while I was still standing. There were creakings and groanings going on that should let someone know that I was weak wood and not going to keep standing, and so it was. Enough strong winds came and wore me down, and eventually, I fell. I fell in the woods. In a woods full of trees and yet it was as if no one heard, and I laid there.

On the floor, in the midst of other trees that were still standing, no one seemed to notice I had fallen. And the world ate me up while I was down there. Critters living in me, making their homes in me, and I was being consumed and rotting while I lay on that forest floor.

But the Lord answered this question for me this morning because He reminded me that He heard me, and He redeemed and rescued me. He took a broken, infested, ate up with bugs and critters living inside tree and made me a new creation. There wasn't much to be done with bad wood that was rotten, but Jesus redeemed me. Has redeemed my time and restored the broken places and rotten places within me. He brought healing to places I never knew I had because they were being eaten while I was still standing. He made me new. This tree that fell, this tree that laid there rotting, this tree that was ignored and overlooked because it fell. No one wants to be around "that tree" might catch its rotten. That tree, a new creation in Christ, He has taken this tree and placed me upright and given me new life, and my wood is no longer rotten and bug infested. He took all those places. I am His work, His wondrous work, and I am firmly rooted now. I know what waters and nurtures my roots and where the sunlight comes from that grows and strengthens me.

I have many verses that are very personal to me about trees, and one drawing on my chalkboard of an oak tree in Psalm 1. There is a reason trees mean so much to me. I am one. So today, if you have fallen on the forest floor and you think that no one hears, friend, you are mistaken. Jesus has seen and heard the fall. Let Him have all the rotten and remake you, new, firmly planted, a work in progress, but in progress is where I want to be. Love loud!

74

SCOOBER DO! Hope all is well! God is good and sits on the throne no matter what circumstances of life swirl around us. He has us. So this morning, my head is giving me some feedback from lack of water yesterday, but I wanted to share a tiny.

I remember being a kid and loving to try and do tricks—card tricks, coin tricks, and loved to watch magic shows on TV. Today, there are many shows and videos about revealing the "trick" performed and how but back then it was a mystery unless someone showed you. As we walk out this Friday, I am wondering today where are you focused? And are you distracted? As much as I loved the tricks, they were just that—an illusion of truth and reality. Get my focus off what was being done to make the trick happen and then redirect my attention when things were readied. I know someone that's really good at illusions and makes David Copperfield look like a baby, the enemy, is a master illusionist, master deceiver, master distractor.

We can be good people and be distracted. We can be doing all the right things and be distracted. We can have a heart of good intentions but really our intentions only get intentional when it's what we want. Lot lingered. David remained in the spring when kings go off to war. Solomon clung to his foreign wives. Eve only saw the tree she couldn't have. Martha was distracted by hospitality. And the list goes on. So today, as you walk out your day, let us realize that the enemy has no new tricks in his book. Been using the same ones, and yet they must be working, or he would have moved on by now. May our focus be intently on being in the Word, being in His presence, saturating ourselves with Him and keeping our eyes keenly on Him. May we not be found lingering where we should be moving forward, not remaining when we should be off in battle and leading, not clinging to worshipping things/people that were never meant or worthy of worship, not turning our focus on all the wonderful things God has offered us to hone in on the "can't" so that we even question His very character in that, not busy doing good things and helping and showing great hospitality when the Lord wants us to sit at His feet and soak in Him.

Where do we cast our time and eyes and works today? Master distractor has his plan. Master over all has His as well. It is our choice. Our hearts. Our eyes. Our lives. Love loud!

75

YAPPLE DAPPLE DO! Up and groovin'! The pillow won the battle this morning and held on a little too tight to my head, so no early workout. I've been burning the candle at both ends for a bit with late nights, so I was asleep before my head hit the pillow. In fact, I had to set an alarm to wake myself up to make a call. That's how dead I was Feeling refreshed and ready to get it done today! Chapel is a beautiful start to my day. Volleyball party tonight, and then I have to rush over to catch the tail end of Bible study and some late-night business stuff. At it.

So this morning, I am soaking in love, in being in love with the lover of my soul. We all long to be in love and loved. It is a deep desire within us, and we seek it, sometimes at great cost. Sometimes we think love is attached to how we "feel" in a moment. We can become too emotion based, and when the emotions turn a different direction or struggle comes, then emotions fly, and our version of "love" is lost. I write this because the first thing my eyes saw this morning were these beautiful words:

> Though you have not seen Him, you love Him. Though you do not now see Him, you believe in Him and rejoice with joy that is inexpressible and filled with glory, obtaining the outcome of your faith, the salvation of your souls. (1 Pet. 1:8–9, ESV)

I am thinking that most mornings, the first thing my eyes behold are the back of a cute head, gray hair all over the place, still with the little-boy cowlick in the back right. I love that sweet head. I actually love that man but today and the days he is out of town working for our family, that is not the first thing I see, and I miss that. We have had a long relationship together. Our first date was July 3, 1983, so it's been awhile. We have been through a lot together—ups, downs, financial stress, joys, victories, raising kids and all that comes with that, starting his business, house buying, more financial struggles, and I could list more. But yes, it's a big but. Today, I love him more than I did in those giddy beginnings. Even though as I rise this morning and I cannot see him by my side, I know. I know like I know I am breathing that He loves me. I don't need to see his face this morning to know that. I don't need to see his face today to know that he is fighting for us and believes in us, and I believe in him. Maybe even more than he knows. I know that when I think about him, it fills my heart with joy and makes me smile. And where does that come from? It comes from years of relationship. It comes from sticking together through it all instead of running when it didn't go my way. It comes from standing together and fighting for our marriage and for each other when times are tough. I don't need to see him today to know that he loves me and is still fighting for us. I believe it.

So this morning, as I read these words about Christ, it made my heart leap. Why? Because I love Him so deeply. Because as much as I love Mark and believe in us and in him, I love Jesus even more. I don't have to see Him with my eyes today to know that He loves me and loved me before I ever knew Him. I don't have to behold a face to know what love is to feel love. I have an enduring relationship with Him and have seen through that relationship how deep is His love and how deep mine has grown. May we have eyes and hearts to behold our One True Lover today. Believe and know that you are His. Love loud!

76

SNAPADOODLES! Up and moving this morning in the early! Ready for a beautiful, beautiful day. A gift. The Lord has opened His hand to me this morning, to you, and given us this very time we sit in at the moment. So my question to you today, "What are you building?"

Last week, in our women's group, which I love, we did some deep discussion on this and dug into what each of us are possibly "building." I will not go into the lesson, but we camped out in Nehemiah a bit and will revisit that book again this week. The question struck me because the Lord has asked it of me, and so I have had to spend some quiet time and reflection in that place. What am I building? Am I fighting for what I am building?

"Those who carried burdens were loaded in such a way that each labored on the work with one hand and held his weapon with the other" (Neh. 4:17, ESV).

The surrounding verses are about how each one was armed, and leaders stood with them in the rebuilding. Why?

Because they were under attack. Why? Because the kingdom of God was on the move. Why? Because naysayers and enemies always come to attack when the wall is down, and they suppose weakness. Why? Because building something is labor intensive. It is burdensome. It is tasking. It is work, and while being attacked, even more daunting. But don't you love that each one was armed? There were ones who were just guarding the builders, but the very builders were armed with swords! Trowel in one hand, sword in the other.

So today, I ask you what you are building because building is work, even more so, building kingdom families, kingdom homes, kingdom seekers is even more tasking and will make us prone to more attacks. And guess what? Right here, we are told that while we build, while we have our trowel in one hand to build our homes, families, environment, we should have sword in the other hand, not lying on the ground where we have to go find it, not across the way, not on the coffee table as a decoration but in hand. That makes us strong and ready to fight, ready to build.

So today, as you set out on your day, this gift, may you think about what you are building and if you are armed to build such. If the enemy is not threatened by what you are building, then he doesn't care if you build it and will not attack. Oh, but, friends, if you are kingdom building, if you are building kingdom homes and families and businesses, get ready! Get armed. And while you are armed, don't stop building—sword in one hand, trowel in the other. Fight! Build! Love loud!

77

SKABOODLES! Up and at it this morning! Legs are singing at me this morning and not a song of joy. All is well, and I can't get better lying in bed, even though my hamstrings would disagree. Ready for a bizriffic week with more to do than a crazy woman, but may I find some quiet time alone with my Beloved each day to keep me grounded and focused.

So this morning, I am thinking about God's grace in my mess and how grateful I am for His mercy and the beautiful people around me who speak into my life. I have done some weeding in recent years. I have found that some people are not "for you," and when those people are a constant drain on me, then my peace and joy are tiny too often. So I am thankful for those people because I still love them, but we can love people from a distance. We can pray for them, and we can want beautiful things for them, but honestly, only God can change a heart. So this morning, I am sitting in thankfulness.

> I give thanks to my God always for you because of the grace of God that was given you in Christ Jesus, that in every way you were enriched in Him in all speech and all knowledge—even as the testimony about Christ was confirmed among you—so that you are not lacking in any gift, as you wait for the revealing of our Lord Jesus Christ, who will sustain you to the end. (1 Cor. 1:4–8, ESV)

As I look in the mirror and see someone who can stumble and trip more often than I wish, I am thankful. I am grateful for a Lord who is abundant in mercy to each of us. Grateful for how He enriches my daily life, wisdom, words, thoughts. And my daily struggle is to focus on Christ each moment, not to let the flesh pull me aside or turn my eyes away. And as I walk in His grace and power. May my life be a testimony to His mercy and also how He can change us, how He pours out His gifts on us and desires that we pour them out on others. So as I have weeded my garden of those I keep close, I am also thankful and have no bitterness to those who have weeded me out as well.

There are times we have to tend our garden, and if we neglect it and are not faithful in that work, then we can find that we are in a true battle with weeds and struggle to spend time with the seedlings we were nurturing. May we enrich others' lives. May we give thanks today for a Heavenly Father that so greatly enriches ours. May we see those people He places around us in this season, and may we tend the garden well. Love loud!

78

FANTASTICAL FUNDAY! Up and groovin' this morning! Ponytail day! Love that I have one, even if tiny. Ready for an eventful day and jam-packed weekend, but know He is in it and with me in it. Last night was such a blessing to my heart. I love the gathering of women. I love to see God in the midst and moving. I love to see hearts on the move and His Spirit in our midst. He is beautiful.

So ever since I was very young, I have always loved stained glass. I remember walking in some different churches and having chapel each week with some windows that had stained glass. I have always been fascinated by its beauty and all the colors. I have always wanted to have a stained-glass window in our home, buy an old one out of a church or whatever, but the price is more than I am willing to pay. When I eventually have the time, I plan on taking a stained-glass class so I can learn how to make one. I even have a "mock" stained glass in our living room, so you get the picture.

God recently gave me a vision one night about stained glass and myself, which I will not share all of it but only part, a part that I feel can speak to all of us and was not just for me in this season.

I was walking out in the outdoors—a beautiful place with open spaces, some trees, beautiful grass, and deep-blue skies with white cottony clouds. As I was walking, God was walking with me, and we were talking about all the beauty, and I was thanking Him for some of the things my eyes were seeing as well as things with my family. His voice was gentle and soothing and, yet, strong and sure. As we walked, we would occasionally see pieces of broken glass in various sizes, various shapes, various colors. As we walked and talked, I picked up each piece, and we continued our journey. After a good bit of time, we came to a place where there was a collection of the glass on the ground, and there we stopped. God began to talk to me about what He was/has been doing in my life. I stood and watched as He put together in midair these pieces of glass. He assembled them into a large "stained glass" window (not shaped like any particular window shape). As He put these pieces together, He spoke of how much He loves me and has loved me through each season and circumstance in my life. As He worked, He revealed to me that each piece of glass we had picked up along the way and the pieces we found at the end are all times in my life—seasons of joy and victory, seasons of darkness where I felt alone and ugly, seasons where I loved well, and seasons where I was selfish. All circumstances, all seasons.

And as He finished the work in front of me, He shone the sunlight brightly through it, and it lit up. All the colors were magnificent and beautiful in a way they had never been while walking and holding them in my hand. As we walked along the path and picked up all the broken pieces, broken places in my life, we came to the end and found all the places and pieces of victory and joy and love. God took all those and assembled a beautiful life. And without the light of Christ shining through me, my life would never be as truly beautiful as it should be, and the beauty is meant to be shared and bless others.

So I look at how we never realize or see the true beauty of stained glass until the light shines through it, and it blesses the one that sees it. When He had finished the work and as the light shown through, He said, "Behold! This is you, dear one. I am using your life. All the pieces. All the hurts. All the joys. I can put them together and make it beautiful, but only because you gave me the pieces. You were meant to let My light shine through you and bless others."

Today, this word is meant for each and every one of us. We each need to give God what we hold in our hands, what we have in our hearts—brokenness, shame, joy, love, hurt. And He can take it all and make it beautiful. He can use it for His glory, and when we hand Him the pieces and let Him assemble them and let His light shine through us, oh, friends, it blesses others. Let us be a beautiful blessing today. Let us be assembled as a blessing and not for ourselves. Without the light, the stained glass is just dark and never fully as beautiful as it was created to be. Behold. Love loud!

79

YABBA DABBA! Up and groovin' this morning! Walking through this day, ready to be amazed! Why? Because God loves me and always shows up, even when I am not looking, even in tiny things, even when I feel forgotten, even when I'm a poo to someone (He gently reminds me that while He could smite me, He doesn't.) He amazes me.

So this morning, I have much on my heart. So proud of my team and how well they played and fought last night. Only one team in the state ends their season on a win, so odds were against us, but they showed heart and battled. Love them!

So thinking this morning about the plethora of things that I am thankful for today. This one may seem weird that I will share, but I promise it is not narcissistic, but it is something that more women struggle with, so I will share. I am beautiful. I am thankful that I can look in the mirror and see beauty. It hasn't always been that way. It was a little easier when I was in my teens and twenties, but as fifty is just a few months away, the mirror reveals wrinkles, spots I never knew I had just months ago (wondering sometimes if I am a leopard), and gravity is winning a battle I cannot fight. And yet I am beautiful. The enemy has pulled my chain on this one. Many times. Many years. I listened to the lies. I bought in to the world's definition of beauty.

The enemy's lies soaked in, and I saw a vision in the mirror that I didn't want to look at, and further, he spoke to my inadequacies in everything. Did I believe it? Yes, hook, line, and sinker. And it was sinking me fast and furious. The nasty lie of comparison was winning the battle. So many women look in the mirror today and compare themselves to someone else, compare themselves to what they used to look like, compare themselves to some things/someone they could or were never meant to be. Comparison is our enemy, a tool of the enemy for sure. Even used it on Eve. "How much better would my life be if I had more knowledge? Good and evil, eyes opened? God is holding out," and she fell.

So today, I have been in this battle many years, my friends. I honestly still struggle with it. I work with young and beautiful women, and the mirror reminds me of my age, but I can say that God has done a huge work in me to see my identity in Him and not always tied up in the mirror. The world says *mirror* and God says Word. Biblical beauty is the only beauty that can increase with age and has no physical boundaries. My beauty is found in fearing the Lord. My beauty is tied up in Him and not myself. So today, I am thankful that I can look in the mirror, and it doesn't work it's undoing magic on me much these days. I find my identity and beauty in who God says I am. I am His. I am His daughter. I am His child. I am a daughter, a princess in His kingdom. Disney princesses and kingdoms don't hold a candle to the way God defines beauty and His kingdom.

"Charm is deceitful, and beauty is vain, but a woman who fears the Lord is to be praised" (Prov. 31:30, ESV).

Be thankful today for the beauty you see in the mirror, and let your beauty increase each day as you grow in Him. Love loud!

80

JUMPING JEHOSAPHATS! Up and groovin' this morning! Ready for a great week to get rolling! This day is here! Loads of stuff going but I know it is going to be a great week!

As I rise this morning, body a little off in time with my natural alarm, I am wondering about walking around out of kilter. I know that anytime we do "fall back" and "spring forward" that it usually takes my body about a week to adjust the "fall" and about two weeks to adjust to the "spring." So I am thinking this morning about what if we spend this entire life walking around out of kilter? Not adjusted? Can't find our zone. What would that feel like? Would we even know we are out of kilter?

I had a dream last night about trying to gather people who were walking out of kilter and didn't realize I was trying to bring them together, and it was the last thing they wanted. They wanted to continue their life in their "zone" not realizing that God wanted to empower them as a gathering and as an individual. In my dream, some came to the gathering, and some ran. Some even ran and hid. They knew that things were not pleasant, but they didn't know how to make it pleasant on their own, and the last thing they wanted was God or someone else to help them. They would rather wander and be "in charge" than relent and become free.

So while my body is working itself straight for the next week, I know what it feels like to be on track, and I honestly know what it feels like to walk out of kilter with God, even to walk out of kilter, knowing I'm out of kilter with Him and thinking that's okay because He's saved me, and that's good enough. Oh, but when we get to a place where we desire with all of ourselves to be His, completely His, what joy and peace! What revelation and obedience! What it feels like to walk in peace and faith knowing that He has me and that my earthly circumstances can't disturb that peace. They can mess up and swirl about me, but my kilter is in kilter because I belong to the Master and Lord of all holds me, and I am His child.

I don't need to fix anything, but I need to walk in faith and trust the One who has me today, tomorrow, all this week, even in daylight savings time. He has me when I'm tired, annoyed, happy, intense—you name the feelings, but they are just that, feelings. May we be grounded in Christ. May we stand firm on that foundation. Even if we don't "feel" just right, may we stay firm in our faith and walk out our trust in our King. Whether lack of sleep, too much sleep, crazy kids, annoying boss—whatever the situation. This is a new day, and no matter how we feel, may we have our compass set on things above, not earthly things. Love loud!

81

YABBA DOODLES! On my runs with the Lord in the mornings, many days, He reveals quite a good deal of insight. Other days, it is quiet. Other days, I am talking probably more than I should, but I always enjoy our time together.

Such was one morning a couple of months ago, we were having some electrical work done in our backyard, so my mind turned to electricity.

Electricity is pretty amazing to me. I'm not a genius, no Einstein, no degree in electrical engineering, not an electrician. This plain ol' gal just has a basic knowledge of the stuff. I kind of feel the same way about God. I'm not a preacher and haven't been to Bible college and don't know the Hebrew or Greek origin of words (doing good to pronounce those actually!). I am just a regular gal who loves the Lord, read some books, reads the Word, done a few Bible studies. You get the picture. Bible scholar I am not.

Therefore, you might be able to draw many more awesome analogies than me, and that's great. I'm just sharing some things the Lord brought to my awareness. Electricity is powerful! It is strong enough to kill you if you come in contact with enough voltage. When toned down, we can "deal" with its power but still can't take a full blast of all that it is (and live). We can't understand or even comprehend God's holiness. He has made a way for us through Jesus to have the opportunity to connect with Him, but in these earthly bodies, His holiness is too great. He has made a way for us to live.

I think it's really cool that when I want to charge my cell phone, I just plug it into the wall socket. When I want to use my toaster, I just plug it in. The electricity is there, waiting. Jesus is there, waiting for us to plug in to Him. Whether I plug in or not, the electricity is there. Whether you plug in or not, Jesus is there. My phone dies without a charge, without the electricity. Short life. Friends, we all die without Jesus. He is the way, the truth, and the life! No one comes to the Father except through Him. I can sit and try to do life by myself. Without all the blessings that electricity brings, I can do life without Jesus and miss out on lots of blessings not just in this temporary life but eternal life.

The electricity is there, still there. It doesn't jump out of the wall and zap you. It waits for you to plug in. Jesus loves us and is waiting on us to plug in, connect to His current. Once we do, He brings such power and amazing things into our lives, so why do I forget to connect some days? Why do I choose to live in the dark?

When I turn on the light switch in my bedroom, the electricity moves into the lightbulb and lights up my room. Will I let Christ flow through me? Will I be a light for Him?

So my questions for you today, my friends, are these: Will you plug in to the powerful current of Jesus? Will you let Him flow through you? Will you illuminate this dark world with His light? Waiting. He is waiting. It just takes you making the first move.

Connect to His current today! Love loud!

82

ZIPPER SKIPPERS! Up and running! Ready for a great one!

So this morning, when I was running and talking with my Beloved, He began to put some things on my heart. He began to talk with me about serving. I was looking at myself and thinking of all the areas or ways I could serve, things I could do but I am not doing, wanting my children to learn to serve, and yet I am not doing a great job of setting an example in this area. Hard look in the mirror on this one! Hurts sometimes.

So while I have my list of ways I "want" to serve, I seem to be falling way short. It's not that I have a list of excuses either. No, actually, it's probably worse. I am just existing. Friends, do you know what I mean? For example, now that I'm off of school this summer, I had all these plans (before school was out) of ways I was going to serve or invite people over for fellowship and things like this, but here it is mid-June, and I have only opened the doors of my home once so far. I am in a routine—get up, run/pray, workout, breakfast, shower, athletic conditioning camp, lunch, relax, dinner plans, social media/watch sports, go to bed. There. That is my every day so far. It's not a day full of evil plans. I'm not killing people or stealing money. It's not a day full of pampering myself, and yet, it's not about God either. At least the whole day isn't. Well, this is where it leaves me standing. We are to live intentionally, not lives with intentions. Let me say that again, friends, because when God said this to me, it hit me square between the eyes.

We are to live intentionally, not lives with intentions. Bam! So the saying, "The road to hell is paved with good intentions," this holds true. Not that we are going to hell if we don't do certain things because it's not a works-associated salvation, and yet if I really love God, and I'm consumed with Him, He lives in all of me, then these things are done out of love (not a checklist). Wanted to clarify that part before I went on further. So I am ready to sit down today and make a list of things I want to accomplish this summer, ways I want to serve, and then find ways, make time, and intentionally make my schedule work around my serving, be intentional about giving my day totally to the Lord and not just being in a routine, and day is over, then month is over, then summer is over, then life is over. Whew! What did I do for the kingdom?

We usually don't just happen upon opportunities to serve and give. We usually have to be intentional about serving;

otherwise, it just passes us by, and we may not even notice. No, I will sit down today and begin to be intentional about living this life and serving others. I won't let my "good intentions" hang in the air because they will get placed on the back burner and be forgotten. I meant to do that but didn't get around to it. I meant to go there, help those, love those, serve those, reach those, but life got in the way.

Friends, we only have one life, so let's not let our routines, our busyness, our life get in the way. Let's live intentionally, and then we'll find that the good intentions take care of themselves. Be a blessing! Love loud!

83

SKIPPETY DO DAH! Up and at it on this beautiful day! Sky is beautiful and ready for an amazing day! Ready for all the Lord has in store for today!

So this morning, I am looking around at things in my bathroom as I am getting ready, and the line of skin care I use has big words on it. (No, I am not promoting any particular brand. There are lots of good ones.) The line I am currently using says *redefine* in large capital letters on each item. So this morning, I decided to soak on that word—*redefine*. I will be fifty in a few months, and my skin (whole body actually) has been moving in one direction—aging. And so as I use this product, it doesn't make me younger at all but works to move my skin of fifty years in a different direction. Don't define what you think fifty looks like; redefine what fifty looks like. At least that's my little take on the idea of the product, which I love.

What does that look like in personal terms for my life? Redefine. For sure I have ideas and a certain direction I think my life should move. I have certain patterns I am accustomed to and things I do daily. My definition is what my life currently looks like in this season. For me, to redefine would mean I would have to make changes. I would have to move forward, bring new things in, do away with some old things that hold me back, not be tethered to anything that is adding weight to where I am going, just like getting rid of old on my skin and moving forward with new.

> "Forget the former things; do not dwell on the past. See, I am doing a new thing! Now it springs up; do you not perceive it? I am making a way in the wilderness and streams in the wasteland." (Is. 43:18,19; NIV)

Behold! I love that we are reminded to not look back and dwell on the former things in old places with old mind-sets living in captivity and bondage. The Lord speaks that He is doing a new thing! It springs forth, not trudges, not oozes, not slowly, barely. It springs! Like a big cat pounces and springs up and out, so God is doing a work that is full of energy and His presence. There is nothing sludgy-trudgy about God. He springs forth. He is doing a new thing. Something that changes, something that is different, something that redefines old mind-sets and former things! That is a blessing, my friends! And the questions for us today are, "Do we perceive this mighty and new work?" and "Are we going to stay with our old definitions, or will we redefine?" Are we so, so stuck in the current and/or past that we cannot ever see what God is doing and wants to do in us? I see His mighty hand moving and that He is making a way in the wilderness and rivers in the desert. Water flowing where there is no water! That's a powerful work! Away in the wilderness where there is nothing, no roads, no signs, but He makes a way.

So get up! Move out of the old and former things that tie you, bind you, hold your positive mind-set at bay or in captivity! God is doing a new thing. He is in the business of redefining. He took a broken, messed up, woman who looked in the mirror and saw mess and muck, a woman who the enemy had pushed down and trodded on over and over. He reached into that pit with His long arm of redemption and pulled me out. He redefined what I saw when I looked at myself. I no longer look at myself through the lenses that the enemy had put over my eyes, but I've cast those off and perceive myself the way the Lord sees me—new, redefined. I'll take it! Thank you, Lord, for saving a mess of a wretch like me! Love loud!

84

YABBA DOODLES! God is up early, and so am I this morning!

I am waking up with thoughts of temptation—not temptation for me but just temptation as a whole. While the enemy isn't using any new tricks these days (nothing new under the sun), he is sly, and he knows our thoughts and what places/things call our name. If temptation were not a struggle, then it wouldn't be temptation. We can be struggling with a certain temptation, and through certain steps we take and keeping ourselves focused on Jesus, we can lessen those strong desires, and eventually, they will not even be a temptation anymore.

I write this from a place as a woman who has been tempted and fallen and repented and turned away. I never write anything from a place as having "achieved it all" or "I'm there, perfect." I am too broken to stand in that lie and, honestly, wouldn't want to stand on a lie. So here I am. This is not for me today but for someone. The world, the enemy will call us. And he makes our "likes" the things we are drawn to, look glittery and glamorous, look like more fun than we think we are having, more luxurious, more, more, more. And he whispers in our ears that to follow Christ means less, less, less. And so we take the bait. We are drawn to it anyway like a bug is drawn to the blue bug light, unknowing that once he gets in there, the very thing that draws him will kill him. And we swallow it. We take it in. Temptation can dangle out there on the line all it wants to, but it doesn't undo us until we bite. We have swallowed it, and now it is in us and has us. The enemy sits and chuckles because we "think" we are in charge. "It's my choice"; "It's my destiny"; "I won't be controlled by anyone"; and here you are on the end of a hook, having completely swallowed the bait. Now what? Are you "in control" at this point? Are you "making your own choices," or are you his puppet at this point?

Temptation calls us with the beautiful woman in the tight red dress. It calls with the handsome man who keeps flirting with you. It calls with the relationship that hasn't gone "too far" yet, but we keep pushing the boundaries. It calls you with sex. It calls with money, lots of money. It calls with putting something in your body for an "experience" all the while knowing that it inhibits your clear ability. It calls you to step across the line that has been right in front of you, as it dangles all those desires in your face. And we step across and find the empty. We tell ourselves, "This is great!" but deep down, we still feel empty. All the sex cannot plug the empty places. All the money, all the drugs/alcohol cannot fill those gaps. All the cheating, lying, or whatever calls you.

Here's what those things do. They hurt. They hurt the ones around you who love you. They hurt you. They hurt the Lord to sit and watch you revel and roll in that filth and not realize what you are doing to yourself and others around you. Sin doesn't hurt just you. There is not enough sex, and no sex that is "great enough" to cover the hurt and pain you will cause to those who truly love you. And the damage is enormous. There is not enough money to buy enough presents and houses and cars and whatever "fixes" you have to fill the empty places and voids that money can never fill. It wasn't meant to. And the same plays out with drugs and alcohol. We push ourselves past and over the edge and wonder why we never truly feel better or joyful or happy, but we need this to laugh and have a good time because we have lost what a real good time feels like. We have turned away from our first love. Jesus.

So as a woman who has been tempted and fallen and risen, I wish I could say that I have conquered this struggle, but the enemy still dangles things in front of me. These days it is much, much less, but I do many things to try and keep myself focused on Christ. Mind and heart and eyes and the temptations don't dart around me as often or pull as hard. I have had to learn to completely turn away from the old. It has cost me friends and relationships because I wanted an intimate relationship with Christ first. And as we place that relationship at the center and in front of us, then all things have to pass through it to get before our eyes, heart, and minds, and we find that as we soak in Him daily, those other things get washed away.

They can't make the cut. Nothing. Nothing on this side of heaven is worth your intimate relationship with Christ. Nothing. Nothing will ever fill us and truly complete us as a deep knowing of Christ will. We can search. We can get our feet wet in trying whatever the enemy tempts us with, but all things under the sun will leave you empty when you pursue them over and above Jesus. He is the only One worth of praise, honor, and our very lives and souls. Period. No need to search. Empty is easy to find. Look all around you. Being filled and having a full life is a submitted heart away. Abundant life. His offer. Will we walk away from the world to take His hand and a better life? Love loud!

"The thief comes only to steal and kill and destroy. I came that they may have life and have it abundantly" (John 10:10, ESV).

85

OODLES AND DOODLES! Up and at it today! Much on the "get it done" list but nothing more important than time with my Beloved.

I was thinking this morning about being a bride. My youngest son is engaged, and they are currently in process of finding a venue and planning a wedding. One of their friends got married this past weekend. There has been much talk in our house of weddings and brides, so when I saw the picture that Randy Caldwell posted yesterday (as he is currently in Israel), it turned my thoughts again to back in the day when I was a bride.

I remember walking down the aisle in a white dress, flowers in hand, so excited. I can't even really find the words for where my heart was in that moment. Looking up at a handsome groom, sweet Mark, smiling at me with such love in his eyes, such sweetness about him. It was moving. He was more than I could have imagined in that moment.

So I watched my oldest son, Josh, as he stood on the platform, awaiting his beautiful bride as she walked down the aisle toward him. His smile was sweet. There was love in his eyes, and his heart was beaming. It was wonderful for a Momma to see.

So this morning, I am coming at you from a slightly different angle on the bride. We are (the church) the bride of Christ. So I am looking at my husband after thirty years of marriage, and I am more in love with him today than I was the day I looked up and he stood at the end of the aisle. Today, as it stands, he knows all my mess, all my junk, all my yucks, my uglies, what I look like without makeup at 4:30 a.m., how cranky I can be, how annoying I can be, how sweet too. But to say that he knows me is no understatement. He did not know me like this thirty years ago when I was his bride, white and shining and beautiful and young. Now he knows the gritty and the good.

So what I am submitting to you this morning is that we all like to think of the church as the bride in a spotless white and unblemished way. And Christ does make all things new, and yet if my Mark stood at the end of the aisle today and awaited me to walk toward him, there would be a depth to our love unlike the giddy love of thirty years ago, a love that knows completely and is deep. And Christ knows His bride, the church. We have blemishes. We are not young and giddy but older and hopefully wiser. We are not white and spotless because of our lack of experience but from Christ cleansing us and setting us free. We hold flowers in our hand, flowers that have bloomed, and are the fruit of a life that has been lived well and has beauty to show for the walk toward our bridegroom down the aisle. So today, I am thinking that while we like to think of a beautiful, perfect, and young bride in a wedding, Jesus puts the ring on with us having known us deeper and more intimately than a young groom knows his bride, and Jesus loves us (you, me, and the church) at a depth that a new relationship could never begin to contain.

So today, may we be beautiful where we are planted, knowing that as the bride, no matter our age, no matter our past, no matter what circumstances have come and gone across the stage, our bridegroom awaits, and He loves. He knows. And that will set us free from any lie the enemy may whisper in our ear. Love loud!

86

YEPPER DEDEAUX! Thought I'd add a Cajun flair this morning. Up and moving on this most fantastic day! My honey comes home today, and I am so excited and ready to squeeze his neck! Missed him like crazy!

So this morning, there are words that I am so ready to hear. "Hello, beautiful." And he will say them gently, with a big, sweet smile on his face, and it will reach and touch my very soul. It's been two weeks since I've seen that sweet face. I've heard those words spoken to me before. I've been called other things along those lines by other people. But when he calls me beautiful, it is like none other on earth. My man can speak to my soul and with such sincerity that I don't doubt for a second his deep love for me. I don't doubt that with all his heart, I am beautiful to him. I might look in the mirror and smile with a little unbelief at times that he could say that with such conviction, but I am oh so glad that he does because somehow, my heart and soul long for it—for someone to look at me and see that I am beautiful despite what the world says. Despite what the calendar says, I am beautiful.

I am writing for you this morning, those who look in the mirror and see less than they want, those who the world beats down and tells you cruel things, those who are still waiting for a man who will truly see you as the most beautiful woman. Jesus is the lover of our souls, and we are ever beautiful to Him. He knows there are broken places, and He looks deep within us and calls us beautiful. He is gentle. He is wonderful. He loves us more passionately than anyone ever could, and yet we so often look past Him and search for the one that will call us beautiful here. And while that is amazing and wonderful and satisfying, if we do not first know and long for the One who calls us beautiful, we will never be satisfied with the man who loves us here. May we cast aside all the glitter and glamour of this life and run to the arms of the bridegroom who calls us beautiful in our darkest hour.

You are beautiful. Love loud!

87

YABBA McDABBA! Up and running in the foggy fog. Hope you are ready for all the Lord has prepared and in store for us today! Embrace it, even if it's awkward.

Much in my head and on my heart this morning about awkwardness. I am writing to you this morning from a place of awkwardness. Ever been in the midst of awkwardness whether by your own choosing or someone else places you smack-dab in the middle of it? Either way, it is not a pleasantry.

I am currently in the struggle of awkwardness by my own choosing. I have chosen to let my hair grow out longer so I can put it up in a pony tail, pull it back and all that jazz. I had long hair growing up but cut it short when I started having kiddos. Easy and kept it out of the way. So here I am at this moment after a few months of growth (not even sure my hair remembers how to grow long anymore), in the ugly duckling stage. You know, the place where it's too short to be short and style and too long to be short and style, too short to put up in a ponytail. This is my existence right now. Each morning, standing in front of the mirror with big sighs. Each day, I pass by a mirror, and it frightens me. What? What? haha! I'm no beauty queen, but I can usually look nice but now. Now I'm in the struggle, and it's real.

So this morning, I had to tell myself, "Hold on and wait." Wait for the growth. Wait and be patient because it can't get long. It can't get to where you are trying to grow it if you cut it now. Cutting is the quick fix. It will make me feel better right now to look better, but I will never achieve longer hair and a ponytail without a heavy dose of patience. Heavy dose.

So if you, my friends, are in a place of awkwardness right now, in a place where you are trying to determine directions, trying to pray through, trying to see the light, trying to see past the ugly duckling stage, wait. Wait and pray. Know that breakthrough is coming. Long hair is just a couple months away. Blessings are around the bend, but we cannot receive those blessings if we give up and cave during the awkwardness. If we lose sight in the struggle, then the glorious breakthrough and blessings we have waited for are cut short and never fully gained. I can achieve a nub of a ponytail now, but that is not where I want to stay, and so I must endure, even in something as small as the length of my hair and my struggle to deal with it in the awkward stage. Prayers this morning because I know that so many of my friends and loved ones are walking in this currently. Hang on! Awkwardness is for all, but may it be short-lived, and may we endure the struggle to the breakthrough! Love loud!

88

SKIPPER DEE DO! Up and hustling about on this early morning! Work is calling!

On the way home from the airport this morning, I was listening to the radio, and two gentlemen were talking about the battles of temptation that men face in the world today. One guest on the show was an NFL chaplain, and he had some good words. So this has me thinking about temptations. Each and every one of us walk in a broken world that is calling our names. Never doubt for a moment that the enemy knows exactly what calls your name and draws you away. It is different things for each of us, but he knows how to set the bait. He's a pro and been doing it for centuries. I would never call myself an expert on anything, but I do know that I have walked in and around my fair share of temptations in this lifetime. I do know that I have jumped into some like full well knowing I am jumping into a burning fire. And I have at times found myself in places where the temptations appeared and caught me completely off guard. So this I will share from my experiences: temptation grows in dark places where light is absent. Dark things grow in the dark. I was thinking back to my college days in botany when I was learning about mushrooms. Mushrooms are a fungi and absent of chlorophyll. They cannot make their own food. They grow this huge mass underground in the dark and damp, and the mushroom that you see is just the "fruit," so to speak.

So when you all of a sudden see mushrooms in your yard and they all pop up in groupings, it is because of the mass system underground that has already been growing and feeding the fruit.

Temptations frequently work this same way—in the dark and damp places. Like mold and fungus, the temptations grow and thrive. If we are not careful, if we ignore, if we play around with it, it can grow a mass underground in the dark. We think it is hidden. We think no one can see. But this dark and ugly mass that we think is hidden from the world will produce "fruit." Yesterday, I wrote about fruit of the Spirit, which is good fruit, but this darkness is false fruit. Fruit of sin never produces anything good, and yet if you live in the darkness of it, you will eat its fruit. Friends, anything done in darkness will come to light. We can try to mask it, cover it, bury it, pretend it didn't happen, but eventually, light will shine in that dark place. I don't run toward temptations anymore. I don't play with fire. Oh, I sometimes get burned, but I have found that when I stay close to the Lord, when I steep myself in His Word, in what He says about me, in remembering I am a daughter in the kingdom, then a few things are in my favor.

Those same old temptations don't call me like they did. I have the power and authority in the name of Jesus to resist the devil and cast him out of where he is trying to pull me/ push me. I turn directly away and walk the other direction not dancing on the edge of the fire ring, wondering how close I can get but not even wanting, desiring to be close to the fire. We all fall. We all sin. We all mess it up from time to time. But when we do, may we turn away from the darkness, not sit in it, not live in it, not dwell in it and let it make a mess in us but run toward God and His mercy. Light conquers dark. Love loud!

89

SUPER ELASTIC DAILY-TASTIC! Up and moving this morning! Ready for a glorious day! Yes!

Been in the trenches a bit recently with stuff going on in my life and so, so many dear ones in battles. This morning brings me to the book of Daniel. I am thinking about delay and about praying through. Staying power.

> Then he said to me, "Do not fear, Daniel, for from the first day that you set your heart to understand, and to humble yourself before your God, your words were heard; and I have come because of your words. But the prince of the king of Persia withstood me twenty-one days; and behold, Michael, one of the chief princes, came to help me, for I had been left along there with the kings of Persia." (Dan. 10:12–13, NKJV)

So I am currently in a season of praying through, doing the things that God is calling me to in my current place, listening closely and drawing in, hearing and knowing what He has forecasted ahead but knowing that delay is part of the process. In our fast-paced get-it-now society, we so often struggle in the wait, the delay. We think we should have what we want as soon as we want it. This reflects in credit issues, financial issues, and long-term issues of not understanding how to "wait well." In a period of delay, we should not be in a position where we claim to be waiting for God but not moving, not digging the ditches and being diligent and excellent in the current place. But over and over again in the Bible, God makes people wait. He delays, always with a reason but delay is part of the process in being a Christ follower.

What I am reminded of this morning as I read in Daniel is that in the delay, Daniel didn't stop praying. The angel assured Daniel that his prayer was heard the first day, but there was much battle in the spiritual realm going on for the breakthrough. So when we look at our lives this morning, our current place, our situation, we have a question to ask. Are we praying through? Are we diligent? Even though we don't receive an immediate answer, will we get up and quit? Will we stop praying? What if Daniel had given up on day 20? We might not be reading this part in the book of Daniel. And so this morning as we pray, pray through. Staying power, praying power. The enemy wants you to give up and stop praying. He wants you to relent. "Oh well, I don't see anything happening, so I guess God doesn't (hear me, care, want to answer my prayer, doesn't want that. You fill in the blank)." No!

Friends, staying power is what brings breakthrough! Praying and knowing that sometimes there is delay for a season doesn't mean we are "off course" or not being heard! There are battles beyond our human eyes and ears, but our hearts know they are being fought on our behalf. So stay. Stay and pray. Pray with power and conviction, and know that the prayers are heard, and you are strengthening the forces. Know that even in delay, you are heard. We must humble ourselves and keep praying. Keep working in our current situation, but pray through and watch. Await the results at the end of the delay. He is faithful. Stay! Love loud!

90

SKIPPERTY DOODACIOUS! Up and at it this morning, feeling the soreness from some neglected muscle groups. This morning, they reminded me who they are.

So this morning, I am thinking about the power of our words. The power of the words we think, we read, we hear, and we speak. Words are powerful, and yet too often, we throw them around without much thought, without thought of the receiver. Maybe without care for the receiver and without thought of the weightiness and depth and gravity that words can carry. And here's the crazy part, negative words have enormous power! People can hear a negative statement once or twice and begin to own it. Positive statements have to be heard about seven to ten times before they begin to sink in.

I have been around positive people in my life, and I have been around negative. I choose to be around positive when the choice is mine to make, but I have worked in places where the people I worked with were negative, so I didn't get much choice on that in terms of who they were, but I did have a choice on what I let inside my heart and mind. I know people who love the Lord, and yet almost every statement I hear from their mouths on Facebook is negative and despair. Is life full of struggles? Yep. Did Jesus promise us a problem-free life? Nope. But the power of choice with what we speak to others, what we pray to God, what we say out loud with our mouths, what we believe about our lives, that's the huge part.

"For all the promises of God find their Yes in Him. That is why it is through Him that we utter our Amen to God for His glory" (2 Cor. 1:20, ESV).

So this morning, as I get ready to head out and walk through my day, I must ask myself what I believe? We are in a current battle, and I can believe that dooms day is here, and we will be crushed. We will be underfoot. We will be the tail and not the head. I can believe that, but I don't. If the promises of God find their yes in him, then how could I? Would I choose to believe otherwise? God sits on the throne. A negative attitude won't change that, but it will change me. I choose today to walk with the positive. To walk in belief of God's promises and not listening and soaking in the lies of the enemy, he's loaded with lies. God is loaded with double-barrel truth that can eliminate any lies. May we walk in belief today that He holds the yes of His promises and that our amen and belief will bring Him glory! Love loud!

91

SCOOBER DEE DO! Up and slow rolling this morning! God is on point, always. He knows. I love my Beloved.

My honey comes home today, so I'm jumping for joy! Been too long and can't wait to squeeze his neck! I can already see the smile he will have on his face. It speaks deep into me still.

So this morning, my heart is soaking in the freedom that revelation brings. When something is hidden from us, we do not see the beauty in it. We cannot understand it. We do not know how to experience it because we never have experienced it. Last night, our women's group traveled to France to order off a menu that was written in French. As we looked at the menu and language that none of us in the group could fully read, we could grab bits and pieces, and a few words were recognizable. It became quite funny, and yet if I was in France and had to eat from what I ordered, I would be quite lacking and wondering. The foods we could recognize were recognizable because we had an experience with that food at a previous time. We had tasted it before. And how would you describe a food to someone they have never before tasted? They could understand in part but not fully understand until they tasted.

"Oh, taste and see that the Lord is good" (Ps. 34:8, ESV)!

God uses all five senses for us to experience Him. His Revelation. God's breath is revelation. Revelation is palpable because it enlightens us to a God who loves us, draws us to Him. So when I am trying to explain God to someone who has had no experience (that they see) with Him is much like explaining a sunrise to someone that has been born blind. I can explain with my experience, and they can understand with their experience, but the two will never fully meet until an enlightening or awakening, a tasting. And once we receive true revelation on who He is, the freedom begins to unfold. Revelation can be flip of the switch or gradual like light in a sunrise, but it will change us.

"The unfolding of your words gives light; it imparts understanding to the simple" (Ps. 119:130, ESV).

So today, may we be enlightening. May we walk in the light and the words that the Lord has poured out for us, His very breath that we behold in our hands, His word is absolute truth. Love loud!

92

ZIPPETY ZAPPETY! Up and running! Lots and lots on my plate today. Mostly piles and piles of clothes and unpacking.

Since I returned from my recent trip to Yosemite, I have been doing a bit of laundry, and the washer has been spinning and spinning and spinning. This took me to a place I have been recently, watching the spin cycle.

I can honestly say that I personally have been in the spin cycle a time or two in my life, but nothing is more painful than watching your child being stuck in the spin cycle. It is heart wrenching. It is a place that even though you've been there, you can't trade places with them no matter how much you may want to, and it's a place that you can't pull them out of no matter how hard you try.

And so I have a beautiful, beautiful child who I have watched over the course of two years getting pulled into an environment that was toxic. And then that environment was a place that she couldn't get herself out, stuck. She had been sucked in and not yet at a place where she was strong enough or fed up enough with the dark and dirty things that take place in that environment to get out.

I have watched people over the course of my life enter environments that were more worldly and less Christ filled, and I have watched people I care about and love, erode. Morals. Things that used to matter begin to slip away. Things that they once held in high value, such as a close walk with Christ, watch those things slip slowly to the sidelines and worldly, temporal, fleshly things begin to take their place. It's not a fast process. The enemy could never get away with it because most people would recognize themselves going that direction. As the Casting Crowns song says, "It's a slow fade."

I don't know about your washer, but we have one of those high-powered, newer versions that spins like a million miles an hour. The clothes come out almost without any water in them at all. If you were an article of clothing in that washer and in the last spin cycle, well, good luck peeling yourself off the wall and getting out. And if you get out, you will have some bangs and bruises and scars from it all. The enemy does that—amps up the speed of the spin. He wants you to stay in there and feel like you can't get out.

So I sit today and write this because I can tell you that my beautiful one has come out of the spin cycle. Much time on my knees in prayer by this Momma, and it sent me back to my knees in gratitude—grateful to a God that hears and answers prayers, grateful to see a beautiful life moving toward Him and His purpose, grateful to see the beautiful smile and see the loving heart that God placed in her being restored.

Are you wanting to break out of the spin cycle, disgust with where you are or overwhelming desire to leave? Disgusted with where you are? Recently, I went to hear Ron Reynolds speak, and he said that for us to be motivated, to change, it comes from within and must be disgust or passion that moves us. We can't leave if we are unhappy. Unhappy doesn't cut it. It's not powerful enough. We can't leave if we are thinking about doing something new or different. It's not powerful enough. So I watched my beautiful become so disgusted with all the toxic things and how it was ruining her life that disgust become more powerful than the hold of the force of the spin cycle. The spin cycle was a powerful force, but it is no match for what God can do when He reaches out to save and overwhelm a heart with disgust by the way you are living. It will overwhelm you with a desire to break the cycle.

I have no words for the tears I have cried and, again, grateful heart to my Beloved for reaching her in a place that was dark and she was alone. If you are in the spin cycle in your life, and your life is on hold, moving in circles but not forward, then cry out! Cry out to Your Beloved in heaven who can hear you! His arm is never too short to reach you, and He can strengthen you to take a stand. He can pluck you out of the spin cycle and break chains, break addictions, break strongholds. He can open your eyes to see that you are in the spin cycle, and that, my friends, is the first step.

You must see yourself in that cycle before you can even begin to be disgusted or have overpowering desire to get out and move forward. It is amazing how God can heal. It is amazing how He can save. It is amazing how no matter how many scars or bruises or cuts and scrapes, no matter how dirty the environment we were spinning in, He washes and cleanses and heals. He pulled me out of something more toxic and disgusting than I ever want to remember, and yet in remembering how bad it was, I am more grateful for where I am today.

Thank You, my Beloved, for rescuing one more. Love loud!

93

HEEP HOP HAPPY DAY! Up and at it this morning! Feels good to run in the dark again. I've enjoyed being up before the sun this week, but I can honestly say that once camp is over, I'm going back to my 6:15 a.m. wake up for the rest of the summer. I work out in the mornings in our game room upstairs. I have been looking at the cue ball on the pool table for a few weeks now and took a picture of it the other day. It's whitish with lots of green chalk marks on it. So I was thinking about when I play pool. I strike the cue ball, and it moves to hit another ball, which hopefully goes in the direction and speed and angle that I want it to, but it really all depends on one thing: how I strike the cue ball.

So I'm looking at this cue ball, and it has the marks on it of being struck many times. I can tell you that some of those chalk marks represent true and solid strikes, ones that lead to the other ball going in the pocket. And I can tell you that some of those green marks represent miscues—times I struck the ball and it wasn't just right, and it resulted in a scratch or the wrong ball going in the pocket or my ball not going in the pocket. I think this is the way of our lives. We can look at ourselves and see the times we have messed up, times we've miscued, times we've messed up royally and scratched or just put the 8 ball in the pocket before it was time. Yep. I think too often so many of us tend to focus on our mistakes, and they can eat us up. We stand and look at ourselves in the mirror and see the faults and stumbles and falls. We see every green chalk mark, and we think that the chalk marks make us bad or unworthy.

But I want to offer it up on a different table, the pool table. Your green chalk marks that you see are not all mistakes. Sometimes, we bare marks of greatness, of striking the right way, doing the right thing, being true, and we forget those. All the chalk marks on us help make us who we are, but we determine if they define us. See, I can look at my cue ball and just see green marks, but I can't tell you which ones went to which shot, but I can tell you that I'm pretty decent at pool, that I enjoy the game, win or lose. That the circumstance of how I struck the ball (good or bad) doesn't define me. It's just a green chalk mark. I am still a white round ball. (No funny comments).

So today, if you are looking at yourself and seeing a life full of mistakes, nope, we've all made them. If you are seeing that, all the green on you is bad. Nope. Just experiences (good or bad). But what you need to see is that you are a beautiful creation. The Creator loves you and fashioned you. And He makes all things beautiful. So don't let what has happened or not happened determine what you think of yourself or how you see yourself. You are His, not a circumstance. Have a blessed day! Love loud!

94

SKIPPETY PIPPETY! Up and at it this morning! So this morning, as I am doing my warm up, I decided to listen to my YouVersion as it read the beginning of Psalm 139 and continuing. There are *so* many good chapters in this book and yet this one is one of my favorites. I am listening, and this morning, my mind kept returning to a few verses, but this one lingers.

"You hem me in, behind and before, you lay your hand upon me" (Ps. 139:5, ESV).

We used to go camping with the kiddos when they were much younger, and we all had "mummy" style sleeping bags. We did a lot of camping in Colorado and were frequently up there when it was cold, even snowing. I used to laugh because at bedtime, they would each get in their warm pj's and get in their sleeping bag and snuggle down then say, "Okay, Mommy, come snuggle me up!" So I would go to each one and pull the drawstring, which cinched the bag up around their head and close to their face. So they actually looked like little mummies. All you could see was these little faces smiling at you, surrounded by a tapered bag.

So this morning as I am thinking about God "hemming me in before and behind," my mind travels back to those days of being snuggled, of times when all the coldness of the world wanted to have its way, and my Heavenly Father tucked me close to Him and hemmed me in. In those places, we feel safe and warm, being hemmed in by the Father. My kids felt toasty, and they loved the fact that Mom or Dad pulled the string to tighten up the sack and keep out the cold all the while feeling loved, feeling held, feeling the hand of someone bigger than themselves watching and taking care.

Today, if we are in places where we feel neglected, where we feel alone, where we feel like the world is cold and bitter and no one cares, I promise you, Your Father cares. He wants to draw us close to Him, close to His chest, hem us in before and behind. I love knowing that when all the mess is coming at me and the world is trying to break me, I have a Father who wants me to know that His hand is on me and He has me. Feel His warmth. Feel His love and presence. It's all around us, hemming us in. Love loud!

95

HAASENFLUGEN! (This means, "Holy cow!") It's a wet one this morning! No rain, just mega fog and humidity when I was running. Had a long run this morning and definitely felt like I was drowning. Where's the air? All is very quiet when it's foggy, so I truly felt like just me and God on the road today. Beautiful time. As I am running this morning and sharing things on my heart and listening, this drowning thing keeps turning over in my head probably because I was living it out right there.

So I am thinking about my walk with Jesus. If Jesus is an ocean, we can put ourselves out in the ocean. It can be all around us. We can swim in it, dog paddle, tread water. We can know all about the ocean because we are in the middle of it. We can be in the shallow end, the place where we want a little bit of Jesus just splashing up on our legs and maybe our torso, but we don't want to go into the deep water. That's too scary! The commitment is a big one in the deep. And we can choose to go into the deep water to have

Jesus all around us, to work and do works for Jesus, but it may be a dangerous place.

Are we treading water to keep ourselves afloat? To keep up a "Jesus front"? Are we doing works that are for ourselves and our gain but we are doing them "in His name?" And so I have been there. But, friends, let me tell you where I want to be in this ocean thing. I want to be drowning in Jesus. Not treading water. Not splashing in the shallow end. See, when we drown, the water fills up our lungs. At that point, we are saturated and consumed with water (with Jesus). We cannot take anything else into our lungs. They are filled with water (living water), and in that place, we die. We die to ourselves. We are no longer our own person, but we become one with the ocean. It has control. That is where I want to live! Dead to my fleshly desires. Dead to my head calling me to do things. Dead to my eyes wanting things and my heart chasing things that are only temporary. Dead to this world and dead to myself. Oh but so alive in Christ! What a beautiful life to live when we are alive and one with Christ, and our souls are His! Abundant joy!

"For whoever wants to save his life will lose it, but whoever loses his life because of Me will find it" (Matt. 16:25, esv).

My prayer for myself today and each one of us that we would die to ourselves and be found alive in Christ! Praise His Name today! Love loud, and drown in the Living Water!

96

ZIPPETY SKIPPETY DO DAH! Up and at it this morning! It's some McCold-O-Rama on my run this morning! The air was cold, but the wind is what got me! Think it picked me up at one point!

"For a man's ways are before the eyes of the Lord, and He ponders all his paths" (Prov. 5:21, ESV).

I've been in much prayer recently about "paths" for my family as a whole, and each of us individually as we each encounter different situations and circumstances. Last Saturday, I went to Blue Wave to get my car washed. It's a pretty cool thing, and I like all the swirling brushes and flopping strips hanging from the roof, all the colored and good smelling soaps. Yep, I'm like a big kid for sure. So to go through this car wash, you have to get your tire lined up just right. Put your vehicle in neutral. Take your hands off the wheel, and just sit back and let all the brushes work. Mark and I are talking about all the groovy going on around us right at the end of the wash when *baaaamp! Baaaaaamp!*

Baaaaaaamp! This loud (I can't emphasize loud, enough) buzzer goes off, red light flashing, and car wash just flat stops. We are shut down. So we sit there a bit, and it kicks back on. Brushes come on but not water, so we have to go through again because my car is covered in soap. As we were getting ready to get washed the second time, I asked the guy who lines you up to get on the track at the start what happened. He said someone didn't put their car in neutral and kept it in gear, which kicked them off track, which shut down the whole wash. Well, that'll preach! ha!

So if I want to be on track, I've got to stop trying to control everything. Let God line me up on His path, put my life in neutral, and take my hands off the wheel! You know. Jesus take the wheel for real because when I try to make my path or do it my way, then *baaaaamp! Baaaamp!* Loud noises, flashing lights, and I just make a serious setback, detour. Yep. Thanks, me. Of course, sometimes, life doesn't come with flashing lights and loud buzzers to let us know we are off track, but for sure, we will see the signs nonetheless. So the second time through my car came out beautifully clean. I was on track, not pushing my agenda or making it happen my way. In neutral (that's when we pray and ask for guidance) and hands off the wheel (we are not in control, and yet we think we are). Friends, praying for us today that we can get our lives on the blue wave system. Haha! God's plan. God considers our paths, and He knows best. Let's let go and let Him guide. Be safe out there as the weather worsens! Love loud and let go!

97

HOPPETY BOPPETY! Up and groovin' today! Embrace the gift of today and use it well.

So yesterday, I drove through the old neighborhood where I grew up. It is over close to a golf course, and we used to frequently get golf balls in our yard across the bayou that people duffed. Anyway, I grew up in this really cool old house. Lots of land and huge old trees, big beautiful house built in the 1930s, trellis leading to the house covered with wisteria vines—just so much beauty in that yard and the old house. My parents bought it and spent all their time and money fixing the place up and maintaining it. I remember when we moved in that you could see the ground underneath the house through the floor boards. It was a beautiful place and full of many wonderful memories for me, and I'm sure for my brother and his kiddos too.

Today, as we drove around the house, it looks almost deserted. Everything is all grown up and unkempt in the yard, just messy. I was brokenhearted because a place that was once so beautiful and pristine is now run down and looks completely abandoned. Sad.

Don't want this to be my life with Christ. If I don't tend to things, keep in close alignment and communication with Him, then things can run down. They can get downright ugly. I need to remember to stay close to Him. Let Him prune the places that need pruning. Fertilize and nurture the places that need that. Put some paint and clean up, just maintaining and keeping the shrubs cut back and not let the muck get out of control. Don't want to let the enemy come and set up camp in my yard, and expect that all that nasty overgrowth and ugliness won't soon take over. Don't want to assume that his mess won't run me into the ground, and it doesn't take long. A little neglecting here and there, you know, this and that don't matter. Then more this, and that doesn't matter, and before you know it, we look like nobody's home. Living in an abandoned shell.

Who lives in us? He doesn't abandon us, so may we not abandon our home, our calling. Love loud!

98

YABBA DABBA DO! Up and at it on this beautiful morning! Rise and sunshine today! Ready to roll!

Lots of thinking and praying this morning with my Beloved. Thinking about how in this world we live in, it is so driven by what we "look" like on paper. How we build our resume, how we look on college applications. Whether we have papers that say we are certified or degreed or trained in something, papers that say we participated in something, and all these other papers that are supposed to show our value and worth. So while I don't feel that papers determine our value as people, they are still the means by which we are judged and valued quite often. While I have been watching this and been victim to it more than once in my lifetime, there are people with every kind of paper, degree, certification, whatever madoodle in town. They are "paper rich." And sometimes, sometimes the paper rich can be as thin and shallow as the paper their certificates and adequacies are written on. So I am looking inward today and thinking about my story.

Is my story written on thin paper? Am I only as shallow as the paper my story is on? Or am I letting God write my story? He brings depth and height and breadth into my being, into my story because my story isn't really my story if I do it right. If I open up and truly become His, then I am His story. That's where I want to be—not thin and all about my resume but all about Him. Praying I raised my kiddos this way as well, even though the world values how we look on paper, praying we all are open to see God's value on our lives and what He sees in us.

> For you formed my inward parts; you knitted me together in my mother's womb. I praise you, for I am fearfully and wonderfully made. Wonderful are your works; my soul knows it very well. My frame was not hidden from you, when I was being made in secret, intricately woven in the depths of the earth. Your eyes saw my unformed substance; in your book were written, every one of them, the days that were formed for me, when as yet there was none of them. (Ps. 139:13–16, ESV)

And so today, if we are feeling like we are insignificant, like we don't matter, like we are invisible to the world, God knows you and sees you and loves you! Your worth is not tied up in documents. Your identity and value is in Him! Love loud!

99

SKIPPERTY DO DAH! Up and at it on this wonderful day! Now ready to get this day rolling!

So the last few mornings and evenings, I have asked God to speak to me before I opened my Bible. Twice (in two different Bibles) I have opened to 2 Samuel in chapter 18 and read about Absalom's death (David's son). My son, Jacob, has a version called "the Voice," which reads beautifully for those of you who have never seen it before. His Bible was here on the end table, and I read from it again last night about Absalom's death.

> Absalom himself encountered David's forces, and as he was riding away on his mule, the animal took him into the thick overhanging branches of a huge oak tree. There his hair was caught, and he dangled between the sky and earth as his mule fled from underneath him. A soldier saw this and told Joab (David's general). Joab took three spears, and finding Absalom still dangling by his hair inside

the oak, he thrust them into his heart. (2 Sam. 18:9,10,14; the Voice)

Now I'm not trying to be a downer this morning, but since this verse continues to come in front of my face, I figure God has something to say. I couldn't help but think about Absalom. Everything was going his way. He was mad at his father David, but his rising army was gaining momentum, and people were supporting him. He must have been feeling pretty good about himself. Maybe even prideful. He had already erected a statue of himself in town. He was probably a handsome young man, and I imagine had beautiful, flowing hair, maybe even more a source of his pride. And yet he rode a dumb animal, and he let the dumb animal take him into the thick brush and overhanging trees. Maybe he was so sure he was going to be victorious that he wasn't worried or mindful of anything that even looked awkward or unsafe. Pride can do that to us. I know. Been there. Done that.

And as this dumb animal takes him into this place, his very beautiful long hair (of which he is so proud) is the very thing that traps him and leaves him hanging, dangling. What does the animal do? Runs off and leaves him there to die. So can you imagine him hanging there? What he is feeling? The panic? I don't know about you, but I can tell you for sure that there have been times in my life where my pride has left me dangling between the earth and the sky. My feet couldn't find the ground, and there was no help for me on my own. Absalom just hung there and awaited his death, and there was nothing he could do.

So today, I am thinking about the pitfalls and traps of pride. It looks so pretty and enticing on the outside, calls peoples' attention to us, and then can leave us dangling. I have walked in the ways of pride, and it is a place I honestly do not care to ever revisit. I have seen my pride hurt me and others I care for and love. It is something we all struggle with, and the enemy knows it, so he places those enticements out there all the time, hoping our dumb animal will lead us right into the forest, and we will become entangled. Taking inventory of myself today and looking in the mirror to chip away any pride or overconfidence in myself that I may have. May our confidence be in our Savior. Enjoy your day, and bless your neighbor! Love loud and walk in humility!

100

MERRY HALLU! That's "happy day after Christmas!" Up and at it this morning and really enjoyed the sweat after a couple of days without it. Lots of thinking and praying this morning as I was running and thinking back over this year and all the happenings. So as I am running this morning, the Lord is bringing some things in my surroundings to my attention, like I've been asleep all this time and never noticed these before today. When I run, I usually do laps around my block, and my block is a big (.7 mile) circle-ish street that goes around a lake in the middle. There is also a green belt around the lake, which is about .3 miles. There has been much going on in our neighborhood this around the lake—people moving out, people moving in, changing seasons, yard decorations, changing yard decorations, cars driving around the lake, golf carts driving around, same people walking/jogging around, new/different people walking around, kids with new scooters/bikes riding, rainy days, cloudy days, months without rain at all, windy days, sunny days, people feeding ducks and turtles, egrets feeding by the lake. You get the gist by now. All, all this stuff and more are things that have gone on just this year around the lake.

So while I sit each day at my breakfast table and write, looking out the back window at the lake, I see new things and similar things and even the same things. But despite all the happenings around the lake, good or bad, there is a constant—the lake. The winds don't make it go away. The lack of rain hasn't made it go away. Whether people come and go doesn't make it go away. So I say all this because I love that God is the constant in my life, like the lake is the constant in my neighborhood. I have had people come and go in my life. I've had circumstances bigger and uglier than I ever want to admit, swirling around me and kicking my tail. I've had days where I'm surrounded by beauty and good things. I've had days when the hurt and pain was real and larger than me, but in those places, I know that God is my constant.

He doesn't leave me or change. He doesn't walk away because it's hard (hard for me, not Him). And He is bigger than my circumstance, bigger than the people who hurt me, bigger than the people who love me. He is my rock. If I get caught up and live my life worrying about who's moving in next door or who's moving out and let people have a bigger role in my life than my Heavenly Father, not a good place for me. Have I done this? Oh, yes! And I can tell you that it is a place I never want to revisit because the pain is too much.

So as I finished my run this morning, there is a house around the corner that has wooden candles with the word "joy" on them on each side of their walkway. One of the joy candles is standing straight up. The other has been knocked caddiwampus and is all looking like it's about to fall over. Don't let someone knock your joy over! Don't let someone steal it or tell you that you don't deserve it or whatever! When I stay God centered, then my joy is up and moving, not determined by circumstance or people. So as you close out this year and get ready to move to another year, let's be ready to embrace the fact that our God is a constant, and that our lives should move around Him and not the other way around. I have a new view of my little lake today. Praying we can all put things in their proper place and perspective as we begin this new year. Love loud!

101

SNAPPER DAPPERS! Up and at it this morning! Who knows what the day holds, but I know my Father holds me so I will run with that. Had a fun evening with a house full at dinner. It always leads to laughs.

So this morning, I am reading in Jeremiah 29 before I get started, and so much on my mind. So many dear friends and loved ones to pray for. Then I get to praying for our home, and the Lord sits me here for awhile. Have you ever thought about your home being a sponge? Think about the sponge in your kitchen sink. So I am praying for the Holy Spirit to fill up our home, to permeate every pore in the sheetrock, tile, and wood. For our home to be so full of the Spirit that even the walls are saturated. And so I am thinking about my home being like a sponge, about it absorbing things each and every day. It absorbs all that goes on within these walls—love, words of kindness and encouragement, words spoken in anger, laughter and smiles, fun times of fellowship with family and friends, quiet alone times.

Our walls are like a sponge, absorbing memories, and all we do and say within our home. When you walk into a room in your house, you can no doubt recall things that have happened in that room like the very walls soaked in the memories, and now they are pouring out. And each memory, each word, each hug and laugh and smile is like drops of water that soak in and stay. And then we add that we want the presence of God within our home as well to fill up each room and each place. For our home to be so saturated with the love of Christ that the very people within the walls are saturated as well, and then the love of Christ is just pouring out of the home and the people because the sponge can hold just so much before it is full and has to let it spill out. Praying that when people come in our home, they feel the love of Christ and are soaking in Him while they are here. Praying that we (our family) can enjoy this time we have together, we are soaking. May we be soaking in His Spirit each day. And if the enemy comes to wring us out, to try and empty us, then may we pour out Christ on this hurting world, and may we stand and let God continue to fill us.

So I am going back to what really struck me in Jeremiah 29 this morning:

Jeremiah 29:14, "I will be found by you." In the preceding verses, God is telling us that if we seek Him with all our heart, we will find Him, but this little part of this verse struck me because it is reaffirming that He is there all along, and we are wandering around, looking for other things and other loves. And there He is. Ready for us to turn to Him. Wanting to pour out His abounding love on us and saturate us. I will be found by you. Yes. And once we find Him, may we be sponges. I don't just want to know who He is and about Him. I want God to saturate me, and may I soak in Him, so He pours out of all I say and do and think. Gracious, I am a work in progress, but I know this about me. I have found Him. Oh, and that makes my heart full of joy and love! Fill up your home today with Christ, and let Him be thick and ever present in your home. Absorb it. Love loud!

102

YAHOOZERS! Up and at it this chilly morning! Glad to be back at it in school and see all the kiddos yesterday. Getting adjusted to a couple of changes in my schedule so today should be a little smoother. Had a great time last night. Dinner with the kiddos then long time sitting at the table conversing about the Holy Spirit, the power of God and ways we have seen Him move. I can honestly say that Mark and I left the table and just sat in amazement at how God has shown Himself so vividly to each of the kids. Revelations. It is incredible to hear your children as adults have their own faith. Faith is something we cannot hand down to our children, and it is not "in the genes" or DNA. We can raise them up; we can pour into them and pray for them every day, but the Holy Spirit will present Himself to them, and it will be their choice to accept or reject. Does that mean because we accept the Spirit that we never sin? No! Never mess up? Never have flesh-driven thoughts, desires, or speak those words? No. I wish! I was laughing this morning because after some time in prayer and listening, I went to get in the shower, and a mean thought passed right in front of my brain. I mean like a ticker tape on display, I saw it, read it, and the best part was I rejected it! I laughed though because the enemy is on his job 24/7, and he doesn't rest, even when you walk out of prayer time he is still coming.

> But I say, walk by the Spirit, and you will not gratify the desires of the flesh. For the desires of the flesh are against the Spirit, and the desires of the Spirit are against the flesh, for these are opposed to each other, to keep you from doing the things you want to do. (Gal. 5:16–17, ESV)

Good gravy! This is so true. And some days, some times, I am Spirit lead, and then other times I fall to the flesh. That always annoys me when it happens, but I can say that I am quicker to recognize it these days and ask for forgiveness. Some days, the biggest things that can get us into trouble are our emotions. They can quickly take us down a path we don't want to be on (at least our Spirit doesn't). It is hard to live a Spirit-led life when we let our emotions have the wheel of the car because quite frankly, they will take us all kinds of places.

I think back to when my daughter was learning how to drive. I love her so much, but she and I in the car together was a mess. When she was behind the wheel, she was surely taking me places I didn't want to go—toward curbs, up in people's yards, and all sorts of incidences I could share. Funny now but not then. So I just sat in the passenger seat and hollered. That helped, don't you know? See me smiling. And times in my life I have done the same thing. Let my emotions have the wheel. Let them drive me to places I never should be and then sit and holler and yell when I end up in the wrong place. Because the wrong one was in control of the car.

Oh, and Jess is a much better driver now. So today, if you find yourself in a situation that is "out of your control" because those do happen, just keep your cool and think about who's driving your car. If it's the Spirit and you are Spirit led, then you'll be fine, but if it's your emotions, then be careful! You could end up running into someone's yard and wrecking your car or worse. Love loud!

103

HOOPETY DO DAH DAY! It's an up-and-at-it day! Wishing this week had gone by slower but no complaints! Grateful to have had this time off with family.

Last year, some of the words God was giving me at the New Year were *abundant blessing*, and no doubt, it was just that for our family. As I have been praying about what this coming year, might hold, He keeps giving me the words *hope* and *Christlike*, so as I think today on the latter and what that looks like, it excites me. I love how when you read about Jesus, He went around doing His own thing, walking in His Father's will, talking with Him in daily quiet time. People were drawn to Jesus. Jesus didn't feed 5,000 and say, "Hey, go out and shout it from the mountaintops about what I did." He didn't heal people all the time and want the press to be alerted. No. Jesus just went around blessing others. He walked in His Father's will and righteousness and loved without condition. He was humble even though He didn't need to be. He was loving and nonjudgmental even though He could have thrown every last one of us into total darkness. He was powerful. He was mighty. He was passionate about what He was called to do. He loved. He healed. He saved. He touched people.

So I am thinking about what it looks like to be more Christlike this year, to love without condition, to bless without broadcast, to be humble, to look at everyone with His eyes—the homeless, the guy on the street corner, the poor, the down and out, the ones who are forgotten, the ones who hurt us. Not just our friends but everyone. So it's big for sure, bigger than me.

Mark and I have been praying this past month for God to fill us to the measure with the Holy Spirit and His gifts, whatever He wants, and to ignite a holy passion within us. So I am praying this year that the holy passion would begin to come into fruition. That I would be His in a new and even more intimate place and completely, utterly His. I pray this over my family for this year, this season. May we all lay down ourselves and find a holy passion that God ignites within us this year. Not our passion, His passion. Just some food for thought today. Have a blessed day, and offer some Jesus love to someone today. Love loud!

104

YABBA DABBA DO! Up and at it and grateful for another beautiful day! How can you not get excited to get out of bed, walk outside under the amazing sky, and spend time with Your Beloved! Can't find the words to explain how I feel about it. Had a great day yesterday and finished it off with a joyful time in the presence of some beautiful, godly women. Sweet! Today, I'm ready for the opportunities God places in front of me today. To bless others. So we have been studying the "full armor of God," and this week we are discussing the "shield of faith" (Eph. 6:16).

As the pastor was talking Sunday about Roman warfare and the Roman shields and how they were made and used, I remembered some of my study in world history as we spent much time on Greeks and Romans. There is much to learn about Roman warfare, but part of what I wanted to share is this: when the Romans were engaging in battle, they would place the new recruits up in the front line (one reason was because they were considered expendable). One of the reasons for this besides the one I listed is that they would gain some valuable front line, face-to-face combat and gain more confidence as a warrior. Another reason was they would place the seasoned legionnaires behind the less experienced to keep them from feeling too much fear and wanting to flee and to know that a strong power had their back. So I'm putting this into some thought today.

As we all stand together in Christ, face battle with the enemy, isn't it comforting to know that a strong power has our back? Friends, this isn't just God who has our back but that we would stand with each other. That those who have been in the battle and have the scars and experience can stand and strengthen the ones walking in anxiety and fear right where they stand. So today, I pray that I will help someone stand. I have been on the front lines (still visit there on occasion) and have the scars left by poor choices and the enemy's little victories over me, but I have come out stronger! I know that Jesus has already won the war, so my battles are small in comparison. We are not finished but works in progress so strengthen someone else today.

> And I am sure of this, that he who began a good work in you will bring it to completion at the day of Jesus Christ. It is right for me to feel this way about you all, because I hold you in my heart. For you are all partakers with me of grace, both in my imprisonment and in the defense and confirmation of the gospel. (Phil. 1:6–7, ESV)

Let's stand and partner with our brothers and sisters in Christ. we are not a bunch of separate groups because we attend different churches. We are one army! Be blessed today! Rise up and lift up someone today! Love loud!

105

YABBA DOOZER! Up and at it this morning! Woo! Got to wear shorts and a T-shirt for my run and workout! Really had much to lay at His feet this morning, so our time was a blessing to my heart! He is constantly asking me to trust Him, and as He asks me these things, then I am placed in situations where I have to trust Him. Oh, I have a choice to not trust, but He is testing my faith. I can talk it, but can I walk it. And so He holds my feet to the fire, and it is hot!

> Let us hold on to the confession of our hope without wavering, for He who promised is faithful. And let us be concerned about one another in order to promote love and good works, not staying away from our meetings, as some habitually do, but encouraging each other, and all the more as you see the day drawing near. (Heb. 10:23–25, ESV)

Gracious! I am holding on to my faith today because I know He is faithful, been there many times, and lived it. As

I am being tested and on my knees with Him, I will strive to hold fast and not waver, especially when it's hard. That's a tough call on us, but faith is more than words; it is action. So today, I am wanting all my wonderful friends who are walking through a fire right now to hold on. Be encouraged! Know that I am praying for you today! Message me, and I will lift you up in prayer! Be strong and courageous as the Lord says in Joshua!

Paul is telling us to not stop meeting together because in community, we lift each other up. We help bear each others' burdens! Don't let the enemy isolate you! He loves to do this. We are not strong standing alone, but when we share, when fellow believers come alongside us, then we can stand united! Then we can lift each other up in love. We can help push back the forces of darkness when one among our fold is weak at that time. But if we are isolated, then no one can help us up or knows our worries or struggles! The enemy always tries to make our struggles about "people," but, friends, it is not people that we struggle with; it is the forces of darkness, the enemy we struggle with!

So today, lift up someone in prayer, someone maybe even in close proximity to you. Bless them by giving them an encouraging word. Pray for them or with them. We never know what someone else is walking through. So today in my struggles, I will lift you up in prayer. I am encouraging you to stay strong, and know that you are loved and never ever too far from redemption or mercy! Love you! Faith is action! Love loud!

106

ZAPPERS! Up and at it this morning! A little windy but still nice run. My motor was a little sluggish this morning but got grooving. Love starting off my day with quiet time with my Beloved. Before the busyness, before all the social media, e-mails, kiddos, job—just life in general. He helps me get to a place I need to be and listen. Some days, He has lots to say—sometimes things I enjoy hearing, and other times, He corrects and gets my heart on the right track. Either way, they are things I need to hear. Funny how that works. It's easy when our friends come to us with praise and pats on the back, and atta boys, but things take on a different light when something is offered up that might be correction but not honestly what we want to hear.

> I charge you therefore before God and the Lord Jesus Christ, who will judge the living and the dead at His appearing and His kingdom: Preach the word! Be ready in season and out of season.

> Convince, rebuke, exhort, with all longsuffering and teaching. (2 Tim. 4:1–2, NKJV)

In most jobs, there is some type of evaluation system in place where we are evaluated by our peers, our supervisors, or the people we manage. Sometimes, we get into trouble when these systems are not in place because there is not a checks-and-balance system. Thinking back to high school on my softball team when our coach had "position challenge" days. A player might have a starting position, but another player could step up on these days and challenge the starter for her spot. Rarely did the starter lose her position, but just the shear fact that someone could "take" my position kept me sharp and working on my skills on the side to make sure I was in step and at the top of my game.

I want to live my life in God's word, listening to His callings, promptings, serving in the places He calls me to serve, obeying Him, following Him, sacrificing, and dying to my wants so much so that my wants become what He actually desires. So looking back over this past year, I would never say that I've done it all correctly for sure, but I am glad that I have followed Him in the hard places. This is probably the second year of my life that I have been gut-level honest in doing that. Looks different. The world isn't pouring out blessings on me, but I don't want the world's blessings. Grateful for God's blessings. Storms, trials, favor, and all of it. Looking forward to this upcoming year. Praying I can better serve the Lord and follow and obey even more than I did this year. Praying to see more evidence of God-bearing fruit in each of my kids' lives. Praying that our marriage is blessed, and our love for each other continues to grow as we stay God-centered and on our knees together. Praying that I lead in my job in such a way that there is evidence of how He leads me and that I am helping young ladies in their daily walk with Him through all the muck of being a young woman in today's world. I am praying that I am humble as a coach and teach my players to be fierce and to lead by serving and loving. Big prayers for the coming year.

The two words I am looking at in a New Year, new season, are *trust* and *fruit*. Please be safe, friends. May God bless your household and pour out love and blessings on you in this year! Love loud!

107

YIPSEE DO! Up and moving on this funday morning! Spending my day with other leaders, renewing and refreshing and preparing for where God is leading. Today is full of great stuff!

So this morning, I was thinking about perseverance. I have been an athlete for many years and coached for many as well. I have seen and experienced firsthand the wonderful attributes that perseverance can produce in someone, and I am not just talking from an athletic perspective. When I was training a few years back to run a half marathon (because I'm only half crazy), I remember the countless hours on the road, running. I remember the black toenails. I remember putting miles and miles on a pair of shoes and having to stay up with fresh new ones so my feet and knees would last. I remember that my outlook in the training process was huge.

I had another friend who was also training during that same time, but she did everything with drudgery and a negative outlook. Wanted to run one to say she had run one but hated everything that went with it. And there is some ugly that comes with training, no doubt, but when we decide to persevere in whatever task at hand, and we maintain and attitude of finding joy in it, even if we have to dig it out, then it can produce strong character in us.

> And not only that, but we also glory in tribulations, knowing that tribulation produces perseverance; and perseverance, character; and character, hope. Now hope does not disappoint, because the love of God has been poured out in our hearts by the Holy Spirit who was given to us. (Rom. 5:3–5, NKJV)

I can honestly say that during some of the biggest struggles in my life, God has walked beside me, reached down and found me, and held me in those places I have endured because of a decision. You can give up and give in. You can stand and fight and persevere. But either, way the ball is in your court, and there will be an end product, so what are you willing to accept for yourself? For your life? As our character is strengthened, then we can see the hope that is out there. When all the mess is coming at us and falling on us, trying to cover us and smother us, we can stand in that strong character that perseverance has produced, and we can see the light, no matter how dim or small the ray. We can see it because of the process we've been through.

So today I am challenging you to make a decision to persevere where you are. You are making a decision, but may the perseverance produce and call out greatness in you that you may not have realized. I can tell you that my friend "out trained" me for the half marathon, but my finish time was much better than hers, and I even beat my best training time when I ran the race. Persevere today, and keep the attitude of knowing that something good is being produced in you. No sorrow but see the joy in the struggle. Hard stuff. Love loud!

108

UP AND AT IT this morning! Moving and shaking right on through the week. Yesterday was a blessed day for more reasons than I can count, and I am so grateful to worship a God who hears our prayers and shows up in big ways to answer them. So I wake up this morning with more blessings at my window, beautiful sky, nice temperature, day with the kiddos at school, practice, and then sweet time with our women's group tonight. Wednesday is good.

Recently, a dear friend was sharing a dream she had, and I wanted to share it with you (per her permission) because I think it speaks to so many hearts today. She has been in a struggle for a bit and had this dream. We have talked about it and prayed about it, so I will share.

She was standing in the middle of this vast field, and there was a fence, but it was far away. As she stood in the field looking around, something dark rushed by her, brushed her, blew her hair and her clothes. She could not discern what it was, but it was dark. As she looked around then up ahead, she saw a huge black bull standing before her with eyes that were fiery red and looking right at her. The bull was massive and just stared at her. The size and the dark, evil look of the bull was shocking, almost scary. She glanced down at her clothes to find she was wearing all red. This should/would send more shock and fear into a person, and yet, she said that her countenance was calm. She felt the peace and presence of God all around her. She knew in her mind that she should be frightened, and yet God's overwhelming presence wrapped her up. The bull charged her and passed over her, and yet she said she could feel it move over her, but she was not injured or trampled. As it passed over her, she just felt God all around her. She woke up immediately after that.

So here is what I want to share with you this morning. The enemy is not the lover of your soul! He is large and powerful and mighty. Is he any match for our God? No. But he can be quite the looming and dark, powerful force against us. He is evil. He is the Father of all lies. He wants to steal, kill and destroy you. Trample you. Overtake you. Crush you. Leave you for road kill. And he is quite capable. See in our own power and presence in this situation we would be weak, helpless and fearful. We are no match on our own against a bull, especially when we are his target and wearing red. When he is after us with all that he is and not seeming to stop. Relentless. I want to tell you that my friend was saturated in God's presence in that moment. In that situation. It didn't matter that she wore red. It didn't matter that the bull was massive, evil and intent on crushing her. God's presence can hold such peace in a situation that seems hopeless. He is our hope. How do matadors battle bulls? With swords. Today, my friend, you have the Word of God as your sword. Offensive weapon in the battle against the enemy. Jesus used it, and if it is good enough for Him, then I think I can use it too.

"We are hard-pressed on every side, yet not crushed; we are perplexed, but not in despair; persecuted, but not forsaken; struck down, but not destroyed" (2 Cor. 4:8–9, NKJV).

So if the enemy is coming at you today, stand in the full presence of God. Let Him cover you and be strong about you. Soak yourself in the Word, and use it against the enemy; he is no match for the Word of God. He may pass over you, but you will not be crushed! He may try and trick you, but pray for godly wisdom. He may try and persecute you, but there is no fear because God is with you, in you, and never leaves you. He may knock you down, but, friend, you are still here—not trampled, not destroyed, not road kill. Rise up. Be grateful today for a God Who loves you and gives you His presence. No fear. Love loud!

109

SKIPPETY SLIPPETY! Up and moving this morning! Breakfast with honey and now he's off getting the preps for ribs for our youngest son's birthday celebration with all the family today. So excited to see all the kiddos today and love on them! Not often we can get all the busy adult lives together in our home, so this is one happy Momma today.

Yesterday was a day full of blessings. I had a wonderful opportunity to meet some women in the area involved in ministry and mingle, lunch together, and some good teaching. Then I was able to watch my girls battle and battle and battle to pull out a win in the bottom of the eighth inning. Does a coach's heart lots of good to see her team go ahead, tie, lose the lead, tie, go behind, tie, then win. I love to see that they never gave up. Even in our last at bat, they still believed in each other and pulled out the win. Had dinner with family and close friends to close out a fun day.

So yesterday in our ministry time, we were in the book of Nehemiah, and there were many great lessons from the two chapters we camped in but wanted to share just one of the takeaways with you. So often in life, we can have "our plans" the way or order we see things need to happen, the way we want things to go, the people we want to line up, the circumstance, or even people we want to control. Our plan, our way. And so often, once we get started going in a direction, we can be finitely focused, which isn't a bad thing, but we must bear some things in mind about our plan or directions.

> Then the king said to me, "What do you request?" So I prayed to the God of heaven. And I said to the king, "If it pleases the king, and if your servant has found favor in your sight, I ask that you send me to Judah, to the city of my fathers' tombs, that I may rebuild it." (Neh. 2:4, NKJV)

So this morning, as I read and meditate on this passage, I am thinking about the direction God has been taking my life. I am thinking that about two years ago, when I went to the She Speaks conference, that I came home thinking I had to have it all together and make it happen on my own. That can lead to some frustration and struggle and some not being sure of what you were called to when you try to do it yourself. I'm a DIY girl, no doubt, but there are some things you must do first in a DIY project before you just jump in and start building. I love that Nehemiah, knowing that his heart is broken and hurting for the people of Judah, wants to go and rebuild the broken and burned walls, but when the king asks him, notice that he prays before he answers.

Yes, I don't know about you, but I have tried to put some things together without directions (often). And sometimes, it comes out okay, but so, so often, I find that if I had received some direction before I began, then the steps would have been easier, and my logic is not always God's way. So this morning, I am looking at where I am and so glad that I finally learned to lay things down to the Lord before I pick them up and go on my happy way. He will fill me with instruction and guidance and insight that I never could have had on my own. And His timing is beautiful. My timing can be forced and failing. So lay down your plans by lifting them up to Him before we step forward. He will meet you there. Love loud!

110

UPSIE DOODLES! Up and at it this beautiful morning! Today is moving and kicking, people, so let's get after it! God is good!

This past Sunday, I heard a great sermon, and part of it was about our walk with God. So I've been on soak mode about my walk, just walking with Him in general. I am out frequently in the mornings on the trails or streets, and I watch people walk. Lots of ways to walk. We can walk at different speeds, have different strides, arm swings, etc. I am a coach, so I am all about biomechanics when I do something athletic. I want to be efficient, want to get the most bang for my buck when using my body and energy. So I see people who have big arm swings, little arms swings, arm swings that twist across their bodies, arms that are doing push press while walking—you name it, it happens. Big strides, small strides, fast, slow, and paces in between, we were made to walk. Think about Adam and Eve. They "walked" in the garden with God. Abraham walked with

God. Elijah walked with God. The disciples walked with Jesus. All this walking is good stuff.

So often, we become complacent in our walk. We think we have to produce something. We think we are just up and moving again today, putting one foot in front of the other without intention. We move, but we aren't getting all that God has planned for us to get in the walk. We might be swinging our arms across our body while our legs are trying to move straight ahead, working against ourselves, making ourselves struggle more than we were made to. I'm no genius but I do know that God wants us to walk in love. When He walked in the garden with Adam and Eve, it was in love, and in that, love is obedience. Think about walking with God and how when we are intentional in our walk. We find an abundance of love, and in that love, we seek to obey. And as we obey, we draw even closer to Him, all while walking, moving forward with intention. You can't walk without trying to walk. In that case, you just stand.

Here's what is so wonderful about God. He began walking with Adam and Eve, and despite their mistake in choice, God still desired to walk with us. So He continues to walk, and years later, Jesus enters and gives us the opportunity to walk close again. God does not hide His love for us. He does not hide His desire for us to walk in obedience with Him. He places so many beautiful blessings in the garden and the tree of knowledge, and He desires our obedience. He does not hide His desire for obedience when He give Moses the Ten Commandments. He does not hide His desire for obedience when Jesus repeats over and over that He is "the way, the truth and the life," and "no one" comes to the Father except through Him. Still love. Still obedience.

God never hides these things from us. He has never been deceitful in what He desires. And we should be so overjoyed to walk with Him. Rise up and put one foot in front of the other each day, and move toward Him and beside Him. Some days will be small steps. Some days will be big ones. Some days, we will struggle to look like we are walking at all. Oh, but may we desire to walk well, to see how much He loves us, to lay down our lives and stop trying to control or force issues and enjoy the walk with our Creator. May we desire today to follow Jesus so close that we are in His shadow, walking in His dust. Obedience is not a bad word. It is walking with a heart of love. Love loud!

111

SCOOBER DOODLES! Up and at it on this beautiful Monday! It's a great day indeed! Today my youngest, is twenty-three years old! Yikes! I'm getting old! What a blessing he is, and what a blessed day!

So this morning, I am reading all over the place, but the Lord keeps bringing me to a few places in the Bible with the same message, so I will share.

Ezekiel 37:1–14 is the passage, but I will only share bits. Please read the entire passage. It's packed with goodness.

> The hand of the Lord was on me, and He brought me out by the Spirit of the Lord and set me in the middle of a valley; it was full of bones. He led me back and forth among them, and I saw a great many bones on the floor of the valley, bones that were very dry. He asked me, "Son of man, can these bones live?" I said, "Sovereign Lord, you alone know." Then he said to me, "Prophesy over these bones and say to them, 'Dry bones, hear the word of the Lord! This is

what the Sovereign Lord says to these bones: I will make breath enter you, and you will come to life. I will attach tendons to you and make flesh come upon you and cover you with skin; I will put breath in you, and you will come to life. Then you will know that I am the Lord." (1–6, NIV)

So Ezekiel was set in a valley, not just any valley but a valley full of bones. The Lord leads him about and asks him what he sees and then asks if the bones can live. Oh, and let's not forget that they are dry bones. I don't know about you, but there have been times in my life where I've been set in a valley of dry bones, a place I didn't choose to walk and put myself in, and yet I found myself there, wondering what on earth I am doing in this place and why God brought me there. Ever been there? Ever been in a place where you feel like you are looking at death, destruction, bones that have been dried up, done, and over? So if you are in such a place today, know that God has something to declare in such a place. He tells Ezekiel to prophesy, tells him to speak, use his speech to speak over the dead things all about him. Not just dead, dry bones.

If we look at dry bones, we see with our eyes no possibility of life being in those bones. We see that because we are looking in the natural. God is asking Ezekiel to not look with his natural eyes but with eyes of faith upon this valley of bones. Can they be resurrected? Can they move again? Yes, but not just move and stand but brought back with flesh and tendons! And then God tells Ezekiel to speak breath into them. Friends, this passage is rich, and my time is short, but He wants you to know today that if you are walking about in a valley and you see dry bones, you are wondering what you are doing there, and how to handle it, know that His hand is on you. You may have been placed there, but you can speak, breathe healing and life into dry bones.

God's Spirit is powerful, so may we walk in such a valley filled with faith and eyes that can see life in a situation that no one else would see life. Today speak life and breathe into all things. Words are powerful and especially the words that the Lord will give you to speak. Love loud!

112

YAPPLE DAPPLE! Up and moving in beauty this morning! Wow! What a gorgeous morning! We have had so much rain and clouds that it's easy to forget how beautiful it is on a quiet, sunny morning! Had a great day yesterday! I am just sitting here this morning with a grateful heart. Grateful for all the people God has placed in my life and how blessed I am to share time with them. They bless me with fellowship, wisdom, encouragement, love, laughter, counsel, and so many other things. On my own, I never could have assembled such an amazing group of friends about me, and yet God has moved His hand, and here I sit this morning, truly blessed by yesterday.

This morning, I was thinking about David being anointed king at a young age and having to wait, about all the incredible things that he encountered—struggles, trials, blessings, and God's favor all before he took the throne. I was thinking about David in this waiting period and how he was constantly seeking God and His guidance, wisdom, and counsel. Thinking about all the muck he endured all the while knowing that he would sit on the throne, but he was under constant attack. Watching him stand and speak in faith over what was happening in his life. Waiting for fifteen years can't be easy. I have trouble waiting for fast-food delivery some days, and here is David waiting for something God has promised him, and if it was fast-food, it'd be a soggy burrito. And yet he waited.

Here's another thing I really love about David. As he is about to take the throne, long wait. Other's would have killed Saul, or asked God where are you? And when is this "king thing" happening? And let's get this show on the road! But here is David:

> It happened after this that David inquired of the Lord, saying, "Shall I go up to any of the cities of Judah?" And the Lord said to him, "Go up." David said, "Where shall I go up?" And he said, "To Hebron." So David went up there. (2 Sam. 2:1–2, NKJV)

So, did David make mistakes in his life and goop it up? Yes. But time after time, we look at David and see that he was a man who sought God's wisdom and counsel. Here he has waited and struggled all these years, as being crowned king was held out in front of him, and yet as soon as he is anointed king, what does he do? He asks the Lord for direction, counsel, and guidance. And notice he doesn't just ask if he should go and then do his own thing. No, he asks if he should go and then where he should go. Then, upon receiving his answer, he goes. Love this!

So often I have found myself laying things down at Jesus's feet or asking God for wisdom with a decision or direction, but I have not been wise enough to ask the second question, seeking more guidance and fully expecting God to provide me with what I need. David was in daily and constant dialogue with God, so I love that he just asks God for "more details please." God answers, and then David obeys and follows what God has given him. The Bible has so many verses about wisdom and seeking wise counsel. I want to lay my decisions down before Him no matter how long I've been waiting and then expect Him to give me counsel. Even if I seek more detail, I know He is listening to me. And may I have a heart that seeks His counsel and desires to follow His wisdom wherever it leads me. So if you are in a place of asking, a place of waiting, in this moment, seek Him and His wisdom. Seek His counsel. He may place answers in your life that are people with godly wisdom. He may speak to you directly, but one thing is for sure. He will not leave you wandering about. Seek and obey. Love loud!

113

HAPPY YAPPY! Up and moving this gorgeous day! God is holding me in His mighty hand so today will not hold me. Join me! A few years ago, the "Got Milk?" campaign was big. Celebrities would take photos or do commercials with milk in hand and a milk mustache for added effect. That was the question of the day, and they did it up right. So people would jump off that and say, "Got _____?" and use that pitch for whatever slogan they wanted. So I was smiling this morning when I got up and was reading the YouVersion verse of the day:

"The beginning of wisdom is this: Get wisdom. Though it cost all you have, get understanding" (Prov. 4:7, NIV).

I love it! The beginning of wisdom is get wisdom, period. If you don't have it, get it. If you want it, get it. If you need it, get it. So many chapters in Proverbs speak of wisdom, the attributes of wisdom, and the value of wisdom, and yet I can tell you that I have lived seasons of my life without much wisdom, just wandering and letting life happen to me and making decisions without wisdom but with just whatever floated through my mind or whatever presented itself. I love this because it is so simple and yet profound. Get it. "If any of you lacks wisdom, let him ask of God, who gives to all liberally and without reproach, and it will be given to him" (James 1:5, NKJV). And understanding will cost you. Experience is valuable and pricey.

So I know I have written on this before, but I am always drawn to it because it is so telling, and I love the book of Proverbs. In Proverbs 9, wisdom is (again) described as a female as well as folly, and they both invite us to come in. We are invited to the banquet table of wisdom, and she has built her house, hewn her pillars, and her home is stable and the feast of wisdom is on the table. We are invited. But our struggle is that folly also sits and calls. Invites. Folly has no banquet to offer—just stolen water and bread eaten in secret. And wisdom calls to us. May we answer. May we "get wisdom." May we hear her call and walk through her doors. Sit at her table and feast. Partake.

If we are lacking, and we ask, more feast is provided, and God will never leave us hungry for wisdom as long as we are asking and eating. Wisdom has prepared a feast for us. Each one of us. We are supposed to get wisdom. I wonder if we get a wisdom mustache when we eat from that table, like the milk mustache? One thing is for sure, the people I know who eat from that table and feast there, wisdom shows up in their lives. Wisdom shows up in what they do and what they speak. So while they don't have a mustache, the traits and characteristics of following Jesus are all over them. Better than a mustache. So today, even though we hear two calls, may we answer wisdom and walk through her door. Dine at her table, and feast on all she has to offer. Wise ones get wiser. I need to get to that table! Love loud!

114

SCOOBER DO! Up and moving this morning! Ready for a great day and all the Lord has in store for today! Looks like this morning will be beautiful, and this afternoon will bring the rain. Had a few verses on my mind this morning but read this one, and it just seemed to fit for today.

> I thank my God upon every remembrance of you, always in every prayer of mine making request for you all with joy, for your fellowship in the gospel from the first day until now, being confident of this very thing, that He who has begun a good work in you will complete it until the day of Jesus Christ. (Phil. 1:3–6, NKJV)

So this morning, I am thinking about what it means to lift someone up in prayer. I want to be so intentional about when someone needs prayer that I lift them up in that moment, that I don't wait until later, but I at least give a whisper to the Father for them. But I love when Paul is talking about being thankful and praying for someone in every prayer. I was reading in a book about how a prayerful heart of gratitude, lifted up to the Lord is like building a monument to heaven for that person. A praying parent who lifts up their child/children every day that those prayers are building and building and building.

What are they building? Generational blessings. Opportunities for the one continually prayed over to be remembered and favored. Not a casual prayer because we can come by those too easy these days (yes, I am guilty). But I love when I can sit in a quiet place and offer up loved ones and friends in heartfelt prayers daily. The fellowship we have with other believers is such a bonding of love and joy, and then being able to truly lift them up is beautiful. What better thing can you do than lift someone you love up to the Lord? I want to be thankful to God for all the wonderful people He has placed in my life!

I want to in every prayer of mine make request for you all with joy. I love the ladies God has placed together in our women's group and the fellowship and love that lives there. I love how God draws us together. He finishes what He began in us, doesn't leave us short, but what a blessing that He places us in community. Community give us joy. Family gives us joy. Deep friendships give us joy. Marriage gives us joy. We are meant to be with people so may we be grateful for those people and lift them up with hearts of gratitude. Every remembrance. Every prayer. God is good. Thankful heart. Love loud!

115

HOPPSEY DOODLES! Bunnies are out in force on this up and at it today! Yesterday was a wonderful day despite a downpours to cancel practice. God holds all things in His hand, so even in a season of rain outs and squeezed schedules, He holds sway, excited because He blesses my soul! Women's group tonight and can't wait to see all my friends!

Reading this week in Mark 5 and so much depth in some of the miracles Jesus performed in that chapter. The one I am sharing today was when Jairus (a synagogue leader) comes to Jesus and falls at his feet, asking Jesus to come lay His hands on his daughter because she is near death.

So Jesus is heading (along with a great multitude) to Jairus's house, and He also heals the woman with the bleeding problem as He makes His way there. Someone shows up from Jairus's house and tells them "Your daughter is dead. Why trouble the Teacher any further?" Jesus turns to Jairus and says, "Do not be afraid; only believe." So Jesus gets to the home and finds people crying and wailing and asks them "Why make this commotion and weep? The child is not dead, but sleeping." And catch this next verse, "And they ridiculed Him" (Mark 5:40, NKJV).

Jesus goes into her room and tells her to arise, and she rises up and walks.

So as I have been camped out a few days in this chapter. I just wanted to speak some empowerment over you today. We see this man, Jairus, a religious leader and someone who should not by the way of religiosity have had a thing to do with Jesus, but, friends, desperate times call for desperate measures. Nothing is more humbling than a sick child, and nothing will draw a parent to their knees quicker. Nothing will make you fall down and pray to Jesus with all of you and not listen to what the world says about whether you should or shouldn't. Your child's life is at stake. Have you ever been in a situation where someone has already pronounced you or your situation as "dead" done, over? You are toast (even burnt toast)—no chance, don't even bother!

I have had these words spoken to me before, and there was a time in my life where I would take those words in and let them sit and soak over my outlook. I'm here to tell you that Jesus can speak life and healing into your body, into your situation, into a circumstance that seems bleak. Jesus walks into this house and hears all the naysayers, all the people who see with earthly eyes and see a little girl who has no chance. Her chance has come and gone in their eyes, and so it's over as far as they can see. Yep. Because when we look at situations and circumstances in the natural, then they can look that way, but when we lay them at Jesus's feet and fall before Him, He can pour out His supernatural into that person's circumstance, hurt, whatever!

Here's another great thing. Jesus speaks that she is just sleeping, and they ridiculed Him. I love this! Why? Because again, it shows that so often, we are not using our eyes of faith our eyes that are earthly and just see natural. Don't forget that Jesus told Jairus, "Do not be afraid; only believe." So what is your situation? What is your struggle? What is your big thing? If Jesus speaks into it and calls you out to not fear and only believe, well, let's do it! Jesus can speak life into anyone, anything, any situation, hurt, pain, circumstance, bitterness.

Yes! So if you are in a place that looks bleak or too much for you, too deep, too dark, too big, too far gone, just know that Jesus can speak life and change what you see. He can change what you feel. He can move mountains. He hold power and sway over death, so why do we fear when something heavy and hard comes our way? Only believe. So here is Jairus begging Jesus to come and lay hands on his daughter near death. Jesus delayed by crowd and another healing. You think Jairus panicked? Hurry up, Jesus! She's gonna die! Jesus kept moving toward Jairus's house even though it might have been slower than Jairus had hoped for.

So today, I am thinking about His timing, His power of healing and speaking life. He can do all things! May I walk today and not fear a circumstance. May I walk today and only believe. May I walk in faith that He has me. He has those things I lift up, and He is moving toward them with His life-giving words and power. Friends, may we remember today that the prayers we offer up are heard and moved upon in His way and in His timing. He is calling. Rise up. He speaks the dead to life. Listen for his voice today! Love loud!

116

YEPPER DO! Up and at it this morning! Legs are jelly, but all is welly. Ready for what the Lord has in store for today! Game day makes it more fun! Praying for some dear ones today.

This morning, I was listening to this song by Hawk Nelson, "Sold Out" and hopping around during my workout. Took the time on the way home to really listen to the words and ask God to soak me in what it looks like. Way back in day, before kids, Mark and I went to a loud concert. It was packed, sold out, standing-room only. The place was wall-to-wall people, and even though we had seats, people stood most of the concert. They put on quite a show, which was good because we paid quite a price for those tickets.

So I am thinking about when we talk about a life that is sold out for Christ, and I hear people say that, and I feel and think the same way. Then I find myself on occasion holding part of myself back, wanting this certain thing to work "my way" and not trusting God for the outcome. I have had some dark places and dark closets in my life that I wanted to keep that way, and God asked me to release them to Him. That took some doing on my part (and some time), but the healing that has occurred since I gave that up is incredible. When we open our arms and give our stadium completely to Him, we put down our performance and let Him move in that stadium the way He sees fit, and we watch it move and flow through the stadium and out the doors. He is the performer, and He doesn't want a tiny crowd, a small seating area of your life or heart.

He can still perform, but the impact of what moves out of the doors and into the world is lessened. He can still perform, but how many lives do we cheat? How many people do we meet and encounter that need us in a sold-out state for the Lord and not just a little piece. God can use all, but how much more beautiful when we open the doors and let Him flood in. Let Him fill us to capacity. Standing-room only, no doubt. And the music He makes within us when we are sold out is so much more incredible than our best effort without Him. Sold out is not just for a ticket holder or stadium, but it is for a Christ follower who leaves the world behind, throws open the doors, and gives up themselves completely, daily. Woo. Rough part, right? So every day, Jesus asks me if I will take up my cross and follow Him.

Jesus replied: "Love the Lord your God with all your heart and with all your soul and with all your mind. This is the greatest commandment. And like it: "Love your neighbor as yourself." (Matt. 22:37–39, NIV)

Loving, sold out. May we walk today as souls that are sold out for Christ! No room for anything else. Jesus has the standing-room only tickets too. Let go! He will do a performance within you, and you will never be the same. Hallelujah! Love loud!

117

YABBA DABBA! Up and moving this morning! Wet and messy outside so practicing indoors today. One thing is for sure, I don't control the weather. God is good no matter the rain or shine!

Mark and I were so blessed to have his grandpa marry us. He was an incredible man of God and such a sweet and loving spirit. He read a poem or two in our ceremony and had many wonderful things to say about marriage that have stuck with me through the years. One of the poems he read closed with this, "It's more than marrying the right person, it's being the right person." I just love that still! I have seen over the years so many of our friends, so many young people, so, so many people I've talked to that struggle in marriage. I have heard women/young women say, "He likes this in a girl. He wants someone more _____ and then they proceed to try to fill in the blank. They try to become what that man is looking for or "wants." And I have seen guys do the same thing. "She wants a man that is _____, so I need to work on this."

I will never by any means claim to be an expert on marriage, so let me state that right up front. I am sharing what I have observed and what has played out in mine and Mark's marriage. We all have rough edges that can be chiseled. We all have places to work on, things and areas we can be a better partner, but we need to look at what angle we approach that idea. When we first married, we had lots of growing up to do, and we did it together. Through some struggles and fights and loud evenings, we started seeing real growth and glow in our marriage when we each stopped trying so hard to please the other person. Sounds funny, right?

Here's what I mean by this: we realized that instead of looking at the other person and trying to pursue them with all we are, we needed to look up to God, and each of us pursue Him with all we are. We had been putting our relationship in a position of worship that was above our worship or pursuit of God. Hard to be the right person when you are focused on pursuing another person, but when we are chasing hard after God and letting Him work in us, then we are in process of becoming the right person, the person He designed us to be. If we each are a cord and trying to run toward each other, we can get things all twisted up out of whack, looking and chasing "things" or "ideals" in and about a person, and we can miss what ties this all together. When Jesus becomes who we pursue and worship, each as individuals, then His cord binds us together and, like a drawstring, cinches us up and pulls us close.

I could never be or fill all the "wants or ideals" that Mark may have had for a wife, but the day we decided to stop chasing each other's ideals and start chasing Jesus was the day our marriage began to flourish and grow stronger. When each individual is stronger in Christ, then we are stronger as a bond to battle all the yuck and muck that comes at you as a couple, and you can stand together and battle as things come against you as an individual. Cinched up together. The Bible talks about the three-stranded cord, and He is the only one that gives marriage true strength and glow. "Till death do you part" may be a long time, and we have the choice on how we will live those days. What we want those days to look like, feel like, and how we want them to impact our children.

You can put on a front for the world to see, but children know what happens behind the doors at home and how we handle ourselves matters. Lay down all the junk, all the pretending, all the worries about what you "look like to the world," and give God reign in your life—each of you—and watch and see how He changes and works and draws the cords together, submitting to His will (that's even when we think we have to have the last word or we think we are right) rather than our own. We will see our marriage glow. We will see that love flow into our children, out of our homes, and follow us. A good marriage is good, but I want a great, godly marriage. He reigns. Love loud!

118

SLIPPETY DO DAH! Up and on the move this morning. Had some quiet time outside with the Lord before the sunrise. I love quiet mornings. Even though there is light outside, all the world is still, peaceful, and beautiful.

Doing bit of reading this morning and ran across this quote by Emily Dickinson, "Forever is composed of nows." So I am asking myself this morning, "What am I busy doing?" Here in this moment, right now, am I living for the Lord? Is what I am doing bringing glory and honor to Him? I can be so worried sometimes about things I need to get done or what I want to accomplish and not that those are bad things, but what is the heart motive behind it is where I need to be. At the time I am writing this, I am forty-nine years old, and I am not guaranteed life to the end of this day, and yet I pray that I get to see my kids all marry, have grandkids (yes!), and get to hug and kiss their little faces, take them places, make brownies with them, go see their games, and plays and see all the blessings I pray for come to fruition for my kids and their kids.

I want to physically be here, but I may not. I want to love on people and point people to Christ by what I speak and the words I live. I want to live a life that blesses others and giving myself away, not a taker or a user. I know that we live our words. I want to put myself in an environment that is encouraging and growing and has leaders that exemplify faith and obedience, not always convenience.

I am hoping that as we begin our week, we will each be mindful of what our nows consist of, living lives of godly character, being courageous and standing in obedience when it is hard because it is easy to stand when the wind isn't blowing full force against you so may we be obedient in the hard places. May our nows consist of being leaders, not Christ followers that run away from challenge, not ones who flee (unless it is away from temptation) but stand strong and fight the battle that is before us. May we know what we are fighting for and who we are fighting against (and it isn't people; it's the enemy), what we are called to do, and who we are called to follow and then be courageous enough to step and actually obey in the now.

So in this now I have, I am seeking Christ and a time to renew my love and wonder with a great God. And this now will fill my heart and keep me encouraged to use each now I have to pursue Him and love well. Love loud!

119

YEPPER SKADOO! Up and moving on this wonderful breezy morning! God is good! Meets us where we are. Even when we are in a pit of despair, He knows where we are and can reach us! He is wonderful!

So this morning, I am thinking about a conversation I had last night and about a wreck I was in about thirty years ago. Mark and I had only been married a couple of months and were heading to Colorado for a camping trip in Rocky Mountain National Park. We left that evening after we both were exhausted. He was driving and got tired, so we pulled over and changed drivers. He put his seat back and fell asleep. And before long my eyelids grew too heavy for me to keep them up, and I fell asleep behind the wheel. I won't go into all the details that happened but will share a few. The biggest one is that Mark and I shouldn't be alive today. The people who found us were so amazed that anyone lived. I will say that all four tires blew out, and I lost control of the vehicle and it flipped over on the roof and proceeded to skid upside down on the freeway for about one hundred yards.

So I have seen these commercials recently where just before the car crash happens, the drivers get out and have a conversation. Both parties realize there is nothing they can do and get back in the car, and then just as it should be impact the commercial ends. I can tell you that as I was trying to gain control of the truck, everything moved in slow motion. I can vividly remember it and feeling each tire blow and fighting the truck to stay upright. I can remember what it felt like to flip over. I can remember how it felt for the roof to collapse around my head and for me to cover my face with my hands as glass and concrete were all around me, seventy miles per hour on the roof.

I remember opening my eyes when we stopped moving and the road being so close to my face that my tongue could almost touch it. Scars still on my knuckles and we had to get my wedding ring cut off. Vivid memories still. But here is what I am thinking in all this. I am not in control. There is that moment of realization in a wreck when your mind truly realizes that you are headed for danger, and you can do nothing to prevent it any longer. It is a sobering moment to say the least. What I am feeling as I have so many dear ones walking through some mess or some in major messes right now that we are not in control. Oh, we have a say so up to a point, but at some point, we must sit back and realize that a greater purpose or cause is being accomplished here. It's an *aha* moment. I could no longer steer the car any direction. I am not saying that we don't have control over our choices because as you can read, I made a poor choice to drive tired, but even in all my recovery efforts, the truck still flipped, and we were skidding out of our control.

We have all these day-to-day things, and we get amped up and caught up in them like they will make or break us. At some point, we see that God is in control. We may have put ourselves in the circumstance, and in some situations, He is the only one who can rescue us. We can't save ourselves. I know so many people who should not be walking this earth, and they are still here—near death experiences. I am still amazed that God reached down and saved me (and Mark) despite my foolish decision that night. He does that. Do I have scars from that decision? Yes. But they remind me what happens when I think I know best. So today, if you are in a place and you are trying to push all the right buttons, smoodge all the right people, trying to line all your ducks up just so, sometimes, our circumstance or choices are bigger than we thought. They might eat us up if we are not in Him if we don't step back and let Him do what He does. May we recognize today we have a God of rescue, redemption, and restoration. He has a purpose for you. How do I know? I am still here. Love loud!

120

WHOOPETY DO DAH! It's up-and-at-it day! I will say that I do some form of squats about every day, but the deadly squats are overhead squats. Who comes up with these? Ha! Ready for today! Whoop! Lifting up one of our sweet ladies in prayer this morning—

Last night, as Mark and I were driving home from Galveston, we were talking about back when we were kids and our parents would go fill up with gas and go to the "full service" side of the station. This meant they checked your tires for air, put gas in your tank, checked your oil, and washed your windshield and back window. As you would drive in, there was a hose the car ran over and made a *ding, ding* sound, and the gas attendant would come out dressed in a uniform and hat and get to work. Our kids have never had this experience, and we were talking about the way gas stations are different today. So I was thinking about full service as we were praying last night. When I lift my life up, when I offer myself to Him completely, I want a full service. I don't want self-serve. Get it yourself. Do it yourself. You are on your own. I want to walk to the cross and lay it down—all requests, all brokenness, all ugliness, all struggles (which by the way is my middle name, Suzanne Struggles, just thought you should know), all strongholds, all weaknesses.

And then Jesus comes in and does His work in me, changes my old heart for a new one, fills me with joy, washes away all the old dirt and muck and grime of the world so I can see and be clean, He gives me strength to walk out each day, and He fills me to the full with His Spirit. So I am reading in Psalm 23 again about "The Lord is my shepherd, I lack nothing." And then in John 10:10, "I have come that they may have life, and have it to the full." Who doesn't want this? Life to the full! That doesn't mean easy street, breezy life full of abundance and blessing, and no hardships ever. No. What is does mean is that I am wanting and seeking to be full to the measure of Him, His Holy Spirit, His love, His demeanor, His giving and kindness. Full.

So may we be mindful today that God is a God of full service. He wants to fill us completely. Change us to look and be more like Him. We have to drive to the right line, full service or self-service, our choice. Today, may we all be arms open and lives laid down as we walk to the cross and remember. He loves us that much! Praying today to be filled with Him every step, every word, every action. Let Him work in us. We will love the results. Love loud!

121

SCOOBER DO! Up and at it this morning in the early! Moving a little slow but glad to be back at it on a short week. Don't think it would be a bad idea if each work week was just four days.

Been sitting out by the pool a bit this past weekend and thinking a bit about swimming, and I've seen lots of beach pictures with kiddos running out and playing in the water. I was thinking about a time when I was little and shouldn't have been in the deep end, but I thought I could swim better than my reality. I can remember going under the water and the voices above the water being muffled. I have been at different times in my life in the deep water, and believe me, I tested it and went further. Tested it and went further and tested it and went further, further until I couldn't touch bottom, further until my own swimming ability played out, and I was too deep. I was under. If we stay out in the deep water too long, we begin to be underwater too much. Underwater too much and we can't hear the voices calling to us. They sound muffled. They are garbled. They are Charlie Brown's teacher.

So there are so, so many great analogies you can make from water, but what if today you have ignored all the signs, all the "Beware of the under current" signs, all the dangerous water signs, and you did it your way and kept wandering out further and staying out there longer and longer, the voices from the shore become distant. The voices above water that come to save you become hard to discern. We can live in a sin pattern so long that it becomes just like every day water around us, and we don't realize that we are creeping out to deep water. The deep water blurs lines and decisions. The deep water, especially when we are under for long periods, makes God's voice harder and harder to hear. Can God rescue us even in the deep? Absolutely! Living proof right here.

But I can tell you that I never want to return to the deep waters. I never want to test myself and show what I can do because it's not about me, how strong I am, or how many people like me, or how many people I can get to agree with me. Not about me at all. If I will spend a little more time each day in the scriptures and in quiet time with my Beloved, then I can hear Him clearly and don't want to wander off or "prove" myself because I have nothing to prove, and deep water doesn't prove me either even if we can swim in deep water, even if we can live in sin. That doesn't mean we were made to.

So if you are bobbing up and down in the deep or if you are down and you know you hear muffled voices but not sure what is being said, keep treading. Swim up. Jesus is calling you to rise and not sink. He is calling you to stop trying to do everything in your own power and for you and to let go and hear His voice. He is speaking. Are we listening? Get in a place today to hear His sweet voice, a place where the noise of the world isn't too loud and waves are too big or overwhelming. Come out of the deep and into your calling. Love loud!

122

YIPSEE DOODLES! Up and moving under the pink sky and tree frogs "barking." So happy to be off today to spend some couple time with my honey today! Weekends can be a whirlwind of craziness, so I'm glad to have some down time today.

So this morning, I was thinking about all the cooking I was doing yesterday, and as I was looking for a cake pan, I ran across a container in my cabinet full of cookie cutters. I don't bake cookies much these days, and when I do, they are ready to bake. Rare that I pull out the cookie cutters since the kiddos are all grown. I am thinking that we generally don't like to be cookie cutters. We don't want to be put in a category or a box or a shape. Well, I am thinking as I look at all the shapes of cookie cutters that I have that there may not be too much wrong with being a cookie cutter. If I am a cookie cutter, then I know my purpose. I'm shaped for my purpose, and my shape doesn't determine what I taste like. That's the dough's job. I'm honestly not sure what shape of cookie cutter I am, but I'm probably the one who has been dropped a bunch of times and a little odd shaped, bent, and if you were a precision baker of perfection, you'd throw me out.

Here's the great part! God makes the dough. He puts in all the ingredients. Sometimes, we let the world add too much of this or that, and that can affect how we taste, but we have the makings for good cookies. When we let Jesus in, then we rise just right. We smell good and taste good to others. We aren't sour or bitter. We don't have too much salt or sugar. And God didn't throw me out. Did you catch that? God didn't throw me out! Grateful! Bent in places, broken in places, oddly shaped. Yep. He still uses me. I still cut cookies, and He uses my shape because someone out there likes weird-shaped cookies and can identify with them. Likes the way they look and taste, so God puts me in proximity to those people. A bent-up cookie cutter.

Here's the thing. I am looking at women's ministry and thinking how so, so often a women's ministry is about everyone being the same cookie cutter. Let's all look the same, talk the same, wear pink hats, make bows and things, eat tea and crumpets, and call it a ministry. And if you don't like all these things then you don't belong. Crazy, right? Yet I have friends in women's ministry all over the place, and we talk about this being a struggle. I look each week at the women who meet in our home. We are all different-shaped cookie cutters. Some of us have some bent-up edges. Some of them are beautifully shaped. Some of them are figuring out what shape they are. But here's the deal: we are all part of God's kingdom, and He has purposed each and every woman for her calling. We all look different and are in different places in our lives. We have each had different experiences. We are all walking through this life together, working, walking toward tasting like Jesus dough. I pray for the day when women can come together and gather and be uplifting to each other, rally around each other, not compare, not degrade, not gossip and slander each other but honestly value that God has purposed that cookie cutter to cut cookies for the kingdom, shaped for the calling they each have and embrace that. No need for pink hats for all. We all are women of God.

So today, if you are looking at yourself and wondering what is your purpose or calling, well friend, look no further. I can't tell you whether it's singing or teaching or administering, but I can tell you that you are called to be His. And in being His, let's build His kingdom. Let Jesus in, and let Him use us when and wherever we are needed or called. He uses our shape and purposes us in that shape for His glory. If you are bent up like me, no worries today! God still uses bent and odd cookie cutters. Taste like Jesus. Love loud!

123

YABBA DO! Up and running about this morning! Lots done already and much more to do but so mindful of what today is. What meaning it holds for me as a Christ follower? I was reading this morning all about this day and days preceding it as Jesus was walking this path toward the cross. I was thinking this morning about the "false" accusations and things that were brought against Him. And I think of His total ability to prove Himself as the Son of God. He could have summoned armies of angels and walked away untouched from the whole mess. But His kingdom is not of this world, so what the people of this world did to Him and said about Him wasn't as relevant as who He was, what He was called to do, and standing in that call no matter what so that people like you and me could have redemption. All are welcome to believe in Him. Thank you, Jesus!

So I was camping out on the accusation stuff because I have walked that path more than once during my lifetime. Both sides actually. I have been accused of things, things where the full truth wasn't revealed because it was meant to cover up for someone. I have been accused when I deserved full on the things being brought up against me, and I have accused without full information based on some hearsay but not what I witnessed with my own eyes. This is what I know about accusing. It is painful. Painful for the person receiving the blows. Painful for you, if you are accusing and realize later that it was wrongful. And yet we still do it. I have come to the place in my life that even if I possess all the information, all the proof that I am being wrongfully accused, I will not fight back. Tired of the fighting back because people will believe exactly what they want to.

All the Jews around Jesus believed what they wanted to even though He had done all the miracles and even said He was the Son of God. They still believed otherwise. He was a threat, and they wanted Him gone. And so it goes. And Jesus stood and realized that His taking all the humiliation and junk that we deserved did more to further the kingdom of God than all the gossip and nasty accusations and religious piety could ever do.

Reading Robert Morris's book about the power of words and I want to be in such a walk with God in my life that if I am going to speak words and they are not bringing glory to God, furthering His Kingdom, encouraging or speaking life into someone, well, then I will not speak them. I know that I will mess up, and my tongue will get the best of me here and there, but I am really doing serious prayer and asking God to work on me in this area of my life. So today, I am looking at our Jesus and how He stood, complete peace of knowing who He was and what He was purposed for despite all the muck of the people around Him wanting to throw Him away and kill Him. Love how He always leads us by example! Today is Friday, full of pain and struggle and harshness, but Sunday is coming! Love loud!

124

SCOOBERLICIOUS! Up and at it this morning! Today is Friday, and that adds to the glitter! The weather has been gorgeous, and I've loved being outside with classes this week! I usually don't suffer with allergies but I've been a little sniffly off and on. Doing great now but a couple of weeks ago, I was a sneezy, drippy mess. It makes me think back to when Mark and I lived in the house where we raised our kids in Sagemont. When we moved in, I was pregnant with Jake, and Jess was only ten months old, and Josh had just turned two, so they were little ones for sure. The house had carpet that was not new, not original but not new, but we were so excited and happy for more room and new neighborhood that the carpet was something we decided we could deal with for the time. We all lived with snotty noses while they were growing (me as well). Then about twelve years after our move in, we decided it was time.

We had the cash, and we needed new flooring. We were do-it-yourselfers so we pulled up the carpet and pad. There was a heavy fog of dust and dirt in the house as we pulled up the old carpet. I mean heavy and yuck! It was gross. We cleaned everything, and I mopped the concrete with bleach. Within a day, we were all talking about being able to breathe. The air was clean, and we could really breathe— no runny noses. We felt so much better, slept better, and lived on concrete for a while until we could afford laminate, but we loved the new environment in our home!

I have been places before in my life, environments that, while I was in them, I could not recognize my inability to breathe. I could not really tell that I was not operating within my gifts or talents or being used the way the Lord wanted to use me, yet I stayed in that place, unchanging because it was comfortable, because to change would require lots of work, and I wasn't sure what else was "out there," so this was "safe." Ever been there? I've lived that with my church life and my job life more than once. Sometimes, when we are in the middle of something, we cannot see or feel how the environment is really affecting us. We have to get out of that place, either rid ourselves of whatever is killing our air or rid ourselves of that environment completely. I can say that when we finally moved to another home, we did not want carpet anywhere in the home.

We remembered what it was like to live with too much carpet and how it collected all the yuck and muck and just held it there, contaminating our very home. So if you are in a place like this, seek prayer and wisdom. Search the scriptures. Ask God to guide you and help you. Let Him reveal the places and things that are the "old carpet" in your life and then the hardest part, removing the old, nasty carpet; taking it out to the trash; and changing the environment you are in. It affects all around you. Take the step in faith! You will be so glad you did! Love loud!

125

SKIPPER DOODLES! Up and rolling out of bed this morning! Had a great day yesterday topped off with a fun night of family. Much enjoyed it! Excited for time with dear ones today!

Yesterday, I was writing about Genesis 4:7 (NIV), "If you do what is right, will you not be accepted? But if you do not do what is right, sin is crouching at your door; it desires to have you, but you must rule over it."

So I am camped there again this morning because the second half of the verse is just as powerful as the first. Anytime God is full out, directly speaking to someone, there is power, so I didn't want to shortchange all the good stuff in the verse. Thinking yesterday about sin crouching at your door and how the enemy lays in wait for us, desires to have us, but you must rule over it. I can look back on so, so, so (keep adding the so's) places, times in my life where temptations have been there, times where they have been huge, bigger than me for sure. Desiring to have me? Yes.

Desiring to consume me, own me, make me its slave? Yes! The enemy wants to enslave us. And sin is oh so enticing, especially when we frequent the environment where we know our weakness lies, and the enemy knows it too. And so we say, "It's okay this once," "No one will know," "If I pretend it didn't happen, then it's okay," "If I ignore it, it will go away," and all the other lies we tell ourselves to justify being in that environment and get caught up in the trap.

It desires to have us, but we must rule over it! So even if we "think" no one knows about the sin, it is spinning a web. It is locking chains on us the minute we fall, but (it's a big but) we have the power to rule over it. Jesus came to destroy the power of sin and death. He overcame them both. Are we Jesus? No, but when we are His, we have His Spirit and power within us. We can cast off this sin. We can "resist the devil and he will flee" (James 4:7). At the name, the name of Jesus, every evil spirit must run. It cannot stand against the name above all names. We must rule it. Does that mean we never sin? No, but we cast it off. We recognize our bents. We run toward Jesus, and His name and presence makes the enemy run.

So today, if you are in a struggle, a battle with some sin slave issues, call out. Call on the name and power of Jesus! He can break those chains and empower you to rule over that sin that wants to devour you. Stand strong today! Rule! You have the power of Christ in you, friends! Love loud!

126

YABBA DOODLES! Up and at it on this foggy day! Fog or no fog, today is here and ready to roll! That makes me excited! Always enjoy sitting out back in the evenings and watching all the activity. Yesterday, I was watching our eleven-year-old lab sit in a crouching position as he was watching a bird in our yard. He was ready. All muscles positioned just so and loaded up, ready to pounce at just the right moment when the bird was least suspecting. Made me think of God talking to Cain before he killed his brother.

> You will be accepted if you do what is right. But if you refuse to do what is right, then watch out! Sin is crouching at the door, eager to control you. But you must subdue it and be its master. (Gen. 4:7, NIV)

This verse always grabs me every single time I read it. God is speaking directly to Cain. Gives him a warning, "Watch out!" I am thinking about times in my life where the Lord has given me warnings flat out. Open your eyes and see kinda warnings. And so often, we wander into sin. We know it's there, and yet we are sometimes in the oblivious zone and sometimes in the pride zone (we can handle it) and sometimes in the "I don't care, I'm gonna do what I want" zone (which is also prideful), and so as God warns Cain, Cain pays Him no mind. This image of evil crouching, waiting to spring on me, pounce on me at just the moment when I am most vulnerable or least expect it, it can definitely wake you up to the complete evil of the enemy. When something is crouching and ready to pounce, when something is "lying in wait" for you, it's not because it wants to give you a happy surprise and hug you. No! It wants to devour you. It wants to kill you and destroy you. Completely. No, "let me mangle you and let you walk away" kind of pouncing, nope.

The enemy wants to steal, kill, and destroy. Jesus doesn't mince words when He says it and calls him the "father of all lies." So my lab Snickers, is a little old and missed the bird last night he was after, but the enemy is not slow and has not "lost a step" over the years. He is quite cunning and deceptive. Be aware as you walk today that he is crouching. Be on guard, and put on the full armor of God this morning as you go out into the world and begin to open doors. Be aware that some doors are not all joy and fun, but sin is crouching. Know what you are walking into, and pray for wisdom and discernment. Love loud!

127

YEPPER DOODLES! Up and at it this morning! Extra joy this morning as my honey comes home today. Lots to do and things rolling around in this heart this morning. Listening to a playlist this morning, and "He Knows" by Jeremy Camp comes on. "Oh the doubt you're standing in between/ the chains of doubt that held you in between, one by one they're starting to break free." So this morning, I am thinking about the "in between" not the Oreo cream filling but the "in betweens" in life that can hold us captive. We can find ourselves living lives of "in between" neither for something or against it, just existing. Just going through the motions. And before we realize it, days have passed; months have gone; years have flown, and we are still "in between." We can walk through life here and finish our race and really never have even run the race. Oh we went on a journey, took steps but never really ran the race with the intention and purpose with which we were created.

It is really a tool of the enemy, and he uses it quite well. Get us caught up in the wrong things, get us distracted, get us thinking about ourselves, our wants, our needs, our fleshly desires, and we will live in the middle, neither hot nor cold.

"And without faith it is impossible to please God, because anyone who comes to Him must believe that He exists and that He rewards those who earnestly seek Him" (Heb. 11:6, NIV).

So what does it look like to have faith? Not just a "Hey, I know God exists. Jesus is the Son of God," and all that, but what does it look like to step into that? The first step is believing, but that is not where we stop the in between. I am thinking that if our faith is real to us, then we will run toward God. That doesn't mean we do it right and exactly on point each day, just as athletes don't have perfect games each time they compete, but if they pour into their craft, fine-tune their skills and pursue the goal, then they run well.

Fall? Yes? But not sitting and staying camped in the in between but getting up and running toward the prize again. That is faith. When we can't see the prize with our eyes but we trust that He is faithful every single time, and we run to it. No camping in the "in betweens." Those are the places we stay broken, unhealed, lost, unforgiven, in chains—just where the enemy wants us, straddling the fence. Not a productive place to be. And so passes the time. Or does it? Today is full of choices, and they are yours to make. So if you are in the "in between," then get up today, and run your race toward the only One worthy of pursuit! Love loud!

128

SCOOBY GROOVY! Up and at it this morning! Yesterday was so good—school, practice, group, late-night talks with family. God is good.

I can't tell you how many conversations I've had the past few days about being a new creation in Christ. It keeps coming up, so I decided to camp out this morning in 2 Corinthians 5. I am loving all the take aways in this chapter. I am thinking about "We live by faith, not by sight" (7), and how often in my life I try to look ahead and see what God has in store. I want to know by seeing, and yet He is calling me to a faith that is just that—faith, trusting that He has me, trusting and knowing and believing in what purpose He has for me and path and that I don't have to see with my earthly eyes. I don't need to see. I need to see with my heart.

So in verse 5, Paul is talking about us being given "the Spirit as a deposit, guaranteeing what is to come." I love this. I get paid twice a month and have direct deposit. The money is there. The deposit has been made, and the money is guaranteed. Jesus paid the price for me, for you, for us. We have been reconciled to Christ, and the Spirit is our deposit, the promise of a life with God now and to come. We can bank on it. We can draw from that account. We can listen to the Spirit and ask for His leading and guidance. And because He has reconciled us, then we are made new, a new creation. The old is gone! Yay! I don't want my old. I've lived that yuck before. Isn't it lovely to be reminded that even though we mess up, maybe even today, we are new. We are in process. We don't have to be able to see the whole picture, but step in faith that God has the big picture and is making us new.

"Therefore, if anyone is in Christ, the new creation has come: The old has gone, the new is here" (2 Cor. 5:17, NIV)!

The new creation has come. We are not waiting on becoming new. We are new. Are we perfect? No. We are new and progressing toward being more Christlike but new nonetheless. When I mess up, I need this reminder that I am new. I need to remember that God has given me a deposit, a promise, His Spirit, and a guarantee of what a slice of life in heaven will be like.

So today, if you are in a place where you can't see what the future holds, what purpose is yours, know, rest, abide in the truth that if you are His, then you are reconciled to Him and new. Cast off anything old the enemy brings back your way. You are new. Now let's walk in newness! Love loud!

129

SNAPPY DO! Up and moving in the foggerific! Rolling forward and ready for today! Each day is a blessing!

I was sitting a bit yesterday in the twenty-third psalm, trying to soak on each verse. I memorized this chapter when I was a kiddo, but I try to go back to those scriptures frequently because for me, sometimes things can just be rote, old hat, and I really not remember the depth with which they were written. Then couple of weeks ago, heard a rockin' version of it at church (called 23), and it just made me circle back to it again. The whole chapter is good, and each verse a blessing, but yesterday, I just really got a hold of the first one.

"The Lord is my shepherd; I shall not want" (Ps. 23:1, NKJV).

I am thinking this morning about all the ways God has shepherded me through my life. He hasn't come out with a whip and beat me (although I probably needed it a few times). He hasn't forced me any direction. His hand has been gently on me, guiding me. His voice has been there for me in the times of plenty and in the dark places, and I have heard it, and it always brings me comfort and peace. If I wandered astray, He would find me close by or on the edge of cliff, and He would bring me back to the fold. I shall not want. I shall not lack. When we are His, we want for nothing. Lack is not what we experience. I am not talking about finances. I am not saying that life doesn't get hard sometimes, sometimes by circumstances, and sometimes by our decisions, but either way, we do not lack as a child of God.

If He was not a shepherd, then He would abandon us at the first sign of our mistakes or hiccups, leave us on the edge. We are prone to wander off and can't see the flock anymore, then wonder what happened. How did we get here? Yep. I've walked those places. I will never claim to be perfect or have lived a life that is above reproach. I am and have been the sheep. Got that part down. Not always making the smartest decisions but always cared for by the Shepherd who calls me home, who guides me gently, who rescues me when I'm in deep despair.

So today, if you are in a place where you feel all alone, where you think no one hears, loves, cares, sees, stop and be still. Be quiet and listen. Enter into some deep quiet time with the lover of your soul. The Shepherd is calling, but we must listen. He will gently nudge us, but we must be willing to move with those nudges and promptings. What else do we need when we have a Good Shepherd? I want nothing. He is my everything. Love loud!

130

SKIPPER DIPPER DO! Up and at it like a sweatball this morning! Today is going to be a good day! Time with my Beloved makes it better! Yeppers!

I was thinking this morning about some of the things I was sharing with my team yesterday about the way we live our lives daily. Years back, I was sharing something with young people about living today like it's your last. I remember another person with me at that time told me to not make the kids fear death. I thought it was an interesting comment and still do. I don't fear death. Death has been defeated, and I am in Christ, so I have no reason to fear. And yet I was talking to the girls yesterday about living a life of intentionality, a life of urgency, not a life that is too busy to see the small things, too rushed, too in a hurry. No, a life of urgency, meaning, that I have today. Good morning. What we have is what we are standing in this moment, not tomorrow, not 5:00 p.m. today. Now.

God is a God of today, not tomorrow, not a procrastinator like me. So I am thinking about this life I live today. It is eternal, meaning what I do today has a lasting impact on eternity. I can love on people, intentionally show them Christ, not judge, not point fingers, not sit and wait, not think I'll do the right thing next year, next week, next month, whatever. Now. This life is but a breath, and I don't know how much time I have left, but I know that I don't want to waste it on myself. I want to live in this temporary world with an eternity mind-set, not a fear of death, not a "oh no, better do the right thing or else" mind-set. I want to live with the knowledge that time is short, and that's not a worry but a want to live well in the time I have been gifted with.

So may we teach and lead people to live out today with intention. Live out today with how much of myself am I willing to give up. Give out love for the kingdom today. I can keep it all in, die, and what have I gained? Nothing. But may I pour myself out today with nothing held back and pray that I am circling up people, drawing them to Christ so that eternity in heaven just continues that relationship. It's a love thing, not a fear thing. So rise today with a focus on urgency, not rushing, but how am I going to live my today, and will I be satisfied with my today if it is my last? Love loud, out loud!

131

YABBA DABBA! Up and moving in the beauty today! All is still and quiet and so beautiful. Had a great break and now refreshed and ready to get back at it. Doing some reading this morning in Revelation and wanted to share.

> What He opens no one can shut, and what He shuts no one can open. I know your deeds. See, I have placed before you an open door that no one can shut. I know that you have little strength, yet you have kept my word and have not denied my name. (Rev. 3:7–8, NIV)

So this morning, I am looking at times in my life where I have prayed and prayed and prayed for things, for doors to open, doors I wanted, doors that held my agenda behind them. And I have watched those doors remained closed in my life. When I was younger, I would still stand at those doors and yank and pull and put both feet on the wall and pull the knob with all my might, all my weight, to no avail.

Thank God! As I have become older (and hopefully wiser), I have come to hold to the fact that once God has closed a door for me, it is for my best and is not meant to be opened. And that I cannot open it. And so I journey on down the path toward what He holds next for me, what door awaits me that is open. That is the door that I want to walk through with Him. He wants us to be blessed. He wants us to walk with Him and not alone through the door because it is His door that is open to us.

I love all the times I have fought tooth and nail to open doors that I wanted, worn myself out in the fight only to venture further down the road to an open door, and what a blessing because I didn't have the strength to battle another door. Ha!

So may we be His today as we walk in this world. May we see what is placed before us on a path, and if the door is closed, maybe just for a season, may we be wise enough to save our strength for the true battles we need to endure and walk with the Lord through the doors He opens. He knows. He knows where we've been and what we need. May we know that He knows best and walk in that obedience today. Love loud!

132

SLIPPERTY DO DAH! Up and at it on a rainy day! Much done so far and scads left to do, including lesson plans (who came up with these things?) and putting up the rest of the winter decor.

So talking with the girl these last few days, week about stuff going on, and we were talking about old Disney movies, which she said how great the new Cinderella movie is, and we have a date to go and see it. So I was thinking about one of my faves—*The Little Mermaid*, and I watched that with my kids probably a zillion times, and I can still quote it to this day. There is one part in the movie where Ursula is swimming around a "garden" of what looks like shriveled souls. These tiny and helpless, pathetic-looking creatures look so lost. I was thinking back to a season in my life many moons ago when I was feeling much like one of those creatures. There was a painful season where I was in a relationship that was abusive at best. It is nothing I care to delve into regarding time or who, but I was in a great deal of pain during that time. I let someone have control over me, sold my soul kinda thing much like the little creatures that Ursula "owned."

I tried to talk with friends around me at that time and heard things like, "Well, that must be who you are then"; "You must enjoy that if you let it continue"; "You are evil or sick or (insert whatever)." And when you are a victim in a relationship, then you are letting the other person control you, have you, own you, answering them at beck and call even though you know you don't want to be doing this. And people judge you. People cast stones. People walk away. I found two who never walked away from me, and both of them reached down into my pit of despair and pulled me out. I was quite a pitiful mess in that moment. Jesus, whose arms and reach know no bounds, kept pouring into my little shriveled up self. And my husband, who saw something I didn't see in myself, somewhere down deep, loved me despite all the ugliness that was in me.

So one day, I had the strength (before Mark) to stand up and deliver a blow, a huge punch to that person who was abusing me. To the rest of the watching world who did not know all the details, all the hurts and pains and behind-the-doors things, it looked horrible like I was trying to hurt someone who was innocent or had done nothing. My scars tell a different story. And so I will always remember a rescuing Jesus and a powerful blow, a day I finally stood up for myself, a day that Jesus's work in me finally revealed to me that I was worth it. I was worth fighting for.

Me. Wow. And so as I have been in the place of working with women for a while now, I know that I have stood where many of them stand today. And I pray we do not judge based on the little glimpse we see through a sliver of glass into their lives. I pray if they are standing up for themselves and finally see themselves worthy of fighting for, then may we support them and reassure them that Jesus loves them. May we love them too. I am eternally grateful for those who loved me through my process. Love loud, truly!

133

YEPPER DO! Up and moving a little slow this morning but happy to be up and off today! Doing some reading this morning about faith, about trusting God in the rough patches and being sure of the One we place our faith in. He led me to the book of Habakkuk this morning (strange, I thought), and then after I read there, He moved me to Psalm, and the correlation was amazing as He always is.

> Though the fig tree may not blossom, nor the fruit be on the vines; though the labor of the olive may fail, and the fields yield no food, though the flock may be cut off from the fold, and there be not herd in the stalls—Yet I will rejoice in the Lord, I will joy in the God of my salvation. The Lord God is my strength; He will make my feet like deer's feet, and He will make me walk on my high hills. (Hab. 3:17–19, NKJV)
>
> For who is God, except the Lord? And who is a rock, except our God? It is God who arms me with

strength, and makes my way perfect. He makes my feet like the feet of deer; and sets me on my high places. (Ps. 18:31–33, NKJV)

So today, if you are in it, walking, trudging, sloshing, treading, trying to make your way in and through a valley, well, there is hope. As I read all the trials, all the struggles of the Israel—no fruit, no food, no herd, no prospering from labor—as we read this, and as we go through these times, we can feel overwhelmed. We can feel that no one is for us, and yet if we look at "I will rejoice in the Lord. The Lord God is my strength." He is our strength in the struggle. That He is our joy in the jumble, the rock.

I love how both places the writer talks about the Lord making their feet like deer's feet and walking in high places. Deer's feet are made to walk in high places. They don't struggle with rocks and climbing or jumping. Their feet are swift and prepared for the terrain. As is our journey, we are being prepared for what lies ahead. Our feet are being readied, prepared to walk in high places with the Lord. That gives me hope when I walk and trudge that my feet are being prepared for better things, for all terrain, for whatever comes my way. Strength in the struggle and joy in the jumble. God has me. Love how His word is timely and true. Always. Love loud!

134

UBERIFIC SCOOBERIFIC! Up and moving this morning! Blessed time last night with women's group and up late chatting with the girl. Loved the crazy videotext my honey sent me while I was in group, such great way to close out a day.

I love how God pours out His wisdom when we ask. I am sitting and listening to my dear friends talk last night and thanking God for His wisdom in our group. I am so grateful that at times, His wisdom comes out of my mouth. Goodness knows my own wisdom couldn't hold a candle and would probably backfire or prove unworthy. Reading in Proverbs 2 this morning, I just want to share the passage because it is so beautiful if you have ever been in a place where you are seeking wisdom and then you watch God come through.

> Turning your ear to wisdom and applying your heart to understanding—indeed, if you call out

for insight and cry aloud for understanding, and
if you look for it as for silver and search for it as
for hidden treasure, then you will understand the
fear of the Lord and find the knowledge of God.
For the Lord gives wisdom; from His mouth come
knowledge and understanding. He holds success in
store for the upright, He is a shield to those whose
walk is blameless, for He guards the course of the
just and protects the way of his faithful ones. For
wisdom will enter your heart, and knowledge will be
pleasant to your soul. (Prov. 2:2–10, NIV)

I am thinking this morning about not only asking for
wisdom, not just sitting and waiting on wisdom like we wait
on rain but seeking it, crying aloud, reading the scriptures,
time in quiet prayer with our Beloved. "Search for it as
for hidden treasure." How would we search for hidden
treasure? If someone told you there was five million dollars
on your property hidden somewhere, what would you do?
How diligent would you be to search for that money?

We would leave no stone unturned, dig up the yard, tear
the house apart, right? And yet sometimes, when we need
advice, encouragement, joy, guidance, direction, wisdom, we
just sit and think we will figure it out. Wisdom is there,
but we must ask. Seek because He wants us to have His
wisdom so may we get busy seeking it. "Wisdom will enter
your heart, and knowledge will be pleasant to your soul."
Amen. That's the life I want. Love loud!

135

FOGGERIFIC! Up and moving in the wet willy fog this morning! Day is off and running. If you are traveling today, please be safe and careful in the fog.

I was thinking back last night about when I was a kid. I always had skinned up knees. I was always sliding, playing hard and getting after it. My mom used to buy these jeans from Sears called Toughskins that had double thickness in the knees. Well, didn't seem to make much difference because I still wore them through. I remember having some kind of scab always somewhere on my body. These days, someone would have called CPS on my parents, but I was just a rough and tumble kid. Tomboy for sure. So I was a girl with scabs. And I would find myself picking the scabs. Ugly to share, but it's true. Just as the skin under the scab is really starting to heal and close to being good to go, a scab really starts itching, and since it would itch, then I would pick, set back the process, maybe make it bleed. Begin again.

So as I was thinking on this whole "scab" thing last night, I was thinking about healing. About times in my life where I've been down on my knees, asking for healing, asking for help, asking for God to move in power in my life. And I would begin to make progress, then I'd pick the scab, reopen the wound, bleed more, relive the pain. Cycle after cycle. Not the brightest crayon in the box for continuing this process, and yet in some places, while I wanted healing, I didn't want it enough to walk away and stop picking. Let the scab itch a little. Leave it alone.

So I was reading in Matthew this morning about Jesus healing people, about Him asking some if they wanted to be healed, about Him telling them and that their faith had healed them. (I'm not saying that if you aren't healed, you don't have faith. It's far, far from truth.) But what I am thinking about this morning is my faith. When I had a scab and it started to itch, why did I have to pick it? Why couldn't I just walk away and let the healing process work, do a work in me? I have to participate in the healing process by being still and leaving the scab alone, by letting it itch. By my not picking at it and reopening an old wound but in having the faith to know that Jesus is doing a work in me to leave it alone.

Then He said to her, "Daughter, your faith has healed you. Go in peace" (Luke 8:48, NIV).

I love this. When we are hurting, when we are lonely, when we are depressed, when we are wounded, when we feel like we are not moving anywhere, making any progress, may we stay in faith that Jesus is doing His work in us. It may itch. We may be tempted to scratch it and then have to start over, but may we endure the itch for complete healing. May we stand in faith the Jesus will finish the good work He began in us, and may we not move in circles or backward but step even in tiny steps forward to His healing. No more scab picking. Let the wounds close and heal. Love loud!

136

SCOOBERTY DO! Up and moving on this beautiful morning! Just makes my heart jump for joy to see the sun again today! Yesterday was a great one, much done around the house and a little time with my honey and the kids makes it better. Ready today for time in fellowship and worship of our Creator.

This morning, I was reading in 2 Samuel about David and Bathsheba. I was thinking about how temptation is always hovering around. The enemy never misses an opportunity to place something before our eyes, pass it through our thoughts, and try and draw us in. He surely knows each person's weakness, and David's was women. I was thinking about how sin can capture us and is never satisfied. David had many wives, and yet he needed one more woman.

"It happened in the spring of the year, at the time when kings go out to battle. but David remained at Jerusalem" (2 Sam. 11:1, NKJV).

So I am thinking about how the enemy can set little traps for us, no doubt, but how we have decisions to make each day, each hour, and the weight of these decisions can be far reaching and affect us for generations, and maybe we only thought of ourselves just in that moment. That's the snare really, thinking of just ourselves. If the enemy can lead us down that path more and more and we find ourselves in those places more and more (those thinking about ourselves and our wants and desires only), then we are easier prey and easier to fall victim. Dr. David Jeremiah says, "Our decisions determine our destiny," and yet so often, we look at some of these decision as trivial, just as the enemy tries to downplay them to us. So I am looking at David and how it began with taking multiple wives even though God had told him not to and how he continued to follow what his flesh desired, all along knowing that God did not want this for him. And as he walked this path, even though he loves the Lord, it takes him closer and closer to destruction and toward decisions that are far reaching—destiny decisions.

This morning, I was listening to Joel Osteen, and he said, "A blessing is always attached to obedience." I was thinking of David, a king who should have been in battle and fighting for his country, and he was following his desires again, which put him in position to see something, look for someone he never should have be looking for/at a wrong place, wrong time. Goodness knows that as I look at David, I can see myself having fallen so many times. I'm called to do certain things, be in certain places with certain people, and at times, I have left my decisions to my flesh, to my desires, and to my wants and not what I am called.

Yep, so I am thinking this morning about the impact of the decisions I make, that each one is a destiny decision and is weighted and has the ability to reach far past me and into future generations. That yes, that will make me stop. That will make me slow down. That will and should lead me to the foot of the cross and on my knees. That will lead me to prayer and to Jesus and asking for guidance and discernment and guarding of my heart and mind. And that will lead me into the scriptures for weapons to battle the enemy. So today, may we look at where our feet are walking and who we are letting guide our steps because each step has power as it is taking us somewhere. So today wanting to walk in obedience and close to my Beloved, to hear His voice over the world, my flesh and my desires. His guidance leads me on the right path. Love loud!

137

ZIPPER DO DAH! Up and groovin' this morning! Breakfast with the honey bear and time with my Beloved is a great way to start my break! The to-do list is in process, and I'm ready to start checking stuff off. So last night, Mark and I were reading together and then we finished up by reading in the Bible about the Pharisees and all the grief they gave Jesus. I was thinking this morning about when I was a kid, our kitchen table and countertops were Formica. Formica used to be the choice product for countertops—not very expensive, looked nice on the surface, slick, easy to clean. But it had its drawbacks too. Don't dare put anything hot on it. Don't dare cut on it, and it stains. So most countertops today are granite or some type of stone product—heat resistant, scratch resistant, they won't really crack or break.

I am looking back at my faith, years ago and thinking about how it used to be Formica—surface faith. Faith that looked good on the outside, but if any real heat, pressure, struggles, trials were applied to it, well then, it was just flat ugly. I would crack, peel, bubble up, come undone from the cheap wood at the core. Yep. I was Formica faith for sure—looked good when life was easy; apply the heat, grape juice, or a knife, any real pressures, and I was undone.

I am thinking about what we look like when our faith is stone—solid, unmovable, unshakable. Apply heat, and it takes the heat, absorbs it, and disperses it, but the heat doesn't change the composition of the stone, and the stone doesn't change. It stays strong. It doesn't crack or peel or bubble up or come undone. There is no false surface attached to a cheap under layer. It is solid all the way through. Cut on it. Spill on it. Then just clean it up. Hard and steady. So grateful for the journey God has brought me on (and I am still on) in becoming rock solid in my faith and that my faith is not wavering, not circumstantial, not related to how hot or cold the trials are, not related to how much mess the enemy brings my way. Friends, may we stand in such a place that we know, like we know like we know, that we stand on the firm foundation of Christ. A foundation that is so solid and trusting and true that we may take the heat and not change because He is our rock.

May we lose the Formica, the cheap surface, showy faith, and get to the core faith that the Lord wants us to have. Faith in Him that He is bigger and more real than anything we encounter in this life, that we are firmly rooted in Him, and that is better than anything we can imagine. Out with the old (Formica), and let's get in with the new (rock solid) faith. Love loud!

138

YEPPER DOODLES! It's an up-and-at-it day! I can smell time off! Much good stuff going on at school today and, hopefully, for you as well!

This morning, I was reading a few places and camped out in Philippians for a while. As I was reading, I was thinking about all the friends and family who are in it right now. Some type of mess and struggle they are walking through, and my heart is with them today.

> Be anxious for nothing, but in everything by prayer and petition, with thanksgiving, let your requests be made known to God; and the peace of God, which surpasses all understanding, will guard your hearts and mind through Christ Jesus. (Phil. 4:6–7, NKJV)

I am thinking about some of the pits I have been in, trying to walk in quicksand, and the more I wiggled about, the worse it got. I remember being focused on my circumstance, being worried, feeling almost defeated and overwhelmed—too much. Too much for just me. I remember when I was a kid singing a song, "I got the joy, joy, joy, joy down in my heart. Where? Down in my heart. Where?" and so it went. The second verse was "I've got the peace that passes understanding down in my heart. Where? Down in my heart. Where?" I laugh because it is such a simple little song, and yet it always makes me smile when I sing it. It always brings my focus back to Jesus off my slimy pit. And, friends, I can't live with joy, joy, joy down in my heart and a peace that passes understanding down in my heart when I've got my eyes on the rearview mirror. When I am staring at my past or looking all around frantically just waiting for something bad to jump out at me.

I think about being in that quicksand, and the more you struggle and squirm, the more it pulls you down; the more it grabs you and you sink, the more you panic. The enemy couldn't make it better if he tried. I also know that if you sit still and stay calm, stay peaceful, get your focus off all the quicksand, and get your focus on the One who loves you and can redeem your soul, save you, then the struggle is not so much a struggle but a matter of how much we are willing to trust. How much we are willing to wait in peace and keep that peace that surpasses everything within us, lifting our requests up to Him without worry but in faith knowing that the rope is long enough to reach us in the middle of the pit with a gazillion-foot radius. Rope still reaches, Jesus is still strong enough to pull us out even if we've sunk to the bottom and have one last breath. He saves us. Joy and peace in the quicksand. Yep. Hold the rope! Love loud!

139

WETSY DOODLES! Time to pull out the boats! Up and moving in the wet, ready for a wonderful day despite the flood. I'm checking my neighborhood this morning to see if anyone's building an ark. If so, I'm getting tickets!

So yesterday, I was reading in Proverbs 31 and then had the pleasure of gathering with a group of women last night and reflecting on these verses in my head as we were together. The chapter is rich, but today, I was holding to this verse:

"She is clothed with strength and dignity; she can laugh at the days to come" (Prov. 31:25, NIV).

As I got dressed this morning, I am thinking about "what" I am wearing. I am thinking about the young ladies that are in my program and about how I clothe myself today. How can and do I lead as a godly woman before them? Today, the world is full of either telling women to step out and be "too manly," overtake and overthrow, or the other extreme, sit back, and let everything, everyone walk over you—doormat stuff. You are a second-class citizen. So I am looking at this verse this morning, and she is clothed in strength. Strength—the ability to resist being moved by a force. Yes, strength—the quality that allows someone to deal with problems in a determined and effective way. Yes. So as we dress this morning, we should be clothed in strength, in being determined to not let forces that are undermining who God says we are, not let those move or sway us! Resist. Push back, not be pushed over. Stand and deal with adversity and not be crushed by it, but stand strong through it. Stand on our rock, firm foundation.

Dignity is a state of quality of being worthy of honor or respect. The ability not to lower yourself to a standard other than what you've been called to, not to let "the world" get under your skin and get a hold of you, pulling you to and fro, a calm in the storm, at peace in the midst of war. In these places, we see people rise to dignity, honor, and respect. We can't fall to every whim or every desire or lash out in anger and expect to be clothed in dignity.

So as we get dressed for the today, put on strength, put on dignity, and walk throughout your day at peace knowing that Christ has you, has called you, is holding you, then you can walk upright and draw others to you and point them to Him. Laughing and rejoicing at the days to come because we are clothed well and we are His. Love loud!

140

YEPPER SKADOO! Up and at it this morning! Ready for some chapel this morning and some women's group tonight! So this morning, I am reading the verse of the day, and it is a keeper for sure.

"I wait for the Lord, my whole being waits, and in His word I put my hope" (Ps. 130:5, NIV).

I am not sure about you, but there have been times in my life where I have been waiting, seasons even, where I have been waiting and waiting and waiting. So as I read this today, I can so identify with these words because I've lived them. I've lived the impatiently waiting for sure. Not proud of it, but it's true. But I've also in recent years lived the patiently waiting. So as I read this today and think about what it means for your whole being to wait. I know that sometimes when I wait for something, I can feel like, "Sure, I'm good. I'm waiting," but then in other areas of my life, I can try to run ahead of the Lord or make it happen on my terms. I may be waiting but not as well as I need, not resting completely. What do we look like when our whole being waits? Sits, rests, soaks all the while at peace. Does our peace mean we've given up? Gracious, no! It does mean that we are full of God's peace, and we trust Him completely. Completely. He is our hope. And since He is our hope, then we don't need to rush ahead. We don't need to help Him. We don't need to give up and move on to other things. We need to rest in peace, patiently waiting because we can trust Him to keep His promises.

So this morning, as my dear, dear friend takes his last radiation treatment, he has been waiting. He has been trusting. He has put all his hope in the Lord because quite honestly, where else could he put it? So if you are in a season right now where you are waiting for God's promises in your life, then wait with your whole self, and let Him know that your hope is in Him. Rests on Him, and you are not on your timetable. Faith walking is not for the faint of heart, not for the weak in spirit. So today, may you rise up and open those hands and heart, and take the plunge of completely trusting the One who holds your life in His hands. He has you. Waiting for You and resting in You where I want to be. Love loud!

141

SCOOBER DOODLES! Up and moving this morning! Ready for a great day! Had a great evening with the family, and we spent time talking about wisdom. So this morning, as we rise, we are praying for wisdom in all decisions and dealings today. There are oh-so-many verses in the Bible on wisdom, and Proverbs has a plethora for sure. I always love the chapters 9 and 10 where he compares wisdom and folly. This morning, I just wanted to share this out of James.

"But the wisdom that is from above is first pure, then peaceable, gentle, willing to yield, fully of mercy and good fruits, impartial and sincere" (James 3:17, NIV).

So this morning, as I know so many people are dealing with so much going on in their lives—so many decisions, not tiny ones either, ones that effect others, effect families, effect lives, long term—I know of no better place to seek wisdom than from the Lord and in the Bible. They never fail me. Now, I can fail me and act inappropriately, but God and His word are true. So as I am thinking and praying for godly wisdom today, wisdom that seeks to find the best in others, wisdom that imparts love and mercy, wisdom that stands fast and firm in the will of God, wisdom that is not self-promoting but God promoting, wisdom that does not conjure up strife but seeks peace and truth. This is the wisdom I pray for this morning. I pray to be full to the measure with His wisdom. "If any of you lacks wisdom, let him ask of God, who gives to all liberally and without reproach, and it will be given to him" (James 1:5, NKJV).

So today, if you are feeling like you are trying to swim upstream, keep your head above all the waves, trying to discern a path while standing at crossroads. Well, let's ask. God is full of wisdom and will give generously, but we must seek it and desire it. Ask, and may He pour out His wisdom on us, and may we soak in it and use it. All for His glory! Love loud!

142

YEPPER DOODLES! Up and at it in the mess! This is good sleeping weather, but work is calling. So today is on the McAwesome chart for me! Mark and I are celebrating our thirtieth anniversary today! When I look back, it's like a blink in some ways, and in some places, it has been a long and beautiful process. Perfect? No. There is no such thing as a perfect marriage. And while our marriage is not perfect, I know that the enemy comes to undo and untie the marriage covenant. How do I know? Besides the fact that I've walked it out, I am reading in the book of John this morning and will share.

"The thief does not come except to steal, to kill, and to destroy. I have come that they may have life, and that they may have it more abundantly" (John 10:10, NKJV).

So as I read Jesus's words this morning, I am thinking about how the enemy comes to steal, kill, and destroy marriages. He attacks our relationships because they are a foundation. If he can get us to forget God, forget putting others before ourselves, forget that our choices impact more than just us when we are married, forget that worldly choices are quick and temporary but hurts are long and deep to heal, to focus on pride, focus on ourselves, focus on what's in front of us at that moment, well, that's when the slipping occurs. I can look back at all the ways he has attacked our marriage, but I can honestly say that finding time on our knees together is where our relationship has strengthened and grown deeper.

We must purpose to be for each other and lift each other up in prayer because we know that we will face battles throughout our day while we are apart, so together on your knees before the Lord is where so much ground can be gained in this battle with enemy. Friends, we have to advance and gain ground in the throne room if we have hope to see our marriage gain ground on this side of eternity. Jesus gives us the invitation of life to its fullest, and I can say that my life with Mark is so very full and blessed. It's not perfect, my kids are not perfect, there's not money growing on trees, we not without disagreements but blessed to the full because we love each other, because I still want to rush home and spend my evening with him, because we love to be around our kids and family, blessed because we love the Lord with all we are and love His presence in our home. Marriage is not a cake walk, but it should not be a drudgery either. Lay it at the feet of Jesus, and ask Him to be the center. Love loud!

143

YEPPER SKIDDO! Up and moving this morning! Ready for today. Team is heading out of town to a tournament tomorrow, so it will be a short week—some games and some silly girls. Life is good. God is good.

I was doing some reading last night when I got home from our game and ran across this:

"Fear. It can mean forget everything and run or face everything and rise."

And so I am thinking about watching my little team this year. Lots, lots of players new to softball, quite a few players with a tad bit of experience, and some veterans from the last couple of state-bound years. What a mix! And we have choices to make each day. We can look at the amount of challenge in front of us and run away, prove others right that we "can't do it." We can think we know everything and have nothing to learn as well, which is a danger in itself. Prideful. The day we stop learning is the day we are in trouble. The tightrope walk between confidence and arrogance is a daily challenge and can lead to complacency, which is another danger.

But today, I want to challenge you in all your decisions to rise. Rise up and face whatever comes your way. Not with arrogance like we know it all and have nothing to gain by listening to someone. Not with timid tiny steps afraid to mess up (because we will all make mistakes) but with boldness.

In the Bible, the Lord commanded Joshua to be strong and courageous three times within a few verses. I think He was trying to tell Joshua something. He will go with us. He is with us, and yet when we sometimes encounter things that are hard, things we have to work at, things that seem to go against us, things that give us push back, we run. So my question to myself and us today is why? Why will we run? Why not walk in bold confidence toward whatever is challenging us? Why fear mistakes?

Friends, I pray we can learn from our mistakes and move forward. Rise. Today, rise and meet your challenges. Make those tough decisions with confidence of who is with you, not just your own credentials. Face everything (yes, everything) and rise! Today is your day. Claim it! Let Him rise up whatever is dead within you and bring your bold courage to the surface. Rise. Face it. Love loud!

144

FOGERIFIC TOODLES DAY! It's an up-an'-at-it kinda game day! Sure hoping we get this game in today! Had a great time running in the fog this morning. It's been awhile. Running and the air is heavy. Can't see very far in front of me. Fog can play with your eyes in what you "think" you see, your ears in what you "think" you hear and where it's coming from. And if you let it, it can lead your mind off in a direction it shouldn't go because our senses are slightly distorted. I could hear footsteps behind me this morning, and yet every time I turned around, no one was there. It was the echo of my own feet. I thought I saw some large black things cross in front of me a few times, but when I got closer, I didn't see anything. Little harder to breathe in the fog.

So as I ran this morning, I was thinking about times in my life where I have been in a fog. In a place where I was feeling dark and gloomy, couldn't see well, wasn't hearing things correctly, my ability to discern well was distorted by my surroundings. Ever been there? So this I can say, if you are walking in a place right now where you can't see far in front of you and all you can hear is the sound of your own feet walking, well, keep walking. God brings people into our lives during the fog that help us walk through. And while we can't see down the road, honestly, we don't need to. We need to be intently listening for His voice within us because the world outside will deceive us, make us hear footsteps behind us and play games with our minds.

When we can just see what's right in front of us, that is plenty. We don't need to see five years down the road. That doesn't mean don't plan or dream, but don't let the fact that you are in a rough, foggy place take you out. God doesn't need us to see five years ahead. Today is our concern. So I have walked in the fog, and I've tried to do it by myself and wandered for a while, unable to make heads or tails of my exact place or which direction. Oh, but when I finally stopped trying to control everything and gave myself completely to my Beloved, then I could hear the Holy Spirit giving me directions, my "best friend," says Robert Morris. The Holy Spirit isn't fooled by what the world holds out in front of my eyes or what my ears are thinking they hear. He is the truth, and He lights my path where my next step needs to be.

"Oh, send out Your light and Your truth! Let them lead me; Let them bring me to Your holy hill" (Ps. 43:3, NKJV).

So, my friends, my sojourners in the fog, let us come to the light and truth that can lead us no matter the circumstances, no matter the weather, no matter the visibility, no matter. Let us ask ourselves as we drive in this today, "Who is leading my life," for we cannot see tomorrow. So who is leading our today? Love loud!

145

WETSY DOODLES! This is some sleepy time weather for sure! Up and moving this morning. Ready for time in fellowship worshipping and praising my Beloved and hearing His word preached today. Reading again this morning in Hebrews and only a few chapters in, but this verse stuck with me today:

"We must listen very carefully to the truth we have heard, or we may drift away from it" (Heb. 2:1, NLT).

One version says, "Pay the most careful attention," and another says, "Give the more earnest heed." This morning, as I am reading this verse, I am struck by how easy it is to drift. It makes me think of being out in the water at Galveston. I remember playing out in the water as a young adult and starting in one place, all our stuff on the beach, kind of camped out. And within fifteen or so minutes, when we walked in to the shore, we would be quite a long way down the shore from where we started and where all our stuff was placed. I also remember when our kids were little and playing out in the water that I kept a close eye on them, and when they started getting out too far or drifting a bit down the shoreline, I would quickly call them to come back in and reset where they were. Drifting is easy. It doesn't require any effort—just a sitting back and losing focus, enjoying playing in the water and not realizing the water is taking us away from where we need to be.

We are usually even unaware it is happening to us, just jumping and playing, just having fun, just living life our way, eyes off the shore for a little bit, and we lose our bearing of where we are and how far we've gone, drifted. Also thinking how we don't drift closer but drifting is pulling away. We immerse ourselves in worldly things, untruth, societal norms. Hey, we're just playing there. It's okay, we know what we stand for, and yet we drift, drift away from the home camp. And we drift outward, not just down the shoreline but out toward the big water, water we cannot stand in on our own, and we are in a dangerous place. Undercurrent is strong out there. Temptations are larger and swirling, and we don't have ground to stand on because we're in over our heads. We started off like little ones, close to the shore, and base camp, Then, over time, our self-confidence, lack of focus, and carelessness eventually pulls us away.

> As a matter of fact, if you examined a hundred people who had lost their faith in Christianity, I wonder how many of them would turn out to have

been reasoned out of it by honest argument? Do not most people simply drift away? (C. S. Lewis)

So I am working to be keenly aware, as the writer of Hebrews emphasizes, to know where I am, what I stand for and believe, and may I row, swim, or whatever effort I need to put forth to work at staying close to Christ. Complacency is drift. I may have to work really hard because my beliefs are going against the tide, against the undercurrent, and against society/worldly views, period. But may I work to be aware and stay close, focused on Christ, and not drifting through life. Too many times the drifting away in Galveston ends in tragedy and so can our spiritual life. Be intently focused. That's where my heart is. May I swim with all my might to stay there. Love loud!

146

YIPPSEE DO! Up and at it on this breezy morning! Much to get done today, and before I blinked, my weekend was full of places to go and people to see. Grateful for the opportunities God is putting in my lap and with how I am spending my weekends sharing with others. Good stuff. I was reading in Hebrews this morning and thinking about the message that was being written to the Jews that had become Christian but, through struggles and trials and all the hard times, were wanting to return to Judaism. I was reading how the writer is trying to convey that Jesus came, and He is, was, and always will be the fulfillment of the prophesies.

So the writer is pouring out all the ways Jesus is the one and for them to stay the course and see it through, even in the struggle. So the struggle is real. I know that it is human nature to return to what is familiar even when it is unhealthy, dangerous, negative, pulling us away from God (or family or whatever is positive in our life); it is comfortable. That's what the familiar is, comfortable. Who doesn't like to be comfortable? I love to put on my pj's as soon as I can every night. Yep. I'd put them on at 6:00 p.m. if I could. But I can tell you this, as soon as I put them on, I'm done. There goes any desire to work or get things done around the house. Once the shoes come off and the jammies are on, I'm in comfort mode. Relax. It's easy-chair time. It is wonderful to be content but comfortable can be a dangerous place. A little rest, a little folding of the hands, so I am thinking this morning about the absolute struggle these people were in.

Running back to the old stuff was easy! No persecution, no imprisonment and all the yuck. Let's just go back to trying to live out the laws, and even if we don't succeed, there is comfort in knowing what's expected and what's to come. So today, if you are in a place where the Lord is pushing you to grow and you are uncomfortable, it's not a bad thing. Don't leave it and run backward, especially every time you start gaining ground against the enemy. He wants you to run back to the old ways, old habits, old people, old desires. He reminds you how comfortable you were there. Easy.

I gain nothing by sitting in my easy chair with my feet up. It's not a position where I can get much done nor do I want to, once I've put on my pj's for the night. If you are being pushed outside of where you are comfortable, God may be trying to grow you. Maybe trying to get you to walk away from things that are toxic and, instead, run to Him. He can fill all those voids and places that are longing and empty. Familiar is not always best. Stretch yourself some. Trust the Lord. Let yourself be a little uncomfortable, and wait to see if He doesn't bring you to a new and better place. Love loud!

147

YABBA DOODLES! Up and moving this morning! Late night after group and kiddos coming home, sitting around the table and talking about life. My body struggles with the late nights, but my heart is filled. This week has been quite eventful for sure. Thinking today about walking with godly wisdom. With His knowledge, not meaning I can "know" all that He knows but that I can be filled with spiritual understanding of His will, of what He wants to direct me toward, of the people He wants me to encounter, of the way He wants me to love and speak to others.

> For this reason we also, since the day we heard it, do not cease to pray for you, and to ask that you may be filled with the knowledge of His will in all wisdom and spiritual understanding; that you may walk worthy of the Lord, fully pleasing to Him, being fruitful in every good work and increasing in the knowledge of God. (Col. 1:9–10, NKJV)

That just sounds beautiful to me this morning, saturated with the knowledge of His will in all wisdom and spiritual understanding. Who doesn't want that? I love thinking about what our lives play out to be when we are steeped in this so much that it is truly who we are, and we bear fruit because we are not just filled but filled to the measure. And as we grow in this, so we grow and increase in our knowledge of Him, spending time with Him, spending time in His word. Thinking about my tea bag sitting in my water and how the water is clear, but upon steeping, it changes to the color of the tea. And the taste changes because the tea bag has done its work. So that when I drink it now, it tastes like tea, smells like tea. It has become tea. Yummy Tazo peach organic tea.

And so being filled to the measure with the Spirit, we soak in Him, and the gifts of the spirit are what others taste and see. We have become the tea. I may not have steeped long enough yet, but be assured that I'm going to keep steeping. No weak tea. I want to be strong and bold for Jesus. Love loud!

148

SCOOBY DO DAH! Up and at it day! Ready for the day! Beautiful morning, so let's go! Women's group tonight is a big bonus to my day for sure!

"I'm ready now / I'm not waiting for the other side. I'm ready now / I still believe we can live forever / you and I begin our forever now / cuz every day the world is made / a chance to change but I feel the same / and I wonder why would I wait 'til I die to come alive? / I'm ready now, / I'm not waiting for the afterlife."

Listening to this Switchfoot song this morning and thinking about what will you do with your day? What will I do with my day? Our forever does begin now. The seeds we sow now are either temporal or eternal. The words we speak either speak life or death. The way we love and pour out God's love on others, that's eternal. Or the way we put ourselves and our desires first, temporal. Won't last. Love, that lasts. People don't last, but the relationships you build and pour into, friends, those last long after this temporal life. Reading a good book and it had a James Dean quote, "Dream as if you'll live forever. Live as if you'll die today."

So what does that look like? Will I spend my day in selfness or otherness? Will I lay my head on my pillow tonight and wish I had done more today? Accumulated more stuff. Went shopping more? Bought more shoes? More stocks? Loved more people? Just thinking about this today. As I write this today, I am forty-nine years old. I don't physically feel "old" or "that old," but when I look at the reality that odds are I've already lived over half my life, well then, what I am doing today? Today, I have lived 17,934 days. I know what I want to be doing with the days I have left. I so desire to pour myself out to others and show them the love of God, what Jesus can do in your life, to your heart. I know that my today better be good. I can make it good. I have a choice. I am confident of who I belong to and that He is by me today.

"I remain confident of this: I will see the goodness of the Lord in the land of the living. Wait for the Lord; be strong and take heart and wait for the Lord" (Ps. 27:13–14, niv).

Eyes open for His goodness today! Don't let the day go by without intentional living. Love loud!

149

SKIPPER DIPPER! Up and at it on this day-off fun day! Full plate today but still so grateful for extra time off!

I was thinking back to when I was a little kiddo. I liked to eat Play-Doh. Yep. My parents still probably never figured out where the Play-Doh was going, but I was eating it. When I was a wee one in school, I liked to color in the lines sometimes, but sometimes, I liked to use different colors and go outside the lines a little. Just be different. I had some of this same conversation yesterday with family, and I am not the only one. So I bring this up because the other morning, I was in a huge hurry to get out the door and be some place. I use an eyebrow pencil to give my brows some color and make them look thicker. I do stay between the lines usually, but on this particular day, I didn't really check myself in the mirror before I headed out. Now let me preface all this with the tragedy that as you get older, you eyebrows thin out. Who knew? This age thing can be quite a challenge! You grow hair in places that you never had hair before, and places like eyebrows where you want hair, it just stops growing, gets thin, and falls out.

So back to the story. I went to this event, obviously looking like I had done my brows in the dark, but no one there said a word to me. They are all lovely ladies and must have figured I had a fight with the eyebrow pencil, and it won. But on the way home, I stopped at Walgreens to pick up something, and people in the store, one lady in particular, kept staring at me. Even followed me over a few aisles to keep looking at me with a bewildered face. I had thoughts of saying some not so nice things because I thought it was rude, but I chose to remain silent and head home. Upon getting home and looking in the mirror, I was cracking up! My right eyebrow (pencil) was a little above my actual brow. Yes. Looked like a fool for sure!

Ha! I say all this because I am thinking that so often in life, we can look at other people and make a snap judgment on that person. We can look at them and think something is wrong with them because they "can't" or "didn't color between the lines." Maybe they eat Play-Doh. Doesn't make them any less worthy of God's love. Think about Jesus. He was an "outside the lines" guy His whole life here in terms of what people thought of Him.

Just because people don't fit in our box doesn't mean they don't fit in. We are all children of God whether we color inside the lines and are people pleasers or whether we color in different colors and use the whole page and are creative thinkers, whether we eat crayons (just purple ones like my youngest), whether we eat Play-Do, or whether we draw a purple turkey at Thanksgiving like my sister-in-law, God uses all our wonderful differences to color this world beautifully. So even if you can't put on your makeup quite right one day, God can still use you. Love loud, and love others!

150

JIGGLEY WIGGLEY! Up and at it this morning! Legs are doing the wobble today! Much good stuff going on today including my honey is coming home today! Yay! So excited! This weekend is jam-packed, but all with blessings. So this morning, as I sit and finish breakfast, I am looking out the windows at all the trees. In our backyard, we have two red maples. Both trees have lost all their leaves (almost) and are full of red buds. They are convinced that spring has sprung. So I am looking, and while this tree is loaded with beautiful red buds, there is this one leaf, one single leaf hanging on. It looks like by a thread. I am watching it blow and spin on the branch, barely hanging on. All around it are new blooms. Buds that are full of promise and convinced that this season they are in is a blessed one.

It is spring, so time to bloom and grow, and be beautiful. But what about my one leaf? It is hanging on, not convinced that spring is here, not having an easy time because the wind can blow it to and fro, and it has to deal with all the elements, and it is not closely attached to the branch. It is barely there and experiencing the full effects of all the weather around it. The buds are experiencing the full effects of the weather too. But they are attached closely to the branch. They are pulled in tight. And so even though the wind blows hard, it does not move them the way it moves the lone leaf, spinning, turning, being moved here and there and trying to hang on.

So I am thinking this morning that sometimes, even when we are strong in our faith and we are being tossed to and fro, we need to keep hanging on by that thread. The others around you may be experiencing nothing but blessings, but you are in the wind.

Here's the other. Sometimes, we can stay barely attached to the branch thinking that is enough, thinking that it will keep us alive and kicking and strong. But we slowly die. The others around us are close to the branch and receiving nourishment and all they need, even though the winds and rains come. They are closely attached. So this morning, if you are dangling in the wind, watching others around you bloom, don't let go. Hang on by that thread. Dangle. Do whatever you have to but stay attached.

You can't get nourishment on the ground by yourself, unattached to the branch. Hang on, spin, but don't let go. So may we stay attached, and may we stay close to the branch. May we receive what we need from Christ and let Him pour into our hearts and minds and veins every day.

All day. Less spin, more spunk. I have watched dead people come to life in Christ. I look in the mirror every day and am reminded of what He has done for me. May we remain in Him! Love loud!

151

YIPPETY SKIPPETY! Up and slow moving this morning! Late nights are whipping me, but I wouldn't trade what's going on for a million dollars. God is good. Praying my girl is in less pain today, and since I think the meds are gone, then I'm sending up some big ones today so she can rest. Had such a blessed time last night in our women's group. God always brings people together who can heal, touch, and walk together each season.

This morning I was reading in John 10 about Jesus being the Good Shepherd and the Gate.

> The one who enters by the gate is the shepherd of the sheep. The gatekeeper opens the gate for him, and the sheep listen to his voice. He calls his own sheep by name and leads them out. I am the gate; whoever enters through me will be saved. They will come in and go out, and find pasture. (John 10:2–9, NIV)

> The thief comes only to steal and kill and destroy; I have come that they may have life, and have it to the full (John 10:10, NIV)

So I was thinking about Jesus's words this morning. I was reading earlier in the chapter about Him saying that no one can snatch you from His hand. I can tell you that I have walked through times in my life where I know I was struggling to hear. I know that God was talking to me, but I couldn't always discern what He was saying and not sure I was getting the full message. I remember being a kiddo and watching some of the *Godzilla* shows, and the people on the show would be moving their lips really fast, but the voice that came out of the speaker did not seem to match up with the words. Ha! Gracious! I have felt like that at times.

God, I know you are speaking, but I'm not sure I am really getting all that. Friends, if you are in a place like that, know that you are not alone. You have already come through the gate, and you hear the shepherd's voice, and no one can snatch you from His hand. He comes to give you life. But spend a little time camped on the verse, "They will come in and go out, and find pasture."

The only times I have found my cure for getting a better/clearer picture of what the Lord was speaking to me was when I would "go out" find a place, a time, carve out some intimate time with my Beloved. Resting in Him is finding pasture. It sure helps me figure out all the things the Lord may be leading me toward because alone, I'd still be trying to read lips. Have a blessed day, and pasture with the Good Shepherd today! Love loud!

152

SCOOBER DOODLES! Up and rolling out of bed this morning. Sleep has been elusive this week for sure. I keep waking up with people on my heart to pray for and seem to be getting lots of little catnaps, which will catch me quick if I'm not careful. Missed a workout this morning with a girlie so that stinks, but we will catch up on Friday. So I know I have written on this before, but it is so much in front of me right now with some dear ones that I can't get it out of my head. I have been camped out in Galatians for a couple of weeks and just keep rereading some of the same verses because there is so much to be gained here. Mark and I have been praying for a while to receive a full measure of the Holy Spirit and praying that we would bear fruits of the Spirit in our daily lives. I have the fruits of the Spirit on my bathroom mirror and look at them each day as I get ready, trying to get myself prepared for the day.

"But the fruit of the Spirit is love, joy peace, patience, kindness, goodness, faithfulness, gentleness, self-control. Against such there is no law" Gal. 5:22–23, ESV).

I have been really looking at the first and last of these fruits of the Spirit recently. I work with young people, and so I see that many of them want to bear these fruits, good fruits. I want to bear these fruits, but if I put all my focus on the love, which is truly what we are called to do but forget the self-control, then I am missing something. They are bookends for a reason. All the things in the middle of the sandwich make it taste good, add flavor, add spice, add depth and vibrance to the life we live. But, friends, if we love well but do not exhibit self-control in our lives, then we will always be lacking, always be wanting. Love and self-control hold it all together. Our being obedient, our ability to reign our inappropriate passions or desires or appetites in and control them, it is the other bookend, and without it, all the books will fall.

Can't have any of the fruits without love. Can't have any of the fruits without self-control, not for very long. So praying today when those things the enemy knows we desire, those things and places that are listed under "my agenda." That today, when those come calling, I am praying we will stand tall in love and self-control and push them behind us. Then may we find all the joy, peace, patience, kindness, goodness, faithfulness, and gentleness we can hold. Love loud!

153

HOPSEY DO! Up and at it this morning! Excited and ready for this beautiful day! Loving this weather for sure! So this week, we start group back up in our house, and this morning, I was praying for our home. I do this pretty much every day but just some thoughts as I was getting ready and praying. I was standing in our bathroom, putting socks on, looking at the floor, thinking about the words I am saying, walking to my closet to grab my pants and shirt, thinking about the words I am saying. Here's my gist, sometimes we can pray; we can ask God for things; and we can do it without really pouring our heart and feelings and true self into what we lift up to Him.

So this morning, as I am looking at the tile under my feet and I thinking, *God what does it look like for You to truly be in our bathroom? What does it look like for You to be in my closet?* I get ready in the bathroom, prepare myself for the day, prepare myself for bedtime. It is a place of preparation for me. A place where I clean myself up and go forth. So when I'm in that place, am I preparing not just my physical body to go forward, but I want God's presence in there with me, preparing my heart to move through my day, preparing my heart for prayer as I get ready to pray with Mark before bedtime. I don't want to run out into the world, naked. I brush my teeth, put on makeup, shower, put on clothes—all these things and more. I get my physical body ready to meet whatever endeavor I am heading toward that day. So surely, I want God with me getting ready in bathroom, preparing the heart, soul, and mind for what is ahead.

I go to the closet and stand at the door, praying for His presence to be in this place. If you saw my closet, you would say it needs Jesus! My closet is a mess. Yes. It is the one place in my life where clutter abounds. I don't take the time to hang up my clothes. I toss them on the floor and just wear them from there. Now I have piles—piles for my athletic pants, piles for my polos, piles for my compression shorts, piles for my T-shirts, piles for my jeans. We all have closets. Yours may be nice and neat, but we all have places in our lives where we don't let the general public see. At this point in my life, I don't care if someone sees my closet. I have lived in places of hiding myself before and worrying what people think, but I don't live at that address anymore. So in all my mess, this room that looks out of control, do I want God's presence in here? Yes! He takes my messy mess and loves me through it.

If there is ever a room I need Him in, it is the one where He can redeem the past uglies that I close the door on and free me. So every day, we need the Lord in all places, not just the living room where we live, and all the guests come and see, but we need God's presence in our places of preparation. Our places behind the doors we close off to the general public, those are the doors we open to Him. So may we invite Him into all our places in our home and all the places in our heart. Love loud!

154

YABBA DOODLES! Up and at it in the early again. Ready for this day, this week, this season to get started. Lots going on, and I know that God is moving and has His hand on what is going on. Saturday I was out in the beautiful weather and sweeping off the front porch and front walkway. It has been awhile since I swept the walk, and lots of fallen leaves all over. As I swept where the porch and walk meet, as I moved the leaves, I uncovered what I carved in the concrete when we were having the house built. "+GOD+" right at the entrance of our home. It made me smile and took me back to the whole scenario when I carved it. Mark and I know beyond the shadow of a doubt that the events that occurred and ways things played out, we wouldn't be in this house without God's move. Much prayer on where we were going and all that, and He directed us in such an amazing way. We prayed over the land and told the Lord that "our home" was always His home, and we dedicated our home to Him to use as He wills and open doors to people and always welcome people inside.

Anyway, I came by the house and carved that in the walkway one afternoon and then again later that same afternoon, I met the construction manager, and he said they were getting ready to float over that. Someone had graffitied on our walk. I explained it was me, and I wanted it there. He didn't understand why and just laughed at me. It gave me a great opportunity to talk with him about the Lord and all the ways we have seen God move and change our hearts. As the build went forward, we had many more conversations about the Lord, and he was always asking questions, and by the end, he was full on believing in Christ. I was just thinking as I uncovered those leaves about whose house it really is and that I need to be more intentional each day about praying for His complete presence in our home because we want Him to abide there.

Life can get crazy. Seasons can come and go, and leaves can cover up your real reasons. Busyness can cover up the real reasons we are doing what we do and for whom we are doing them. Who knew sweeping leaves was going to get my heart and mind redirected toward whose home I live in. All we have comes from Him. Love loud!

155

SCOOBER DOODLES! It's Monday! How did it get here so quick? Up and at it this morning! Glad to be back at it. Monday feels like a start-over day after not hitting good workouts on the weekend. Ready for a wonderful week ahead and, hopefully, some days out on the field. Lots on my heart and mind this morning, so listening to YouVersion while I worked out this morning and heard so, so many beautiful truths. The Bible is such a beautiful book! Full of wisdom and truth every time. Yes, every time, I am in a situation or trial or circumstance or have questions or concerns, I can always go to His Word and find what I need. Sometimes it slaps me in the face, and I will need that on occasion. Sometimes it enlightens me. Sometimes it guides and offers wisdom. Sometimes correction, but one thing is for sure. It is true and relevant. I heard David Jeremiah say yesterday, "Everything God wants you to know is in the Bible."

I enjoy reading. I read books whenever I can get my hands on them. I don't always have time to read within a book each day, but I will always carve out time for reading/hearing God speak through His Word. Part of what I read this morning are the verses below:

> Do not merely listen to the word, and so deceive yourselves. Do what it says. Anyone who listens to the word but does not do what it says is like someone who looks at his face in a mirror and, after looking at himself, goes away and immediately forgets what he looks like. But whoever looks intently into the perfect law that gives freedom, and continues in it—not forgetting what they have heard, but doing it—they will be blessed in what they do. (James 1:22–25, NIV)

So as we get up each morning and read the Word, as we spend time in prayer and conversation with God, praising and loving on the Holy Spirit and thanking Him for what He does. And after doing all these things, may we not walk away and leave these things where they happened. May we take them with us throughout the day. So today as I am thinking about teaching girls new to softball how to hit and making the transition from drills, whether stationary or live, to an actual game is huge. It is not easily done for them to take the same skill set and walk out and now use it in a game. It takes practice. It takes replicating "game" situations at practice, but there is still nothing like live game experience.

Today, as we walk in Christ, this is our live-game experience. What we do and say and cast out there is real, and it is our way of living out Christ in front of this world. I don't want to spend all this time and get all this joy from being intimate with my Beloved and then leave it in the room. I want to take it with me all day, every day. So may we all walk today and remember whose we are and to whom we belong. Game situations can be live and intense and exciting, but may we stay the course and remember who has us and who has prepared us for this. Love loud!

156

OODLEY DO! Up and moving this morning! Ready to spend the morning in fellowship and worship of our Lord! Started out foggy this morning but turned into a beautiful day! It is funny because I was asking the Lord before I opened my Bible this morning to show me what He wanted to speak to me today. I turned to three different places, and all three pages talked about trusting in the Lord. I know our pastor is starting a series today about "In _____ we trust," and so I am guessing that I'm not getting out of the "trusting God" message today.

In my health class a couple of weeks ago, we were learning about good character traits, and trust was at the top of the list. I was telling the kiddos that of all the traits on the list, trust was listed first for a reason. All the other traits either stem from trust or the relationship can have all the other character traits and exist, but without trust, it will not thrive. It cannot be intimate without trust. And so I am thinking this morning that so often, we tell God we trust Him, and yet we still walk the way we want to walk. He might have lead us in one direction, but we may not like that direction. That direction might be hard to walk. That direction may not be convenient, or it doesn't allow us to do what we want to do. And so we don't follow. We don't trust. In word, yes. In action, no. Trusting is hard. You are opening yourself up for someone else, giving them a piece/part of you, and then hoping that they will treat it tenderly and with love and care. And we trust things. We trust people. We trust that our hearts will be valued and held dear. And sometimes, we find out otherwise.

If we trust in pleasure and flesh, it is but quick and fleeting. It leaves one wanting and longing for the same thing again, but it does not satisfy or fill one's soul. It is consumable and will consume you. If we trust in people, no matter how good they are, at some level, they will hurt us, and no matter how much we may love each other, they cannot fill our soul. They were never meant to complete us, but we search in the way that they will. There is only one who completes us. If we trust in money, we will find that it too can be fleeting, temporary. No matter how well we invest, it can be gone with one fail swoop. And quite frankly, we cannot load it up and take it to eternity, so maybe we need to look at how closely we hold it to our hearts. If wealth was complete satisfaction, then the wealthy and famous we see would all be content and peaceful. Money is not evil, but our desire and greed for it can leave us empty.

I will love You, O Lord, my strength. The Lord is my rock and my fortress and my deliverer; My God, my strength, in who I will trust; My shield and the horn of my salvation, my stronghold. I will call upon the Lord, who is worthy to be praised. (Ps. 18:1–3, NKJV)

Preserve me, O God, for in You I put my trust. (Ps. 16:1, NKJV)

Trust in the Lord and lean not on your own understanding. Prov. 3:5, NKJV)

And so, so many more verses about trusting. So today, I am thinking about in whom do I trust? Surely not myself because I can be a big mess sometimes. Surely not my money because it honestly is not mine from the start. I'm just managing it for a little while. Surely not pleasure because that is as empty and false as believing there is a "no calorie chocolate cake that tastes good." Surely, I am not trusting in people. Although well meaning, they will always fall short because we just do whether we mean to mess up or not. We are not worthy of that level of trust. God, who loves us always, is the only one worthy of our complete and total trust. Open our hands and heart because He wants what is best for you and loves you like no other. Love loud and trust!

157

GOODNESS GOOD MORNING, my Beloved! I know you are up and at it and ready to have a great day! I know that we have both had a lot on our plate lately. I know that when I look at things currently going on in my family, with kiddos, with work, well, it can be overwhelming. When I have too much to do or too much going on, I get worn down and worn out. That's when the enemy decides it is prime time to attack and hits me with it. Sometimes a big blow and, other times, a multiple of small things, but I can be sure of this: he is coming at me. I'm never sure the way in which he will attack me, but I can smell him coming (usually). This sounds funny, but my dad was born and raised on a farm, and when we would go outside sometimes, when I was growing up, I remember him saying, "Stop, I smell a snake."

I thought this was funny because I didn't smell anything. I remember thinking he was crazy, but many times, we ended up seeing the snake he smelled. In my book, the only good snake is a dead snake. I know this isn't true, but I'm sticking to it. I can say that I always felt safe when I was with my dad, and we were outside knowing that he could smell the snakes before they were able to get too close to us.

My friends, just thinking about that makes me think of our Father. He walks right with us. He smells the snake all along. He warns us of the snake ahead of time and even eventually helps us learn what the snake smells like and signs of a snake being close. He wants to protect us from the enemy, but He also wants to empower us to recognize the smells and signs of the enemy. No, we won't get it right every time. Sometimes, we will smell the snake and still head straight into the situation. Other times, we will see or smell the signs, try to avoid it, and still get bit. But, oh beloved friends, when we actually smell the enemy, recognize his rotten schemes to steal, kill, and destroy us, and then we turn away and take cautious heed, and miss the situation. Well, we have made some strides in the right direction.

So wake up today realizing you are a conqueror, a conqueror in Christ. We can't do it on our own. It takes His teaching, leading, guiding, and His sacrifice to give us this power. Stand strong today! Smell the snakes! Know that when Jesus returns, He will finish the job and cut off the head of the serpent and end his evil. Snake killer supreme! Until then, know the enemy is coming, but stay convinced that we have already won the victory through Jesus. Amen! Love and blessings! Love loud!

"In all these things we are more than conquerors through Him who loved us" (Rom. 8:37, NIV).

158

GOOGLEY MOOGLEY! Up and at it this morning! Gracious! Didn't stir until after 7:00 a.m. My body was like part of the mattress! Finished a run/workout while my honey did his workout in the pool this morning. Beautiful day to be in the outdoors in the weather! Always have things to do on the to-do list, but I'm making sure I enjoy this weekend as well. Weekends are usually full, so I am feeling the pull to slow down this weekend and love on some people.

> Count it all joy, my brothers, when you meet trials of various kinds, for you know that the testing of your faith produces steadfastness. And let steadfastness have its full effect, that you may be perfect and complete, lacking in nothing. (James 1:2–4, ESV)

So this morning, as I am running and I thinking about trials, about some of the recent ones in my life and ones from years back, nothing is "beautiful" when you are walking through the trial but what it is producing and shaping in your life is moving you toward beauty. I have coached for many years, and it is always disheartening to see a player quit. When the going gets rough, workouts get hard, playing time decreases, feelings of not being treated fair, coach doesn't like me, players don't like me, or a myriad of other things, then sometimes, a player will quit, give up, stop trying. Sometimes you can see them quit before they actually ever step foot in your office and speak the words. They have lost hope.

Whatever it was they were banking on, pouring themselves into, has gone sour or differently than they expected, they just stopped trying. A circumstance has won. A situation has triumphed. The victory never belongs to the one who tells us our circumstances are huge, and we should give up at the first sign of trouble. Oh, but to those who persevere, oh what wonderful things can happen. Steadfastness—how to hang on when it's tough. How to push through when it's not easy and everything says stop—steadfastness. I want this. I hope you want this as well. We want it for ourselves and for our children.

We tell them that life is hard; life isn't fair; things don't always go "your" way, so may we help equip them toward that. May we help them learn to stand in steadfastness and faith when all things are flying coming at them or us. May we set examples and not collapse and break. We may wobble. We may stumble, but may our weak legs keep standing, and in that standing, they will become stronger, steadfast.

Thinking about children being ripped out of homes being asked to denounce their faith in Jesus, denounce Christ and live. Profess your faith and die. And so they, little children, proclaim their faith and face death, staring it in the face.

May we raise our children to have steadfast faith. If we don't raise them to be steadfast in the small things, then how, how are they to be steadfast in the big things? The life-changing, life-defining moments. So this day, if you are walking through the muck and yuck, or your child is walking through it, walk with them, teach them, raise them up to stand and stay the course. Be steadfast. We never know how huge this will be at some other point in their life. May we lead and parent well. May we be examples of steadfastness. Love loud!

159

HAPPIER SNAPPIER! Up and rolling along! Loving life and smiling at the day in front of me! I'm a get-after-it kinda girl. I'm not much of a sitter. I'm a goer and a doer, so I like to have things lined out like to have a plan, "a where to go, when to go, what's going on" type of plan. I can fly by the seat of my pants with the best of them, but if I had my preference, I'm a planner.

So most of my life, I've made lists, written things out, what I need to accomplish and by when and on what day and sometimes even what time. When Mark and I first got married, I thought I'd help him out and make lists for him too. Yeah, that didn't go so well. Ha! Mark likes to plan too, but my lists and his lists were often very different. I continue to plan things and make lists. That hasn't changed, but I just don't do it for others anymore. Well, with all this "experience" planning, you think I'd be good at it, right? If I plan to accomplish certain things in a week, sometimes monkey wrenches come in and mess things up. Lots of monkey wrenches and all that jazz. Well, what if you have made big plans, life plans, you have a Plan A schedule and scheme going on for your life, and then through a turn of monkey wrenches, decisions, circumstances, hiccups, you find yourself outside of Plan A? Not just on the fringe but on a different coaster ride than the one you started on? "How'd I get here? And what do I do now?" are probably just a few of the questions we begin to ask ourselves.

I thought I knew how many kids I was going to have, how far apart they would be in age, what I was going to coach straight out of college, where I was going to college, what district I would teach in—and the list goes on. I've stood at all these doors with answers in my hand—my answers in my hand, my perfect "plan A" answers. If everybody would just move over, then I could get this rolling and get myself on the right track, carry on with my Plan A.

Do you hear that? That's laughter. So God has laughed at my Plan A. He's asked me why I think my plan is best? Why did I stand at each circumstantial door with my Plan A held tightly in my hands? I remember at different times absolutely being in tears and on my knees because Plan A wasn't the answer. I thought I'd messed up royally, and God couldn't use me because it didn't all line up with the way I thought it was supposed to, so I must be useless to Him. I mean, how can God use a broken girl with a broken plan? Friends, I can honestly tell you that God can use you and wants to use your life. I am on my plan D, E, F, or whatever.

I have been sidetracked and off course, more than once, but God has A plan. Do you get that?

See, we have a Plan A that we want to work, and when it doesn't, we so often think we're done or too far gone, but God, the Creator of the universe, has a plan, and a plan of God's is better than any Plan A, Plan B, Plan Z that I have. So when do we stop fighting and just give it up? When do we open our tight little fists with our neatly typed answers and turn them over to Him? Today. Today is the day to stop trying to make it work your way and let God use your broken self and rocky path and turn it to a beautiful life—a beacon that shines for others. Does that mean we are perfect? No. Does that mean we won't shine because we are broken? No.

I heard a quote before that says, "God's light shines beautifully through the cracks in broken vessels." So I am standing here without answers for where I'll be in two years, what I'll be teaching, if I'll be teaching, if I'll be a grandma, if I'll be writing and speaking—without answers. And you know what? I'm fine with that. Honestly, I'm resting peacefully without answers. It's such a freeing place to be. I hope you'll join me! There is freedom in letting go. He has you. Love loud!

160

LUCKY DUCKY DUCK! It's a movin' groovin' day! Are you ready? I hope so!

So I am thinking today about what it means to be "in process." I am looking right now at my body. I have done a decent job at taking care of it, but I have neglected things as well. Some from lack of knowledge at that time, and some from just shear "it's too hard to be that good." For example, when I was young, in my twenties and even when I started coaching, I would go outside all day and play in the sun with the kiddos, no makeup or very little, and there was no sun protection in makeup then. So now here I am at forty-eight, and what used to be freckles when I was a kid doesn't look so great as bigger "age" spots, sun spots.

I know I can put bleach-type cream on my face but not really thinking that is too healthy of an alternative, so I am a leopardess. In regards to my eating and exercising, yes, I get up and run every day and for a few miles, but I don't always have time to do resistance/weight training, and that catches up to me quick. To make matters worse because I like to eat clean and healthy, but sometimes certain things, foods can call my name. Brownies call my name. Things along this line. I'm a sweet-a-holic for sure, and when I am self-disciplined and full of self-control, then this really isn't an issue. And then, honestly, that isn't often enough. I mean, if I really due diligence and fight the battle (and it is a battle), then I can overcome. But if I'm completely truthful, there are some days, sometimes, I just want to eat the brownies, even knowing that I will look at my belly in the morning and say, "You fool!" and be annoyed with myself. I choose the temporary pleasure of the taste over the long-term fulfillment of making the right choice.

Been there? We probably all have. Now, moving past the food/exercise and applying this to my spiritual life. I am a work in progress. I can look at myself and some days, sometimes, I get it right. I want to walk so close and don't want to say the wrong thing or let a hurt get in the way. Choose peace over turmoil. Love my enemy despite my head saying, "Smack 'em right upside the head!" or whatever my goofy brain conjures up at the moment. Yes. Those days, those times, they are good! When the Holy Spirit in me is speaking and I am listening and obeying, those are good times. I am a forward work in process, progress. But yep, there's a but. There are times when I choose wrongly, when I ignore the Holy Spirit. I have let the flesh win the battle.

I am here to offer a couple of thoughts on those times. First off, we so often tend to see our fallen moments and hold them up, looking at ourselves as failures, as broken people, as men and women who are too flawed. Besides wanting to tell you that idea is far from true, that idea will also hold you captive. Been there, done that too! But I want to offer you something today. You are a work in process, and the process is progress. Let me say this, if we never fall, we never learn how to get back up, how to finish well, how to strive and push through. Yes, friends, if we live a life without trials and without failings, then we are not progressing. I can tell you that in my experiences, in my times of falling down, even digging my own pit and walking right into it, I have moved forward in my walk with Christ because of those experiences.

If I just pretended my life was perfect and I didn't make a mess of things, that my kids were perfect, and my husband was perfect, then I'd be living a lie. And please tell me how a lie can help you grow? It can't. Only in the truth can we grow. We can stumble, fall, get up, and learn to walk better, stronger. Think about a baby learning to walk, and then see for yourself. See your life, and see that you too are moving forward because you fell down. I'm not saying we should purposely sin or choose wrongly and go hog wild. I am saying that when we are completely His, we will be a work in process, and our desire and His desire is progress. I am not where I want to be, but I am not the same woman I was ten years ago. And I want to thank Jesus for that! Stand up today and see the process and the progress no matter where you are! Love loud!

161

SKIPPERY SLIPPERY DRIPPERY! Rain drops. They are falling on my head, and I'm calling for an umbrella, please! Or a poncho. Or a pontoon boat.

There is one thing we have not lacked around here lately, and that's rain. Everything is drenched, filled up, saturated. So I am sitting here, looking out my bedroom window, watching the water drops on the window screen and the window. Always something to see.

The rain is still falling in big drops but more softly now. I am watching these drops on the glass. Most of them hit the glass and run down to the bottom quickly. Some hit the glass and cling there for a few seconds before moving down, and some sit for a few seconds, like wanting to stay, only to be hit from above by more drops on their way down the glass, and so it goes with them. Not many raindrops on the window.

Now I am watching the raindrops on the screen. They hit the screen and almost cling there. Some gather more drops to themselves and become a big drop. Others connect with other drops and make patterns on the screen. The screen looks like a wet community. Lots of drops all doing something, and all different, and together they cover my window.

I am thinking about my life when I was younger, much like the drops that hit the glass. I was going somewhere, and I was going there fast. When I hit or fell, it was usually against something hard, and I never slowed down to think where was all this fast and furious leading me. It was leading me down. And because I was living without thinking of tomorrow or consequences or anything beyond what was in front of me, then I was on a fast track, a fast track down to nowhere. There is nothing to cling to when you are on the slick. The enemy wants it that way. He greases it up and then pulls you in, and you are fighting and trying to grab a hold of something that will slow you down or stop you, but there's nothing on that glass. You just slide down quick and fast and pick up all the dirt along the way. And when you hit bottom, there you are. Not with a community but you feel all alone. You feel like you must but the only raindrop that was blind enough to hit that window and fall hard and fast. You see no one else on that window with you, but you can see lots of drops at the bottom. The ones who went before you, and there they are. And there you are now. In a puddle.

On the screen is community. On the screen are drops clinging and holding on to something much bigger than them. As the wind blows, it just moves the drops. Moves some closer together and some further away. Moves some into neat patterns that look like the screen. They are not running down, falling down but holding on and staying together. They are not in a puddle on the bottom; they are together. They are many drops, but stepping back and looking at the whole screen it is pretty like little diamonds all over the window.

When we become a Christ follower, then we live in community. We all look different. Different sizes and shapes. Different giftings. Different callings. And yet when we cling to Christ and understand that the church is universal not just one corner of the screen but an all-encompassing vision of what Jesus wants to do in this world, then we can step back and see all the diamonds on the window screen. We no longer look at individuals differently based on where they go to church or what gifts they have. We no longer see the picture as just being about us. That's what happens on the window with just glass and no screen. We can step back and truly appreciate what each drop is offering, the beauty that it brings to the screen, its purpose and how the clinging to Jesus and each other makes the screen beautiful. Jesus has a beautiful bride, and each one of us has gifts and callings that make us vital to the church shining like diamonds, shining bright in a dark world.

So may we embrace each other. May we lift each other up. May we pull together. May we see the value that each person and each church has to offer as the bride of Christ.

So glad that I have a Savior that took this puddle of girl and made me new. And so now, I cling to the screen in hopes to pull together with others and paint a wonderful picture of Jesus and His love. Love loud!

162

RAIN-O DRAIN-O! Up and swimming in the streets today! It's a wet one, but my lawn could always use a drink. Today is about being prepared, like rain boots.

So I am not a fashionista by any means. I am usually quite behind the trends in what I wear. I guess it's because I'm usually a T-shirt-and-jeans girl, that my wardrobe is lacking in the trendy area. Oh, I have a few trendy things, but I can tell you that about a year ago, I decided it was time to clean the closet (like a for real cleaning), and I had my twenty-four-year old daughter help me, and that she did. She pulled some of my clothes out and let me know that those haven't been *in* fashion for quite a while. Haha! So I rid my closet of the out-of-date stuff, which left it looking rather anemic, but that's okay.

So since I am trying to be a little more trendy, I decided that I wanted a pair of rain boots. Now not just any old pair of rain boots, but I wanted a cute pair with some kind of print that would go with my anemic but trendy wardrobe.

I got on line and started searching for these boots. Most of my friends have some, at least one or two pairs, so I thought I could snag one pair to start and maybe later get another. I honestly planned on spending about $25 to $50 for the boots. Yes. If you have already bought rain boots, then you are laughing at me as you read this.

But so is my journey into fashionhood. Well, I spent an entire morning looking online, on discount shoe pages, on sale pages, on name brand stores—you name it. I looked there. And do you know what I found? Rain boots in all colors and styles and designs with prints and flowers and plaids and plain and even some that looked like paintings. Who knew? At first I was almost overwhelmed by the selection, but I later was overwhelmed by the prices. Good gravy! I saw some rain boots that were $325! Yes. They were plaid. They were $325. I'm sorry, just still trying to wrap my mind around that one! And let me tell you there were many in that price range!

And you might ask why on earth am I talking about rain boots? So this is what I am thinking today. A rain boot can be beautiful—all decorated and printed in awesome patterns and designs, and it is still a rain boot. A rain boot can cost $50 or $350, and it is still this, a rain boot. So what really do we want rain boots for? I wanted a trendy pair that was cute, but I also live in a very wet climate, so I thought it would be a good idea. After all, rain boots are made to keep our feet dry. That is their purpose. So I am thinking this morning about people.

We come in all colors and sizes, and we can be all gussied up and fancy pants on the outside. We can be plain Jane and only come in one color. We can be from one end of the spectrum to the other in what we look like on the outside, but know this: we have but one purpose. Our purpose isn't to be the most beautiful, the most fancy, the most expensive, the mostest of the mostest on the outside stuff. No, our purpose lies in what we were created to do. And no amount of fanciness on the outside or what we "think" we are worth monetarily matters or bears weight toward that purpose.

And what is our purpose? Our purpose is to know God and to love Him with all that we are. Our purpose is to love Him so much that we desire to obey Him. Our purpose is to live lives that bring Him glory and honor and praise. And in all this, we may share this purpose with others. Because quite honestly, if we do this, well then this purpose is singular. It encompasses every area of our lives because it is our life. To know God in such a place that it is not just head knowledge but a deep knowing from the heart, a love, and when you are in love with God, you want to pour out your life for Him, live for Him, please Him, point others toward Him because you are so overjoyed with the love you have found. And when we live lives of love, pouring out God's love on others, then, friends, that brings glory and honor and praise to the Father.

So no matter what we look like on the outside or what we think about the outside, the purpose is what matters. No matter how fancy the rain boot, it is a boot to keep your feet dry. Let's not spend our lives getting caught up on the outside, but let's celebrate our purpose. Let's get out in the rain and yuck and muck of the world and fulfill what we've been called to do—making disciples. Love loud!

163

DOODLES AND OODLES! Singing in the sunshine and running with some giddy up! Today holds much potential, so I am ready to run into oodles of what the Lord has out for the day. Who knows? Not I, but trusting.

So thinking this morning what does surrender "look" like? We sing, "I surrender all," and so many songs about surrendering ourselves to Christ. And I can tell you that it's easy to stand in church and sing these words. But what does surrender look like outside the church walls?

When I am in a situation where my body is pulling me, my mind is pulling me, and my spirit is standing and fighting back, those are the hard times. Those are the times we are called to surrender. The tug-of-war of being a Christ follower is that we know our spirit should win this. We want, down deep, we want the spirit to win, but we can push the Holy Spirit down. We can ignore it because the flesh is strong. As a Christ follower, we hear the Holy Spirit rise up and tell us to walk away, be silent, offer encouragement and not ugly words, not go there, and so on. He wants us to draw strength from Him, and yet, if we aren't in regular communication, dialogue, soaking in the Word and spending time with Him, then it is so, so easy to pretend we didn't hear that voice. Ignore it. It's not saying what I want to hear, so.

I wish I could sit and write this telling you I have never been here, never let my flesh win the battle, but I have too often. Paul writes:

"This is a faithful saying, and worthy of all acceptance, that Christ Jesus came into the world to save sinners, of whom I am chief" (1 Tim. 1:15, NKJV).

So I sometimes look at Paul, this incredible man of God, that has the same struggles as me, but this is not an excuse for me to continue sinning. Oh well, if he can't do right, then I sure can't. No. Surrendering to the flesh is easy. We are to battle the flesh and surrender to the Spirit, to God. We are in a tug-of-war! All the years I have coached, and done field days, tug-of-war is the premier event. It's the one who has so many involved. The kids are planning strategy and even the people watching are on their feet and cheering for one side or the other. And that's just what's going on here. We are in a daily battle with the flesh. We are telling our bodies/minds to do a certain thing, and the enemy is enticing us to do something else. We can make plans. We can strategize. We can think, *I'll never do* _____.

We can think we have all the willpower in the world, but the enemy knows us. He knows what calls to us, and he uses those very things to pull us. He puts the quick little strong pullers at the front of his rope to get a quick advantage on you, get you leaning the wrong way so he can get you off balance. Hopefully, we have some fight in us. Hopefully, we are strengthening ourselves daily. We can have all the strategy going on, but if being stronger in Christ isn't part of that, then the battle is easily won by the wrong side. But in daily walks with God, talking with the Spirit, listening to Him, then we have an anchor in this tug-of-war. You know, the one always at the back of the rope. The big guy, can't be moved. Yep. God is on our side. He wants to help us. We have every opportunity to win this battle. Our anchor won't let go of the rope and leave us flying across the line and into the pit of muck. No. He will hang on. He loves us and wants beautiful things for us. He wants us to live a life of victory. But instead of surrendering, handing over ourselves completely to Him, have we let go of the rope because it is too hard to pull any longer?

See, we think it's easier to just give in, surrender to sin, and yet we don't understand how that is robbing us, killing us, destroying the victory that God has for us. We decide we need some cheap here-and-now version of what feels good victory. Just like the temporary little trophy we get for winning a baseball tournament, a tug-of-war at field day, a bowling tournament, and we'll find that those temporary things collect dust. They break. They are cheap and empty and shallow. Then we are chasing some other pleasure. Some other empty because that one didn't satisfy, at least for very long. So are we going to keep chasing our tail like a dog? We laugh when we see it because we think it's crazy but chasing these temporal, earthly, fleshly desires that are empty, it's the same thing.

I hope that today, you realize you are in a tug-of-war. I hope you have not only planned well but also equipped yourself for this battle. Spend time in God's word and with Him so He can strengthen you for what you will encounter on the front line. And know that He has your back. He is the anchor. He will hang on. It's our job to not let go of the rope. Love loud!

164

SKIPPETY DO DAH! It's a up-and-at-it day! Today has lots of moving parts, so need to get busy before I run out of daylight. Ready for some amazing things the Lord has in store for today and trusting Him in the process.

So this morning, I am reading in Genesis chapters 6 and 7 about Noah. We have read the story of Noah many times, seen half-baked movies about Noah, read children's stories about Noah, and so on. But today, I am coming from a different place with the Noah story, thinking this morning about marriage and what it looks like to be Noah's wife. Noah for sure walked his days in obedience and righteousness, but have you ever thought about what it would take as a wife to walk alongside a man of such obedience?

Today in society, it is so easy for people to throw marriage out the window. For people to walk away from a covenant, a commitment, a vow, and the promise was to each other and to the Lord that you both would work and strive and do everything necessary to maintain and hold sacred those vows. So people today have taken out "till death do us part" because that is too hard. Today, people prefer marriage to last until they find something better, or the struggle is deep and walking away is the easier thing to do. So I am looking at Noah's wife this morning—a woman who stood by her man when the rest of the world around them thought he was crazy. She stood by him and supported him. I imagine she prayed for him. She held tight to his hand knowing that he was righteous and being obedient to the Lord, but she lived in the world that was giving huge push back to their life. And she stood. And she stayed. She didn't walk out the door and tell Noah he was crazy because by the way it looked, he could have qualified. Piles of gopher wood, measurements, instructions on how to build and animals to fetch, yep, she could have looked at her husband and gone along with the rest of the world, the lost world, the world that was drowned (as sin does to us).

So my question for us today is, "How many of us, as wives, would stick and stay?" As women of God, when our husbands are called to walk in places that aren't "normal," when they are set apart and listen to the Lord and walk closely with Him, and He calls out a different path for your man, would you stand? It is easy to say we are committed to our marriage, and yet do we, as women, do the things we are called to do? Do we stand by our man when times are hard? Do we hold his hand? Do we lift him up before the Lord in prayer in a strong and powerful way, not weak and barely mentioning him in our daily prayers? How committed are we as women to our marriage? When our husbands walk in obedience, then we are doing the same when we stay and stand boldly beside him, calling out to God on his behalf for him to continue to have the strength to stand in the hard times. May we be those women. Not runners. Not faders. Not pretenders. None of those last in the trenches.

And when you stand, ladies, know that it is not easy, and the enemy will come against you and your family but stand. Stand while your man builds that boat while there is no rain on the radar. May we be set apart and not like the rest of the world, and yet may the world around us see how we live, and may it draw them. And may we point them to our Beloved. May we look to His word for teaching and wisdom and truth. So today, I am standing by my man, building and ark in the clear blue sky and knowing that God has walked with us through thirty years, and we aren't done yet. He still has plans. Mark is still obedient. I will still stand. May we hold tight to our marriages. Love loud!

165

YEPPER DEE DOODLES! Up and rolling out bed this morning. Alarm was a "what's that noise?" After a five-day cruise, finishing up the tail-end of a semester and kiddos are prepping for finals.

So this morning, I am soaking in this verse. Not a verse that I read or cling to from a materialistic view but from a place where the Lord desires to bless us.

"Delight yourself in the Lord, and He will give you the desires of your heart" (Ps. 37:4, ESV).

So my question to us this morning is, "What are the desires of your heart?" 'Tis the season. To be or not to be, that is the question. So while we prepare our hearts and homes for Christmas, we must be closing out this year looking back and looking forward. We look back to appreciate the things of the past year and to learn and prepare to move forward. 'Tis the season for many to begin to look to new beginnings and what kind of year it will be. To ask ourselves the question of what will I do differently this year. So as I am soaking this month in some quiet time with my Beloved, I am seeking wisdom for moving into the upcoming year and what He has prepared before me and to be readied to walk into that calling. I hear so often people use this verse thinking that God wants to just open the bank accounts of the world and pour it into their laps, and we are missing some of His heart with that idea.

When He is our delight, when we wake up and desire moments with Him, when we get a little break away time and He is our longing and thought, when we seek Him throughout our day, not just at meal time prayer or just on Sunday, well, we see that He is our delight. And as a Good Father, He longs to give good gifts to His children. We are a royal priesthood and kingdom walkers, so His blessings will find us when He is our desire. And blessings are not "life is perfect," but many blessings come through the struggles. And we stand on the other side of those struggles and look in the mirror and see a person we didn't see before—someone who gained ground, someone who pushed back the kingdom of darkness, someone who walked knowing that God's very Spirit resides within them and that gives some authority and power and strength (not ours but always His).

And the desires of your heart begin to align with Him because you are so deeply in love with Him. So today, may we seek His face, long for His presence, go deep. He will never disappoint. As I look to move forward with new, I know that He is my first desire, and I know that my path and steps are ordered, and I know that He desires to bless. Trusting that whatever that blessing looks like, He is shaping me into a woman I was not five years ago. So I run to greet Him and desire my Beloved more than air. He is my blessing. My desire. Love loud!

166

YEPPER DOODLES! Up and groovin' on this beautiful morning! Ready to head out the door to school, but God has been calling me all morning. Good conversation with my Beloved and wanted to share.

So this morning, I am soaking in thinking about the time that I have been placed here. I could have been born in the 1800s or pick a time, could have been born in another country in another time and all that jazz. But the word for each of us today is that we are called and placed here in this season, for a purpose.

> Behold, I send my messenger, and he will prepare the way before me. And the Lord whom you seek will suddenly come to his temple; and the messenger of the covenant in whom you delight, behold, he is coming, says the Lord of hosts. (Mal. 3:1, ESV)

As we prepare our hearts and minds for this Christmas season, may we also bear in mind that we are placed and called. John the Baptist was sent as the messenger, the one to prepare the way, the one to proclaim the Messiah was coming. Prepare. So on this December 1, many are preparing homes and decorating and shopping, but are we preparing ourselves for whom our souls long for? Further, as we prepare for Christmas, may we realize there is more than Christmas season.

> If you remain silent at this time, relief and deliverance for the Jews will arise from another place, but you and your father's family will perish. And who knows that you have come to your royal position for such a time as this? (Est. 4:14, NKJV)

So this morning, as we sit and look at not only the season of the year we are approaching with Christmas celebrating the birth of the Savior but looking at the very place and time in which we have been placed, place matters to God. He is not a God of chance or happenstance. He is purposeful in everything down to the last minute detail. So why would we take casually our placement of time and location? So why would we fill our lives each day with "us stuff" and not "other stuff"? Should we just walk through life existing each and every minute, letting life happen to us? Or should we open our eyes and see that the season of preparation is upon us, that God is birthing and purposing our lives for something more than we see with limited vision.

May we remove the veil and may our lives reflect His glory and power and might today, right now, in this season. Not all about presents, not all about hubbub, not all about us. Let us prepare our hearts and minds today, not just for Christmas but for our calling! May we step into seeing that we have been placed where we are for such a time as this. Love loud!

167

SCOOBER DO! Up and at it this morning! My body is still working on 6:30 a.m. being off work wake up, so the alarm didn't sound pleasant this morning but jumped up anyway. Ready to be back at school and seeing all the bright faces! God is good. Much and many to give thanks for Him today.

So this morning, I was reading in many chapters in Psalm but kept coming back to 103. So much in the chapter but wanted to camp in a couple of places as we are all up and heading out to work/school today.

> Bless the Lord, O my soul; and all that is within me, bless His holy name! Bless the Lord, O my soul, and forget not all His benefits; who forgives all your iniquities, who heals all your diseases, who redeems your life from destruction, who crowns you with loving kindness and tender mercies, who satisfies you with good things, so that your youth is renewed like the eagle's. (Ps. 103:1–5, NKJV)

There is much more in this sweet chapter about all the Lord has done for us, but the first five verses are an amazing start! I love how David calls out of himself twice to "Bless the Lord, O my soul" in case you weren't feeling it the first time, in case those of us reading didn't grab the first one. Bless Him. Let our souls bless Him. Let our souls cry out to Him, not just in our distress and anguish and trials but in our seasons of smooth sailing. Let our souls raise up and praise His Holy Name. With what? "All that is within me." And may we be so mindful as we kick start this week—cyber Monday, Christmas shopping, Christmas programs, Christmas parties, Christmas services, Christmas gatherings with family and family and family.

Let us be mindful of all His benefits—the healing, the redemption, the restoration, the casting off of our sins, the mercy, the steadfast love, the provision, the renewing, the abundant life. So today, may we find it oh so easy to bless the Lord with all that is within us. May our souls truly rise up and give Him a shout of praise. We are not lacking. We are not the cast-offs. He is our shepherd, the Good Shepherd. He is our Father, the Good Father. He is our King, the King of kings. Bless the Lord, O my soul! Love loud!

168

YAPPLE DAPPLE! Up and moving slow this morning! So much to do in every day stuff. Trying not to get too excited yet, but leaving Saturday morning for our first ever cruise with some amazing people! Ready for tonight and all the wonderful ladies who will walk in the door for women's group. God is good!

So yesterday was full of several conversations that revolved around wisdom. Wisdom is one of the places I didn't frequent much when I was younger. The enemy does a good job of masking deception; mediocrity; lies; good-enoughs, feels-good now; intelligence as an idol and many other things as wisdom. His worldly wisdom is no match for godly wisdom, and yet it can sound good, and people can walk right into the pit and be captured. Sometimes we can even live in the pit of worldly wisdom for years. Sometimes people die in that pit, never knowing they were deceived or trapped in the first place. The enemy does the job of making it look like wisdom—masked, disguised, a front, but underneath the mask is pride, heartache, brokenness, destruction, and a path that leads to death. Proverbs has much to say on wisdom as well as James and other books of the Bible.

"Whoever walks with the wise becomes wise, but the companion of fools will suffer harm" (Prov. 13:20, ESV).

Thinking this morning about who we let speak into our lives. Do we seek wise counsel? Do we go to Scripture and search to confirm or find truth? Do we rush into decisions? Do we make decisions based on our emotions, which are fleeting, ever changing as the wind blows? Or do we stick and stay in the counsel of the Lord in prayer? Do we lift up our decisions and concerns to Him before we step? I have a handful of people who I allow to speak into my life—my husband and about four women I trust. They are godly and wise. They seek the Lord's face in prayer. They search the scriptures, and I can see the way the Lord is with them and upon them, so they are my trusted counsel besides my time with scriptures and my Beloved.

May we lay aside earthly things, earthly "looks good," earthly wants. Friends, may we pray for wisdom each day. May we seek and desire it. May we seek Him first, and above all, may we cry out for wisdom as we walk in this world. His wisdom is true and beautiful and life giving, freeing! He will freely give. All we need to do is ask. Asking again today for wisdom. Won't you join me? Love loud!

169

FANTASTICAL FUNDAY! Up and getting busy on this beautiful morning! God is good! Today is school then pack for the cruise! Trying to contain the excitement for about eight hours! Amazed and grateful for this opportunity!

So last night was a warrior night for me. So, so many to pray for that every time I fell asleep, more would come to me. So many dear ones suffering loss and struggles right now. So many dear ones in need of healing and someone to hold a hand. The enemy is doing his work, and yet, God is doing His as well. Can we keep guns away from evil ones? No. And while the media may make fun of prayer and God, may we all remember that God works through so many people and prayers are heard each and every day. We do not even know what kinds of evil have been deterred or thwarted because of prayer because it is something you can't "see," and yet to those with the veil lifted, it is as evident as you seeing your face in the mirror. You can behold it. Last night, our lesson was on patience and perseverance, and such is our plight in this time. I will never do a full lesson in my writings. You will have to come to group for that, but I will share a tad.

In Greek, the word *patience* means cheerful endurance. And while so often we endure trials and circumstances that are huge and like a hurricane, the winds and waves are felt by both a ship in harbor and a ship on the seas, but ships are meant for sailing, and so by our patience in affliction and by our perseverance, we can find ourselves being made more mature. And more mature happens by our choice. We have a choice to learn from our trials and experiences. Live the same experience twenty-five times over and over again and again through the period of twenty-five years, or live the experience once, and gain knowledge and wisdom from that experience for twenty-five years.

> For this very reason, make every effort to add to your faith, goodness; and to goodness, knowledge; and to knowledge, self-control; and to self-control, perseverance; and to perseverance, godliness; and to godliness, mutual affection; and to mutual affection, love. For if you possess these qualities in increasing measure, they will keep you from being ineffective and unproductive in your knowledge of our Lord Jesus Christ. (2 Pet. 1:5–8, NIV)

So today, as we endure, as we are actively patient, as we a pressing through with perseverance, may we gain these fruits in increasing measure. For through these, with these, we change the very environment where we do life. And through that, we change the world. So whether or not anyone sees what the power of prayer can do will not phase us. We can persevere, and our faith will prove out. God is good. Indisputable truth. Love loud!

CPSIA information can be obtained
at www.ICGtesting.com
Printed in the USA
FFOW05n0459220916

9 781683 333593